PRAISE FOR TOME

'Great horror narratives should be tense, strange, gory, and creepy, and Tome delivers all that within the first two chapters. Jeffery walks a fine line between reality and mayhem, between the darkness of the world around us and the even darker stuff hiding just beneath it. If you like your horror mixed with murder and inner turmoil, Tome should be at the top of your reading pile.'

Gabino Iglesias author of Coyote Songs

'A mesmerising glimpse into the abyss of small-town horror worthy of Stephen King; lifting the lid on the ugliness that lies beneath the surface.'

Tracy Fahey author of *The Unheimlich Manoeuvre*

'*Tome* is a truly horrifying novel, flowing with a dark lyricism that echoes the best moments of Clive Barker, Shirley Jackson, and Jack Ketchum. It is awash in the uncanny, dripping with Lovecraftian chaos, driven by a mortality and curiosity that lingers in us all. The tension and appeal of this books is a hypnotic spell, cast with a gleaming eye, a siren song we cannot turn away from, leading to a certain demise. This is a powerful book written by an emerging master storyteller.'

Richard Thomas, Thriller Award nominee of *Breaker*, and *Disintegration*

'Jeffery has crafted a truly dark look into the deep crevices that slither just below the surface of the town and the people of Juniper. Tome is a follow up that grows more horrific with each turn of the page.'

Steve Stred author of Ritual

'Ross Jeffery's work evokes the insidious menace of past masters. Prepare to be scared.'

Kealan Patrick Burke, Bram Stoker Award-winning author of *KIN* and *SOUR CANDY*

ALSO BY ROSS JEFFERY

Juniper

Tethered

For my beautiful daughter Eva

- You make me proud every day. Just keep being you as everyone else is already taken... you're perfect don't ever change -

First published in Great Britain in 2020 by The Writing Collective. Copyright ©
Ross Jeffery 2019

ISBN: 979-8647-50407-4

Cover art from Pixabay.

Created in Canva.

Cover designed and formatting by Ross Jeffery.

TOME

JUNIPER BOOK II

ROSS JEFFERY

'There are some secrets which do not permit themselves to be told. Men die nightly in their beds, wringing the hands of ghostly confessors, and looking them piteously in the eyes – die with despair of heart and convulsion of throat, on account of the hideousness of mysteries which will not suffer themselves to be revealed.'

Edgar Allan Poe
(*The Man of the Crowd* 1845)

PROLOGUE

L ight fell into the room from the single small window, the moon outside a large incandescent plate in the sky. Perched on the side of his bed, sweat pouring from his body, Jasper Legg gripped a book. Knuckles white, pages crumpled in his grasp.

He sat wrestling with an unseen foe boiling up within him. His mind was present, but occupied by the internal struggle, and did not fully register his surroundings. Legg reached a hand up and scratched his stubble. His face pained, haunted like those gaunt faces that stared out from the chain linked fences beneath the sign of Arbeit Macht Frei... but Jasper still had work to do before he was a free man. He slid his hand from his face to the back of his neck and gripped the muscles, slowly but powerfully massaging the ever-present ache. The book slid from lap to bed, where his hand gripped it just as tightly.

Rain thundered off the cars parked outside and slashed through the leaves on the trees. The drainpipe overflowed where moss and leaves hadn't been emptied and the water dripping became an axe chopping wood on the window-sill. It formed an orchestra of static noise, enough to drive most insane. Jasper was already at that destination.

Crazy Town: Population One.

The book stayed on the bed as he stood, knees cracking as they extended. He strode over the rough concrete floor to the window, the dirt of a hundred dead men cold beneath his bare feet. He stretched onto tiptoes to gaze out at the town asleep in the distance. Lights punctuated the town's dark silhouette, as if someone had punched holes in a piece of card held up to a bulb. The little dots reminded him briefly that somewhere life was still moving on, without him. Darkness had not won out yet.

Jasper's eyes were drawn to the water tower, the moonlight bouncing off its monolithic structure. In the moon's glow, he could see the red and white of the American flag which decorated the dome. His fingers traced the name of the town etched below the flag.

JUNIPER

The sight helped ground him when he felt lost and alone. His thoughts, although jumbled, were gaining a kind of clarity.

A face appeared in the shape of the trees surrounding the prison, where the moonlight was erased in the thick canopy. It was a face he could never forget. His first. Jasper's eyes continued to rove, following the streetlights until he found the place he'd shot Gregory Nelson. Nelson had been sitting at his seat in the town's bustling watering hole and Jasper didn't take kindly to someone like that getting one over him in his town.

Jasper had followed Gregory Nelson out into the night after he'd refused to give up his seat and Jasper's constant goading hadn't had the desired effect of starting a brawl. Jasper figured this Gregory was one of those equality types, an entitled, defiant sonofabitch. Jasper had stalked Gregory while he was walking down the 701, hugging the shadows, slinking in and out of ditches like a rattlesnake. When they had got far enough from town, Jasper'd made his move. He'd drawn up alongside Gregory, pulled Gregory into a ditch and shot him six times in the head. Once would have been enough, but Jasper wanted to destroy him.

When the police had finally found him a few weeks later, there wasn't much to identify the body. Coyotes, or some other wild animal, had been feasting on what remained of him. The skull was completely missing, carried off in the night as a trophy of some sort. His body was a tattered mess. They found his wallet in his jeans pocket, the only thing they had left to identify the body. In the end, the death was put down as a possible hit and run. Wrong place. Wrong time.

There were other landmarks in Juniper that drew Jasper's attention: the town square, where he'd slashed a stranger across the face; the bar where he'd been thrown out more nights for causing various disturbances than he'd been let in; the town hall, where he'd smashed the window by putting a trash can through it when they'd refused his right to freedom of speech. He'd been telling people how it really was, how jews and blacks were taking over and that the townsfolk needed to purify Juniper of this cancerous horde before it was too late.

But it was the building out toward the swelling river which now held his attention. The dilapidated, charcoaled, roofless skeleton of the building where he'd been apprehended.

Jasper had been found at the burning property like some macabre magician that'd just appeared out of smoke. He'd been swaying in time with the undulating grey and black tendrils. The officer that had found him on the scene stated Jasper had been in some sort of fugue state, an unholy rictus etched onto his soot covered face. His eyes were reported to have been vacant, the only thing living in them the dancing flames suspended in glassy clarity. He had been remanded into custody while the town waited for the fire to be put out and an investigation of the scene to be completed. Many folks had a feeling he'd be arrested for arson, but would soon be out to terrorise the town once more, a lot of shit was slung his way but none of it ever stuck. How wrong they ended up being.

When the smoke had cleared, and the firefighters had dampened the inferno, the authorities made the grisly discovery of seven bodies, charred and shrivelled up like long dead flies on a window ledge, arms and legs drawn in to what remained of their bodies. It became clear that many despicable acts had been carried out by Jasper. The prosecutor at the trial had pronounced Juniper to have its very own Ed Gein to put them on the map.

Each corpse had been decapitated. The heads were never discovered – Jasper had giddily announced he would be taking that secret to the grave. The remains, all unidentifiable, were picked over by investigators like vultures over carrion. They had found short, sharpened poles which appeared to have been imbedded in the flesh pre-death, through various orifices. Teeth marks had marked the bones. It became clear once the bones had been washed those marks were not made by wild animals, but the beast that was Jasper. Large steel nails jutted out of the crispy, carbon rich flesh of those bodies that had been discovered near the outskirts of the blaze, a sadistic game of pin the tail on the donkey had been played on those who'd tried to crawl from the flames. The psychopath had had fun with them before finally snuffing out their lives.

Jasper lowered his frame, slipping down from tiptoes, ankles clicking as they were released of the tension that had held him there during his reverie. He robotically slunk back to his bed and collapsed onto the hard mattress. He reached under his pillow and pulled out a letter. As Jasper turned it over in his hands, he stopped and began to stare at the address written on the front. He held it, fingering the script, tracing the ink with his fingers.

Something moved behind him. His fingers tightened against the enveloped letter, crinkling the edges. He glanced frantically over his shoulder and observed the walls of his cell. The solid beam of ivory light carved up the darkness of his dwelling, separating it into Above and Below. The darkest corners of the room seemed to swell, as if something were lurking, breathing within them, its bulk falling with each exhalation.

He tried to pierce the black voids as he stared into them, but fear gripped him. His neck hurt as he stretched further forward, trying to locate the sound, a sound that seemed so out of place. Unsure if he were dreaming or not, Jasper tried to filter out both the noise of the rain which continued its downpour in sheets outside his window and the dissonance of other tiny sounds fighting with one another to be heard.

"Heeeerrreeee..."

The voice seemed to claw through the gritted teeth of someone unseen, a breath that continued until the word had been exhaled and abruptly ceased.

Jasper shook his head; was his mind playing tricks on him again? He couldn't pinpoint the noise. It appeared to start in the upper corner of the room and finish in the lowest corner, moving through the utter darkness. He reached behind him and picked up the book.

"No. Not now..." he blurted out, as his fingers flipped open the book, his hands shaking as he placed the letter between two pages.

Jasper threw the book down on his pillow. "It... it's too soon, I thought I had more time... I thought *we* had more time?"

His utterance was met with silence. He turned back to the darkness, his eyes desperately trying to adjust to the contrast of light and dark in the room. He rose from the bed and took a tentative step forward.

"*Sssstttooopppppp...*" The word came out like a rattlesnake ready to strike.

Jasper wobbled, his body slowly retracting his hesitant step forward. "What do you want with me?" he croaked into the void.

Silence.

"What do you want from meeeee?!" He screamed with a ferocious persistence until his lungs gave up and his words drifted away into a rasping wheezy cough, which brought him to his knees, spluttering until he steadied himself. Jasper lifted his gaze, noticing a wisp reaching out, almost like smoke, dancing toward him in the light. Then, as suddenly as it was discovered, he heard something skitter away from the light and the tendril was gone. The skitter climbed up the wall and retreated to the left side of the room, the darkness swelling as if a body had just dropped into a pool of water.

"*Come into the... light, Jasper...*" The voice was smooth like whiskey, an enticing and intoxicating call. "*Come Jasper, let... me gaze upon you once more.*"

Jasper took another faltering step, this time into the column of light. He stood captive within the beam, his shadow blocking out the light that spilled in through the window, allowing more darkness to spread to the left side of the room, where the voice resided – for the time being. Jasper could feel the air to his left being whipped into a frenzy from something thrashing about in the dark. He shuffled slightly and a shard of light broke the darkness, spearing its way through the gloom, sending the stalking presence scuttling back to the depths of shadow.

"Don't try to ssseek me out... you must trust me, Jasper... do you trusssst... me?" The voice came from the darkness again, pained, as if the light had hurt it.

"I... I do. But you... left me."

"Don't quessssstion, Jasper... you must only obey. That... is what I ask of all... my children. You musssst trust your master. Our work here is almost... complete. Are you willing to trust me... again?"

Jasper turned back to face the wall, blocking out the light yet again. He steadied himself, a soldier at attention awaiting orders that he would follow blindly. "I... I am." The words tumbled from Jasper's mouth without his intent, but he was soon aware of the weight of those two small words when they fell into the room and were ravenously devoured by the black void.

"Goooood..."

Jasper's unease was as palpable as the shadows grew thick and eddied around his legs, informing him it needed attention, that it needed *something*, its hunger tenacious and unrelenting.

A methodical tapping, as if the legs of a giant millipede were rippling down its body in waves, crossed the floor. Jasper felt hooks latch on to his pants then begin crawling their way up his body. The darkness pawed at him, climbing higher and higher. He could hear it breathing as it neared his neck, but it was cold, like a winter's breeze. It sent a shiver down his spine. Fingers continued to latch on, moving within the darkness; it felt as though a colony of tarantulas had crawled over him. The concealed being stopped, a weight upon his shoulder.

"Move forward..."

Jasper moved through the light, his own shadow concealing the tormentor until he passed out of the bifurcating beam spilling through the window. The being came alive within the safety of the dark, scuttling and groping the other side of Jasper's head, moving around him like water.

"Ssssstop here. Listen to... me, obey what I... tell you..."

Jasper's mind flashed to a vision of Annette, and he wondered if she'd felt this fear when he had forced her body to become ramrod straight by hammering a steel pike down her gullet and out the other end, the rod imbedding in the ground a human scarecrow for eternity.

"I want you... to hit the wall..."

Jasper reached out to the wall, judging the distance in the darkness. He could feel the photos and newspaper articles he'd tacked to the wall, a gallery of all his little atrocities. He shuffled to the right, feeling brick underneath clammy fingers. Jasper pulled his hand back, and punched the wall.

A crunch echoed in the room. He winced at the pain; something was broken, he was sure of it, but he couldn't stop. He was powerless to deny his aggressor. So he began to prepare for another punch, arm cocked and ready to fire again.

"Tut... tut... tut..."

Jasper heard the sounds begin in his right ear and warp into his left. It was all around him, ensnaring him within a blanket.

"Again..." spat the darkness.

Jasper was about to release his coiled arm to strike the brick, when the voice interrupted.

"This time... with your head."

"My... head?" Jasper whispered back.

"... do you disobey... the one who leads?"

"No... I..."

"Then... Again!" The voice shouted, formed this time of many voices, but answering as one.

Jasper planted both of his palms on the wall, the cool brick matching the cold breath at his neck. He could feel the darkness *breathing,* deep powerful breaths, like bellows blowing rancid air over him.

"NOW!" the voice commanded, and without further thinking Jasper pulled his head back and swung it into the brick. He felt the sickening crunch as his skull connected with the wall, his teeth chattering in his head with the contact. In a daze, he pulled his head back. It felt as if parts of his head were being left behind. Something warm trickled down from his forehead, snaking down his nose, dribbling over his lips and wetting his chest. He shook his head to clear the new fogginess, and like a dog shaking its wet fur, he released a torrent of blood that momentarily blinded him, stinging his eyes. He reached up a hand to wipe away the blood, feeling a deep and ragged crevice snaking across his forehead.

"Again..." the voice commanded, and Jasper followed the call. His head met the wall. Something cracked.

"Again..."

Jasper swung his head forward like a hammer. He felt his orbital socket connect to the brick with a crunch. His legs wobbled beneath him. Blood streamed freely from the gaping cuts that covered the meaty jigsaw that had been his face. His head lolled to the side, a punch-drunk boxer waiting for someone to throw in the towel, but he knew the towel was never going to come. There was no one in his corner, just a venomous, controlling, baying darkness – willing him to ruin himself, again and again and...

"Again..."

"I... I... can't..." Jasper slurred, as if some internal wiring had come loose, a computer unable to boot up.

"You can... and you will... again. Again. Again!"

With a surge of energy, Jasper wrecked himself upon the brickwork, blood flying with every recoil and thudding connection. His left leg buckled beneath him and he collapsed to one knee, his hands sliding down the wall. His other leg buckled and he was now kneeling in a warm, slick puddle of his own making.

"One... more time..." the voice trickled out.

Jasper, exhausted and folded before the wall as if in a prayerful lament, placed his arms behind him so he wouldn't be tempted to stop the carnage even if he wanted to, leaned back, and with one final effort, using every ounce of momentum he could generate, swung his head like a sledge hammer. Skull met brick for the last time as he collapsed into a twitching bloody mess on the floor.

The many hands of darkness consumed him, tearing what glimmer of a soul remained away, piece by rotting piece.

CHAPTER 1

F rank Whitten was decidedly not a morning person. But the smell of coffee seemed to drag him and guide him out of his stupor like a ring in a bull's nose. He had no other option but to follow its bitter scent. He stretched and felt the bed next to him, his hand padding at the vacated side where his wife would usually be. It was cold. She had always been the morning person and the bed had long been empty, but as of late it always seemed empty when he wanted her. He pushed away from her space.

As Frank perched on the side of his bed, he could hear the rain typewriting against his window. It was relentless, and sometimes the wind would pick up as if someone was hammering those keys in a burst of madness. Made him think of Jack Torrance. He glanced at the clock more out of habit than necessity. It was just after six, the same time he woke up every morning. He was a man of routine, and kept that routine no matter what. Frank reached over and turned off the alarm before it had a chance to scream.

He rotated his wrists as he reached to rub his neck. After a few circles, he moved his hands along his shoulders then down to his chest. His muscles strained and groaned under their sudden activity of massages. His calves burned when he raised his leg to stretch them out. With a deep sigh, he skulked into the bathroom where he pissed rusty urine. He'd known better than to drink all that booze last night, but work had been hard and he'd needed a way to relax. Guilt ate at his subconscious as he gave himself a shake and flushed. The cramping in his stomach made him debate taking a seat, but he was on a very precise schedule and there wasn't a minute extra for his innards to decide if they wanted to excrete themselves or not.

He walked over to the sink, turned on the hot water faucet, and waited for the heat to push out the cold. The cabinet squeaked as he opened it to pull out the shaving cream and razor. Staring at his reflection in the mirror, he pulled the skin down under his eyes, seeing how completely bloodshot they were. He stuck out his tongue and inspected it, half-expecting to be greeted by a rug of fuzz. He began massaging his cheeks with the shaving foam. When the water warmed, he began to shave. He should have stopped at the second can, but got carried away, just like every time before, and one full six-pack later, well... his body was letting him know just how fucked he was. He sighed as he tapped the razor against the sink and wiped his face. Frank pulled a bottle out of the cupboard and took a huge swig of Pepto Bismol.

He could always start over... again.

As he wandered into the kitchen while buckling his belt through his tan uniform pants, he narrowly avoided the chair leg that would scuff his otherwise immaculately polished black boots. The sore head was joined by the sting from nicking himself, tissue adorning the cleft of his chin and near the corner of his mouth. Truth was, he needed a new razor, but his wife wasn't going to be getting him one anytime soon.

At least there was the siren call of caffeine. He shambled over to the coffee pot of hot, molten goodness and poured himself a wake-up call. His mug was where his wife usually left it, by the answering machine, and a note – that appeared to have been scrunched up and then flattened out again – informing him she had gone out for an early morning run and not to wait for her before he set off for the day.

Frank reached up and pulled back the sheer curtain over the kitchen window. The rain was rushing down the pane. "Damn crazy woman. Gonna catch her death in that." He blew over the top of his raised cup and watched the steam billow off the other side before taking a sip. He noticed yesterday's newspaper was open at the table and he sat down to read.

Half an hour later, Frank rose from the table. The coffee and the Pepto Bismol seemed to have soothed his aching stomach and throbbing head, at least for the moment. He'd been doing the cross-word but was stuck on "Casually unconcerned (10 down)" so he left the paper folded to the puzzle and circled it for his wife to finish when she got back from her run. As he put his pen in his pocket, he thought about scribbling his wife a note about pulling a double and not to wait up for him... but he knew she wouldn't see it, so he didn't bother.

Frank approached the front door and reached up to the coat rack, removed his brown jacket and slid it on, zipping it up tight. Each morning played out like Groundhog Day- same shit, different day - but he loved his routine and wouldn't change it for the world. He opened the drawer to the dresser in the hallway and withdrew a shiny pair of metal handcuffs, clipped them to his belt and then reached back in and withdrew his state issued handgun. Unclipping his holster on his belt, he slid the gun in and re-clasped the leather catch. The last item he pulled from the drawer was a gold badge. It was in the shape of a shield and had *Juniper Correctional* embossed in black letters across the front. He rubbed it on his trouser leg to buff it and make it shine a little more, then hooked it onto his jacket pocket. As he took one last assessment of all his gear, his heart whispered a wish for just one morning where his wife was still home before he left. He sighed and opened the door, plunging out into the rain.

It was only a few yards from the front porch to the car, but Frank was totally drenched as he fell into his Honda. He wondered how his wife would be coping in the rain. She'd be a bedraggled, muddy mess by the time she got back. Frank slammed the car door and sat there for a moment, trying to shake the rain and the guilt he felt for drinking again. It was a conversation he didn't want to have with his wife, and pulling a double was a way around that for a while, but as he thought about the eventual confrontation, about his wife's sad face staring back at him, the ache in the pit of his stomach returned, and it wouldn't leave him however much he tried to ignore it. It only got worse as he thought about her faith in him, in his ability to stop.

Frank never had faith of his own. He'd borrowed his wife's for a long time, offering prayers to a god he was unsure existed, but the belief in his wife's eyes made him yearn for that type of steadfast certainty. Recently he'd made inroads with the groups, or *meetings* as they called them. After attending for a while, he was following *The 12 Steps*, managing to scale each one and in the end, offered himself to this higher power that welcomed him with open arms. It had been working. He felt he could cope; he was carrying less of a burden and things were more manageable. He was getting better, but this time every year he wobbled and fell off the wagon. If his wife found out how bad things had got, she'd be spitting feathers.

The rain thudded onto the roof of the car, sounding similar to the enraged prisoners hitting their cell doors after an imposed lock down, deafening and growing all the time. The window was a watery blur as the torrents of water flooded down from the roof. Frank glanced up at the rearview and noticed that he still had that damn tissue stuck to his face. He pulled the little pieces off, smarting from the sting as they tore away from their bloody moorings. The drinking was just a blip, he reassured himself. A bump in the road. He just needed another meeting, but he'd have to do that after work, so he just offered up his mantra to the hammering rain.

"Lord, grant me the serenity to accept the things I cannot change, courage to change the things I can, and wisdom to know the difference." Frank put the key into the ignition and the car spluttered into life.

Ten minutes later, Frank pulled into the parking lot of Juniper Correctional. He'd usually walk from home, but this whole week had been nothing but torrential rain, and gloom seemed to be constantly draped over the town of late. However much the sun tried, it couldn't seem to shift the veil of darkness.

Frank parked in his usual bay, continuing his daily routine. He checked his watch. It was a point of pride with him to always be a little early, and never, ever late. He deeply exhaled as he sat contemplating the day set out before him, down to the minutest of details. Frank was a stickler for routine, and the next point of it was in a few minutes, with morning rounds. He waited a few seconds longer, enjoying his current oasis before he commenced his double shift. The car blowers had warmed his body and had begun to dry his clothes. Frank huffed to himself as he prepared himself for another drenching on his jog into the facility. Then he opened the door and bolted for the prison.

He buzzed into Juniper Correctional. The heavy door unlocked and creaked open on its rusted hinges, and he slid inside.

As the door clicked shut behind him, it was as if someone had hit the mute switch. The thundering, slashing, crashing of the rain was no more.

Standing there in the sudden silence, he could make out a whirring noise. He glanced up and watched the camera rotate over him in the holding cage as he stood there dripping like a drowned rat. A light on the camera flashed red as it pivoted back when Frank began waving. There was another high pitched, prolonged buzz, and he opened the cage. It swung shut when he released it, and he scooted along to stand opposite the Plexiglass window with a small bank style hollow in the counter. He pressed the bell on the desk. A sign next to it read *"For service, ring bell. For a black eye, ring it twice."* It had been taped down numerous times, but the yellowing tape was peeling up at the sides again like mouldy bread.

"I'm coming... I'm coming!" a hidden voice shouted, out of breath. A harried looking woman appeared at the glass a couple of seconds later. "Oh... Hi, Frank. Clocking in?"

"Yeah." Frank reached into his pocket and pulled out his cell phone, wallet, and car keys. He plopped them into the drawer. The drawer retracted and Frank's belongings materialised on the other side of the wall. "Busy morning, Nevaeh?"

"No, not really, just stuffing my face. Breakfast... er, my dinner anyway. My mother dropped off some blueberry muffins last night and I just can't get enough of them." Nevaeh removed the items from the drop box and placed them in a locker behind her. She returned to the window with his set of keys for the day. "You might wanna get changed. You look like a drowned rat. Oh, and here." She slid a baton under the window. "Looks like you left yours at home, and the Chief's on the war path."

"What now?"

"Does he need an excuse?"

"Yeah... you're right. Thanks for the heads up. I think I've got a spare jacket in the locker room." The drawer opened and Frank removed the huge bunch of keys. They jangled as he clicked them onto his belt.

"You have a good day now, Frank!"

"I'll be covering for Jenkins this evening. I'll make sure to drop off my overtime on the way out. You wouldn't be able to expedite the whole process, would you? It's the anniversary at the end of the week, and I ain't got a pot to piss in."

"Well, I'll see what I can do..." She gave him an innocent wink, but something in her eyes was sad. "I can't promise anything though, Frank." She paused a moment and said, "You okay? Things good?"

"Yeah... Everything's good. Thanks, Nevaeh. You take care now!" Frank turned to walk away then quickly doubled back to the window, catching Nevaeh stuffing her mouth with a massive piece of muffin, the blueberry staining her top lip as crumbs fell onto the paperwork below her. She stared back at him like a child caught stealing cake.

"One last thing..." he proffered, and Nevaeh swallowed hard. Frank knew she loved gossip, so he motioned her towards the glass with his hand as if to confide in her. Licking the crumbs from her lips, she leaned forwards. He whispered, "Make sure you save me one of those!"

A while later, Frank was standing with the other officers on the middle deck of the cell block. The buzzer sounded, followed by the mechanical clanks of the cell locks releasing. The doors to the "pens" as the inmates called them, opened with a rusty screech. Each inmate was locked up at night, many by themselves, though some had company. It wasn't uncommon to find various prisoners transferred into one cell or out of another. But roll call was the same each morning: same drill, same time, same routine. Frank loved the formality of the whole thing.

Inmates staggered out from their holes, stretching, rubbing their eyes, firing glances that tried to maim those they wanted to cause harm. They walked up to the railings which overlooked the concourse below.

Prisoners were required to stand with hands on the top rail until a full room check had been carried out and a roll call performed. Frank took the lead, as he did most mornings when he pulled the early shift. He loved every part of his job. He was extremely mindful of the rules, but he treated each inmate equally and took pride in knowing that was what they liked about him, even the brutes that could snap him like a twig. They knew that he was fair, had no favourites, and was above corruption. Frank was the son of a marine. He had learnt how to look after himself, and the strict lifestyle he'd grown up in had taught him the importance of listening to authority even when he didn't agree. He tried to share that with the inmates, that he knew it was tough but they had to knuckle under to make it through.

Frank observed the other guards mingling on the platform. He felt their eyes on him, judging him for being such a taskmaster. Some had pity in their gaze and it suffocated him for some reason. Frank wanted out, so he began walking down the line, keys jangling at his hip, his feet clanking on the meshed metal apparatus that served as a bridge.

"Morning, Jim."

"Frank."

"How's things, Michael?"

"Been better; you fancy letting me out today?"

"Fat chance, but I like your tenacity. You keep asking and one of these days I might just open those gates for you myself."

He paused as he approached the next cell. "Sid, you lose weight?"

The inmate had a post-coital glow about him. "If anything, I think my wrist might be getting bigger," Sid replied, his brow slick with sweat.

Frank moved past more inmates, exchanging pleasantries. He stopped just before the last cell. No one stood in front of the open door. He checked his clipboard. He knew who was in there, but wanted to make sure they hadn't been swapped out in the night, or moved to isolation or the medical ward.

"Jasper?" Frank called. There was silence. He placed a hand on his baton. A silent thanks winged its way back to Nevaeh. His sidearm would only escalate here but the baton ensured order. In all his time at Juniper correctional, he'd never once had to draw his gun, but he'd be a fool if he thought he would never need it. The moment that thought crept in was the moment a guard ended up leaving in a zipped-up bag. He'd rather be judged by twelve than carried out by six.

He edged forward. "Inmate Legg. Step out onto the gangway, now!"

The remaining inmates craned their necks, staring at the current showdown of wills. A murmur erupted from somewhere around him. The air thickened with palpable excitement over a potential fight.

Frank began to peer around the edge of the cell door. His body was tense, ready to draw his service weapon at a moment's notice. "You better be pretty sick in there or have a dead good excuse!" He stepped into the doorway and immediately lurched to the side. His brain seemed to automatically compartmentalise what he was witnessing, shutting down the reality he was seeing. Nausea swept through him like a ship tossed in a storm.

Frank turned back to the audience of Juniper's most repellent men. Each wore a look of expectancy. The other guard on Frank's floor had begun yelling at the inmates to stay where they were, as he hustled around the perimeter over to Frank. There were hushed voices and keys jangling as guards leaned out from below to look up at the upper railing. The guards on the row above stopped their idle chatting and glanced down at the sudden noise and movements below. Frank held up a hand, informing them to stay where they were. He rubbed the back of his head.

The guards stared at him expectantly, waiting to leap into action.

Frank cleared his throat. "We've got another one!"

CHAPTER 2

The entire cell block was a hive of activity. Guards armed with mops and rags, buckets of hot water, and plastic bags, walked between the lower floor, where they emptied the dirty water and refilled with clean, back up to the second, where they passed other guards taking out more buckets. As Juniper Correctional was struggling financially, it had fallen to the guards to take on more responsibilities. The cleaning crew had been the first to go once the budget cuts came. Jobs that the populace didn't want usually went to the immigrants that were hungry for work. But, as is so often the case, they were the first ones to get the boot when times got tough. No severance pay. No warning. Just told that they were no longer needed. Warden Fleming was also kind enough to call the local PD on the day of the cleaners' dismissal and have them all corralled up and sent back to the border, deported and dejected. Immigrants got kicked out, and guards got kicked in the ass by a Warden drunk on being seen as fiscally responsible.

The small cell was bursting at the seams with six guards fret-

ting over washing the walls. Frank stood near the door, observing
the erasure of the carnage that had taken place within. For once, he
let the younger guards do the grunt work. He figured since he
normally did the hard work, they could do this one. He crossed his
arms as he looked from one side to the other.

To the left of the cell door was a canvas of ghastly brown
smears, handprints long since dried, and several indentations in the
crumbling brickwork. The wall was flecked with small shards of
white that glinted in the light. It was easy enough to decipher what
they were when Frank's gaze travelled down the wall to the beginning of Jasper's body on the floor. The face was crumpled in on
itself like a spoilt pumpkin. His eyes were poached blue eggs in
gory holes. What was left of the rest of Legg's body lay in a brown
puddle of solidifying fluids, his limbs splayed around him like a
parody of a crime scene chalk line. What puzzled Frank the most
was how Jasper had managed to shred his skin so completely
before he'd smashed his head in.

Two guards emerged from the cell with grimaces tightening
their faces. Frank walked inside, stepping around another two
guards busying themselves with the corpse and the body bag,
which was lying on the floor near the bed. The task had been
made even more difficult by the frantic searches for life they had
performed upon arrival, which had made their hands slick.
Wasn't like the body could have drawn a scream, let alone a
breath. Anyone could see Legg had been dead a while from the
bashed skull, but some of these officers were still green, and so
they followed procedures to the letter, regardless of whether it
made sense or not. Frank did have to respect the adherence to
the rules. For a few of the newbies, he thought it may have been
the first dead body they'd ever encountered. *They'll soon get
used to it working here,* Frank mused as he stood at the head of
the bed. Those green officers would soon be gone anyway,

replaced by crooks on the take. It was the Juniper prison cycle of life.

Frank turned to face the wall, observing that one spot was clearly the epicentre of the carnage. It looked like someone had hung a disturbing Jackson Pollock on the wall. He fought the bile rising in his throat. Whether it was from the horror show or from not eating, he couldn't tell. His lips puckered.

"Y'alright, Frank?" one of the officers asked.

"Yeah... sorry. Officer Petty, isn't it? I was just..." Frank shook his head. "It doesn't matter. You need a hand?"

"No, it's okay, we've got this. Thanks." Officer Petty and the guard with him started to reach under the body, trying to find somewhere to lift it from.

Frank turned to walk past as they laboured to lift the stricken Legg. He heard a squelch as they pulled the body from its gory fixings. He glanced over his shoulder and saw the guards share a look. Jasper's head had rolled to the side and juices that had pooled in the crater where his face should have been dribbled out on to the floor. It was soon followed by a wet thud as they dropped the remains into the body bag.

"Fuck!" cried the other officer. "Got fucking brain and shit all over my shoes!"

"I think you'll live, Larry" muttered Officer Petty.

"Whaddya think drives someone to do something like this?" Larry began wiping his boot on the bedsheets, leaving bloody skid-marks on the yellowed sheets. "What was going through his head?"

"The wall," Frank said dryly, as he turned to them, a faint smile on his face. There was a moment as the officers tried to figure out what he said. His words seemed to hang in the air, like the smell of death that lingered in the room, then the joke seemed to land and they began to laugh. Frank assumed they were laughing with him, but they could have quite easily been laughing at him.

Officer Petty shook his head with a small grin. "That's a good one, Frank... But, really, what would drive someone to end it like this?" He stooped to grab the zipper, pulling the flap over the flattened head, and sealed the two poached eggs within the darkness.

"Hard to say." Frank scratched his chin. "I mean, what drives people to do the unspeakable acts that get them thrown in here in the first place, finding themselves in this stewing pot of hatred and disregard?"

Petty stood up and glanced over to the wall. "But you must have some idea. I mean, you've been working here longer than I've been alive! No offence, of course."

"None taken." Frank shrugged. "I don't know. I think a person could drive themselves crazy trying to reason it all, trying to fix people. Sometimes there ain't enough sticky tape or Band-Aids that can fix those type of deep-rooted wounds." He walked over to the bloody carnage sprayed on the brickwork. "Y'know, my wife once said something to me, which, when I think about it now, is quite profound. It's something I live by, something that I try to do each day. It'd do you guys good to learn it, too. She said, 'Everyone you meet is fighting a battle you know nothing about. Be kind. Always.'" Frank reached up and pulled one of the photos tacked on the side of the cell. Blood had splattered across the faded picture of a young baby in a woman's arms. He studied it.

"That is profound," Officer Petty agreed. He nodded to the photo. 'What do you have there?"

"No idea. But it's one of the only personal effects Jasper had; must have been important to him... I guess it should go with him." Frank turned and handed the picture to Petty, nodding down to the cocooned body. As Petty bent down, nausea gripped Frank; he didn't want Petty to open the bag again, didn't want to see those eyes looking at him. Petty unzipped the bag, placed the photo inside, and all three men avoided looking directly at what lay within. Frank moved across the room, turning his back to the bloody endgame of Legg.

Larry cracked his neck. "Right, gotta get this down and processed."

"Yep. Finish this and get back to the day."

The way they spoke about the dead made Frank feel like his wife's wisdom had fallen on deaf ears. They were treating Jasper as a task instead of a person. It irked him, but he let the moment go without scolding them.

Petty called over his shoulder, "See you around, Frank!"

The two officers picked up the body bag and began shuffling from the room, as if they were carrying a roll of carpet that sagged in the middle. Legg's liquid, heavy mass bumped into the door several times as he was removed from the last room he'd been alive in. Lifting him high, they dumped him onto the waiting stretcher as someone would dump a bag of dirty laundry. Their voices grew faint as they wheeled the body off and they disappeared down the gangway.

Frank was alone. He couldn't recall the other officers leaving, but at some point they must have, busying themselves with grunt work. He didn't have long before other living bodies came in to finish the clean up and get the room turned around for its next occupant. Frank glanced down at the stains on the sheets that Larry had left. He twisted his body to lower his head and look under the bed, trying to find something that would explain Jasper's final moments. He didn't want to kneel down in the massive pool of blood, so he craned his neck further. There was nothing out of the ordinary: a few hidden sweets, packs of cigarettes, a Playboy magazine – contraband, but who'd care now? He left them where they were, knowing that the clean-up team would see that they were put back into the populous at a cost, or for a favour.

As Frank straightened up, he noticed a book tossed on Jasper's pillow. It had a dark cracked cover with an extremely faded title. He could see it was dog-eared and torn at the edges, yellowed pages like smokers' teeth. Frank stepped over the gelling blood pool and picked it up. He opened the front cover and noticed numerous stamps on the first blank page.

Property of Shady Mountain Mental Hospital

Property of Oswald Federal Mens Penitentiary

Please Return to Huttinson Island Public Library

Property of Maine Sex Reassignment Clinic

Property of Juniper Correctional Facility

Frank flipped the book over and shook it out. He flipped it back upright and thumbed through, pages flicking past in a blur. No contraband. As he clapped the covers shut, he walked over to the window and stared out. The rain obscured his view and the clouds were dark and menacing. He turned back to the room and noticed a letter had fallen to the floor. Blood seeped into the porous envelope. Frank stooped to pick it up, and tried to wipe the blood off with his hand, but only succeeded in smearing it. He turned the letter over and noticed an address on it.

Two guards entered the cell, each with a bucket of water and mop. Frank slipped the letter into his back pocket, squeezed past them, and headed down the metal walkway, keys jangling at his side while shouts from the locked-up inmates rang in his ears.

CHAPTER 3

Slumped in his green leather office chair, Warden Hezekiah Fleming tapped thick fingers on cracked armrests. He scratched his head, further scarring the bald spot that was already raw. He inspected the skin under his fingernails before wiping the sweat from his puffy face. It wasn't even after ten in the morning, and he had already been through a hell of a day.

Fleming sat at a desk that dwarfed the office, oak and ostentatiously decorated. Hunting trophies littered the surface as well as the tops of the filing cabinets around the room, forever stuck in ridiculous poses. A woodchuck perched atop a cabinet glared at incoming visitors; he'd bagged it one day when he'd been out roaming around the prison's perimeter. A small confederate flag was grasped in its paw leaving no doubt to his Dixie allegiance. But just in case it wasn't clear, Fleming had hung a full-size flag on the wall next to the door, for people to see as they left. A line of squirrels stood sentinel on his desk next to the overflowing ashtray and marbled name plaque, which sat front and centre on his desk. He was the Warden, and no one was allowed to forget it.

Paperwork lay strewn out before him- APBs from other systems, bills, incident reports from the days and weeks prior. He only kept it scattered to make others think he was very busy. As a rule, he was only ever busy drinking. He glanced to his left to take in the bank of monitors. They'd been installed to give him the opportunity to keep an ever present and dutiful eye on proceedings within the prison without ever having to leave his seat. Why should he be out there with them when he could observe from the comfort of his office while sipping on scotch? The guards, however, knew that the cameras were a part of the busyness front, so he could always be ready if someone approached his office, and allow him time to slip the bottle of scotch back into the drawer.

He scanned the images, flicking at random intervals between differing angles. The prisoners were still in their cells since the morning's discovery, an imposed lockdown until the dust had settled. The guards milled about, chatting, going about their other many duties.

Fleming turned back to his paper pile, slowly moving his body over to his desk drawer and reaching in for his secret, usually-filled-with-scotch glass. He drained the remaining dregs before picking up his pack of smokes. Letting the momentum of his turn roll his chair around away from the monitors, he stopped in front of the floor-to-ceiling window which was the main feature of the room. He placed a cigarette in his mouth and searched his pocket for a lighter. His finger stroked the engraving. *Warden Fleming, for Thirty-Five Years of Service.* Leaning back in the chair, he flipped open the lid, rolled the lighter down his trouser leg in a swift and deliberate motion, the wheel spinning and igniting the gas. Out of habit, his fingers drummed against his leg to tap out any lingering spark with a hunger for pant fabric.

The yellow flame wavered as if afraid to meet the cigarette's end. His hands were shaking from deprivation of scotch. He'd only had two and he usually had had four, and what with the additional stress of another dead inmate, his nerves couldn't take it. He needed to kill them and kill them quickly. He craved something to dull the feelings and delay the paperwork, the phone calls, the police investigation, not to mention Juniper Correctional's upcoming examination. But, before he allowed himself a drink, he'd have his cigarette first.

He inhaled deeply as he slipped his lighter into the breast pocket of his jacket, and gazed out of the window, licking his lips, enjoying his nicotine cuisine – he knew that worries would follow soon enough. The smoke mirrored the grey fog twisting around the rope dangling from a suspended pulley arm, a bygone of Juniper's rural history.

When the prison had originally been constructed, the roof of the building had been designated as the spot where deliveries would be taken in and stored. Former heads of the institution figured there would be less chance of attempted prisoner escapes if deliveries never truly came into the grounds. The old pulley system, a type found in the eaves of barns all across the country, still stood at one end of the building like a hawk's beak jutting from the prison's otherwise sheer face. One of the history books the old cretin of a librarian had loaned Fleming had mentioned that the pulley arm used to also double as a gallows from time to time, used for hanging runaway slaves and sympathisers who needed redemption. Fleming's office sat directly below the intake room, and he was constantly aware of the oversized hempen scythe reminding him of the dead space above and the carnage below.

Supplies had not been the only thing delivered by the long arm outside. Times past had made use of the pulley to bring in medical equipment or to remove the dead from the access window. Bodies had been carted up to the attic and then lowered onto a stretcher outside a waiting hearse. But in all the years of Juniper Correctional's existence and of all the things to go out, no prisoner had ever used the pulley to escape. It was, frankly, a miracle.

Fleming watched the rope swing for a while. It was like watching a grandfather clock ticking, illuminated by the warm glow from his office lamps, which starkly contrasted with the scene outside. Rain was avalanching down his window, as if he were sitting in his Mustang at the car wash. It was unrelenting... but strangely calming, and that was exactly what he needed right now.

As Fleming observed the rain falling, his mind wandered further from the present. He'd started the head-honcho job when he was twenty-seven years old. "Too young!" doubters had said, but he had enjoyed proving those fuckers wrong. He'd been proving people wrong his whole life in Juniper. Absent parents had left him to drag himself up from the stereotypes and disdain heaped upon trailer park trash as he had been. He'd worked cash-in-hand jobs for the various shop owners who'd taken pity on him. Pity that had only been tolerated as long as it helped - helped him save money, helped him get the schooling and training he needed to make something of himself. He'd been his own fucking role model, showcasing how hard work, determination, and persistence could pay off. In Fleming's first year, he'd sworn to be the poster boy of the correctional world, the youngest and most cut-throat Warden this facility had ever had. Local pastors taught on the virtue of sparing the rod and spoiling the child but he scoffed at that. Every prisoner was one of his bastard children and he'd correct them when needed.

When Fleming had taken over the running of Juniper Correctional, Jackson Delmont had been the Warden incumbent who had been a sleazy lawyer of the worst kind - defending the scum that landed in the jail. Delmont had pretty much run the correctional facility into the ground, and with that many of the inmates. What money had funded the prison, Delmont would waste on various luxuries, because at that time no one would dare tackle the cantankerous Warden. People needed to eat, Juniper Correctional was the second biggest employer of the town after agriculture, and no one wanted to bite the hand that fed them, even if that hand only dropped scraps from the table. Scraps were enough. For a time, at least.

Delmont's end came when he was found after diving off the roof of Juniper Correctional headfirst; no suicide note, no family, and no obvious reason. But the rumour-mill could never be kept from churning. Some of the inmates had said it was a guard who'd pushed him. Others had blamed the weight of an extortion racket. One had even mentioned blackmail, an aggrieved ex-prisoner unhappy with late night callings in the dead of night.

For the town of Juniper, Fleming had been a breath of fresh air after the cesspool that had been Delmont. He had dragged Juniper Correctional out from its languid pit of despair by implementing an entirely new rule system. The inner workings of the prison had been updated, making things more streamlined, and he'd introduced a more person-centric approach to both guards and prisoners alike. The town warmly embraced their white knight saviour of the run-down establishment.

Fleming sighed between puffs of smoke as he drifted back to his current predicaments. His eyes landed on a photo of himself on the wall, all eager to take charge. His thick Southern accent pooled out of him like the smoke clouding his head, "Where did that time go?" He'd done it, he'd risen to the top, but he felt like he was about to be tossed aside by the town like a pus riddled bandage. *What happened to me?* he wondered as he stared at that strapping young man.

Shaking the thought from his head, he rubbed his stomach, diverting his eyes from the man he once was. He stubbed out his cigarette in the ashtray. A thick cloud curled over the edge of the bowl, tendrils creeping out from the grave of cancer sticks toward his chair. Fleming frowned. There was only so long he could push off the paperwork; he'd have to face facts soon enough. He reached into the desk and pulled out the bottle of scotch. Being behind in his drinking was a bigger concern than being behind in paperwork.

He lifted the glass to his mouth, slurping at the warming fuel. Still unsettled, he reached for his cigarettes. The gold lighter repeated the lighting ritual, rolling down his leg. The flame flickered as it touched the tobacco. Once it caught, he blew out a cloud of smoke and extinguished the light, snapping the lid closed. He placed the lighter on the desk and began shuffling the papers around, putting them into two piles - one to act on now, and one to worry about later. The cigarette wobbled between his lips. Fleming shuffled it around until it was snug in the corner of his mouth and the smoke trailed up the side of his face, whilst his hands were busy moving paperwork from one pile to the next. Ash dropped onto the paperwork and was briskly brushed off to join the stained carpet. There was a circle of grey around his rotating chair, like a line of salt used to ward off evil spirits.

Movement caught his peripheral vision. He turned to the monitors and noticed Frank, the most senior prison guard, striding toward his office. Fleming hated that sonofabitch, not that he'd ever let on why. As far as Fleming could tell, Frank just thought he was the usual aloof, cantankerous boss.

Fleming quickly downed his liquid courage and stowed the cup back in the desk drawer, sliding it shut. He grabbed some paperwork just as the monitor showed Frank raising his hand to knock on the door. "Come in!" Fleming called, his voice rough and authoritative.

The door began to groan open. Fleming straightened in his chair, trying to convey an air of authority. A halo of not-yet-dissipated smoke lingered in the air around him, like fog over the Juniper fields in the early morning.

"Sorry to bother you, Warden, but I thought you might like to see this." Frank marched up to the desk, his sudden movements creating ripples in the smoke within the still office.

"What is it? Ah'm extremely snowed under." Fleming snorted in exasperation at what was being handed to him. "A book? Ah don't have time for -"

"It was in Jasper's cell." Frank firmly placed the book into Fleming's stubby hands.

"Who?"

"Inmate Legg, sir," Frank replied.

Fleming realised the guard was standing at attention, all straight and stiff in body. He leaned back and steepled his fingers. "Ahh... Inmate Legg. Yes, Ah was just looking at the incident report." He paused and frowned at Frank. "Ah wish you'd stop growing attachments to these inmates, Frank. It's a weakness of yours. If you were my dog, Ah'd beat it out of you." There was an uneasy pause, in which Fleming thought about how much he'd love to beat that smug look off Frank's face, but he had a good thing going and didn't want to mess that up for a moment of brief insanity. "Call them bah their prison name. Saves a whole lot of confusion, don't it?"

"I'll try to remember that, sir."

Fleming turned the book over in his hand, observing the cracks in the aged cover. "What's the point of this, Frank?"

Frank gestured to the front. "It's what's inside, sir."

Fleming opened the book to find a letter. The envelope had what looked to be blood on it, so he tilted the book and allowed the envelope to fall onto his desk to avoid touching it. He placed the book to the side, and used his dagger styled letter opener to flip the envelope over to try and find the address. Fleming saw the dark

brown stain on the front that obscured the destination. Bloody
fingerprints and a smear where someone, Fleming assumed Frank,
had tried to wipe it off. "What is the meaning of this? This was
evidence, but now it's fucking ruined!"

"I believe it fell from the book whilst we were clearing the cell,
sir. I picked it up, but as you are aware," Frank nodded to the incident report on the desk, which he'd filed only a few hours previously, "it was a pretty bloody scene in there. The letter fell in some
of the blood and I was just trying to get it clean."

"Have you read it?" Fleming asked as he flipped the envelope
so the closed flap stared at the ceiling.

"No sir, I brought it straight here when it was discovered."

"At least you managed to do that correctly. Did anyone else see
you make a piss poor job of co-lecting evidence? Anyone... ah, see
the letter?" Fleming twiddled his dagger.

"I don't believe so sir... why?"

"No reason... just... well, y'know what the rumour mill is like
in this place. We don't want anyone saying you've been tam-pering
with evidence. Your secret's safe with me." Fleming picked up the
envelope, no longer bothering to keep it unsoiled. The dagger slid
silently through the sticky bond and severed it. From the corner of
his eye, he could see Frank eagerly waiting to see what the letter
contained. Fleming placed the small knife down on the table and
slid out the letter. It was one sheet, folded three times. Writing was
scrawled on both sides in jagged letters. Fleming began to
unfold it.

The phone rang.

The sudden high-pitched shriek made both men jump.
Fleming placed the letter on the desk in front of him and reached
for the phone. The writing looked like a spider had stepped in ink
and crawled across the page.

"Yes." Fleming barked into the receiver. "Oh... right. Don't keep 'em on hold any longer, go on and patch 'em through." The hard edge of Fleming's voice disappeared. He felt flustered and apprehensive, sweat breaking out on his clammy face. Fleming covered the phones mouthpiece. "That'll be all, Frank," he muttered. "Go on your way. Ah need to take this call - big boy stuff."

Frank stopped trying to crane his neck and read the letter. "Yes sir, of course. If you need anything..."

"That's all, Frank."

CHAPTER 4

Frank turned to walk away.

"Frank..."

"Yes sir?"

"Take this... Err - drop it off at the library, will you." Fleming snapped the book shut like a Venus fly trap. He extended it across the table in a shaking hand.

Frank trotted back and tried to take the book from Fleming, who seemed unwilling to let it go despite his request. As Frank prised it from his grasp, Fleming blinked as though he'd started from a dream, and returned to shuffling the mountain of papers on his desk again. The phone was nestled deep within the folds of fat on his neck.

The book felt cold in Frank's hand. He tucked it under his arm and turned once again to leave the room, but slowed his pace to the door as he wondered who was on the other end of the phone. Whoever it was, they'd really put the shits up Fleming by simply calling. Inevitably, he reached the door, and could only begin to close it behind him. Frank felt like a butler addressing his host before leaving.

He lingered as long as possible, slowly, slowly closing Fleming's door. It let loose with the kind of squawk heard in a B-rated horror movie. Fleming glanced up, beady little eyes glaring at Frank. The Warden shook his head incredulously, very obviously wondering why Frank was still in his sight and gesticulated wildly for him to shoo. Frank just made out the opening of the conversation as the door finally clicked shut.

"Yes, this is Warden Fleming... Yes, Ah'll hold for the Marshal."

Marshal? As in, the Feds? Frank wondered why the Feds would be calling such a rural prison. Had there finally been enough death to warrant a bigger investigation? Frank was one of the few guards who had survived Delmont's rule. If the Marshals were poking into the suicides of Juniper Correctional, they had to suspect foul play. Frank wasn't sure if he could handle anymore corrupt bosses.

Later, at the end of his shift, Frank became aware that his musings had kept him so occupied he'd forgotten he still had possession of the book Fleming had asked him to drop off at the library. He was losing time again. His wife would make him go to the doctor if she had any idea how bad the gaps really were. But instead of being able to sink into her arms, the library would have to hold him now.

There was nothing that Frank enjoyed more about his job than visiting the library after lights out. The place was on the third floor, deep within the prison walls. Huge, oak barricades stood sentinel, guarding the books from the grey corruption. In Juniper Correctional, they were a stark contrast to the perpetual metal, flaking paint, and crumbling bricks. Frank would note flakes of plaster collecting at the edges of the walkways and corridors regularly while on his rounds and would come back to clean them. But he never noticed flakes near the library. The doors seemed like gods issued from another time, when deities protected their creations from the scourge of a wild world. They reminded Frank of himself, ushering in the remnants of good in even the worst of mankind.

Though the doors were closed as he approached, a pale orange light poured through a crack. It made his heart warm just seeing it. After lights out, when the cells were bathed in darkness, the corridors seemed to swirl with a deep bluish ink, reminiscent of an ocean after sundown, cold and bleak. It seemed that the library was somewhere else; somewhere light and airy. Once inside it was like walking around one of those rich folk places out by the river that had been built on the blood of slaves and cotton pickers. Frank often mused that the town's founders had built the very foundations of Juniper on top of the corpses of those too weak to survive or those that tried to flee. The town had its fair share of secrets, many stored on the shelves of the prison library - although racism and slavery weren't one of them. They were worn as badges of honour by many of the townsfolk and even the inhabitants of Juniper Correctional. Frank found it abhorrent, and for that he was labelled by many as a "sympathiser." To him it wasn't sympathy, it was marriage.

He glanced out of one of the long rectangular windows near the ceiling. The rain was still hammering down. Small, circular windows, made of thick pieces of reinforced safety glass with wires set deep within, were the only eye level breaks in the concrete. *A prison within a prison* Frank mused. From the porthole which overlooked the parking lot, he noticed Warden Fleming clambering into his car. The Warden must have turned the ignition as the lights blinked on. The rain formed translucent cables, reaching all the way from the dark clouds above and tickling the earth as they trailed back and forth, blown by the wind. Frank watched as the cables seemed to reach for the car. Eventually the wipers came on and the Warden headed on home, or wherever the hell it was that men like him went after work.

When the red lights of Fleming's car winked at him as they disappeared around the corner of the external wall, Frank turned back from the window. Fleming leaving meant Frank was now the most senior person in the prison. Well, apart from Stanley Bryson, the prison librarian whose age was something all the officers took bets on. Some had him at sixty, some at ninety, but Stanley never let on. Personally, Frank figured him to be at least a hundred. But Stanley always had a knack of turning the conversation away from himself, as if he didn't like people prying or paying him too much attention.

Clearly a bit less fortunate, judging by the dirt under his long and cracked fingernails, Stanley had long ago taken on the task of running the prison library. Having lost his wife to a cancer that turned her innards into a knotted mess and his children having drowned on dry land from pneumonia, he occupied his time with trying to educate the minds of those trapped within the confines of these walls. He offered them freedom through the words which were trapped in books, giving them a way to leave their cells, a reprieve from their sentence for as long as it took them to finish a story. They could be sailing on the seas aboard the Pequod or fighting off evil in the Overlook Hotel, even living out a prison escape fantasy with Charrière's autobiography. The world was at their fingertips - provided they could read.

Frank pushed the door open. He could hear Stanley inside, shuffling around the bookish cell and muttering to himself. It was a relief to hear him moving. Over more recent months, Frank had started catching Stanley reclining in a chair, completely out of it. It was one of the only times he didn't look like a droopy plant; when he walked, he looked like his spine had had enough with gravity and the weight of his head was dragging him down to the grave. In a chair, he was able to sit a bit more upright. But his mind, sharp as a tack when he walked the corridors offering books, was never as sharp with his seated body. Even the times Frank dropped a book on the desk, Stanley never moved. If he ever decided to report it, the Warden would happily consign Stanley to being released from his duties, and then the old man would have nothing left. Fleming would be consigning Stanley to the grave if that happened, so Frank kept it quiet, placing books on the desk and pulling the door shut on his way out. Even still, with all his ailments, all his wear and tear, he continued to serve Juniper Correctional in the best way he could, an Igor kept alive by some hidden elixir that only he knew about.

As Frank thought about it, he realised he'd never seen Stanley leave Juniper Correctional, or arrive. He was just an eternal presence in the building, a corporeal ghost. Frank wondered if Stanley even had a home to go back to at the end of a working day.

Though the door swung open freely, the hinges cried out their disproval at being moved. What had been a small hint of light suddenly flooded into the dark hallway. Frank regarded the library in the same way as many of the inmates - a little Eden where they could come to find themselves, but most of the time it was to lose themselves. This meant it wasn't without its issues, as small scuffles occasionally happened, though they were nothing that Stanley couldn't control. He, in a strange way, held more power and more sway over the inmates than the Warden ever had. He held the keys to this palace, and he alone decided whether or not inmates got to stay; not even the Warden stepped over Stanley's threshold. The threat of never crossing that magical threshold for the entirety of a sentence was too much for many to bear. He was one of the only men in Juniper Correctional that everyone truly respected.

Frank strode inside across the threadbare Persian rugs that littered the floor. The wear was more focused under the four tables that sat in the middle of the vast room, and so decrepit you could see the wooden floor peeping through from the footfall of the thousands of inmates who'd sat in the stiff-backed chairs writing letters, devoured words, travelled to far flung corners of the earth without ever leaving their seats, or cells for that matter. The tables were etched with names of those long forgotten, scratched into their dark wood with homemade shanks. It was befitting that the names were kept here, in the library, acting as a census of the lives that had passed through the veins of this unforgiving beast.

In the evenings, Stanley would light candles, making it cosier than the grandmother's house of Little Red Riding Hood. It was a fire hazard, and against protocol, but as the Warden never showed an interest in the library, Stanley did as he pleased. Banker's lamps shone on each desk, with the brass fittings intricately engraved with fern leaves and other fauna.

But it was the sheer number of books that always took Frank's breath away: row upon row of titles from every conceivable genre. Sometimes, when Frank was alone in the library, he could almost hear the shelves groaning under the weight of the words trapped within. They reached from the floor to the ceiling, as if they were the foundations of the room, columns of books that held up the roof.

Stanley was perched up a ladder, stretching a paper thin arm out and placing returned books carefully back on their shelves. There were two that caught his attention held in the crook of Stanley's arm; a book called Scratches and another small volume called Crossroads. Stanley's hunched torso meant he had to climb higher than the shelf as he couldn't stretch enough to reach above his head. Frank thought he looked like a Cellar spider, all arms and legs and with a little body in the middle. The ladder rattled as Stanley reached out to the crevices. It was showing its wear too, protesting loudly each time Stanley reached out. The wood had originally been edged in brass but the metal had been worn off from constant use, leaving translucent veins of reflective metal to match the translucent veins seen through the skin of the librarian.

Stanley spotted him as he returned his arm to his body. "Oh... Frank. Sorry didn't see you there. You enjoy watching an old man work his fingers to the bone?" The skin on his exposed arms folded like crumpled parchment as he pulled them closer to his torso.

Frank chuckled. "Sorry, Stan, I didn't want to startle you. Don't want you having a heart attack and falling off that infernal contraption."

"Bless you, boy." Stanley held each side of the ladder and then placed his feet on the side rails and slid down to the floor. His feet connected to the wooden boards with a thud. "Still got it!" Stanley wheezed, before beginning to cough. It was a dry, hacking retch; his face changed from its usual deathly pallor to a scarlet mess, veins swelling across his cranium, bulbous and flexing between each cough.

"Can I get you-"

Stanley waved away the concern from Frank. He shuffled towards his desk, coughing and trying to hack something up. Frank couldn't help but think that the noises Stanley was making sounded remarkably like his mother. Cancer turned her lungs to soggy sponges full of brown gravy and even the day she died she'd never seemed to finish hacking it up. Ten years later, it was still a sound he'd never lose the intensity of.

Suddenly, Stanley loosened the blockage and gasped like a fish out of water, his face shifting back to its usual malnourished sallowness.

"Everything okay?" Frank asked.

"Oh, yes; it's just a little cough. Guess my body is reminding me I'm not forty any more, or even fifty at that." He blinked up at Frank. "What brings you here at this hour?"

"Well, I was-"

Stanley interrupted as if he hadn't heard Frank. "Has that paralysed streak of piss left for the evening?"

"Who?"

"Fleming. Has he gone, d'you know?"

Frank nodded. "Yeah. I saw him driving off just before I came in."

Stanley reached behind his desk. He tapped a pack of cigarettes against his palm and then pulled out a single tube. He lifted it with a trembling hand and placed it between his thin, dry lips. "Do you have a lighter?" Stanley asked as he pawed his clothes, looking for where he placed his.

Frank reached into his pocket and sparked his lighter. "Here you go." He held the flame out for Stanley.

Stanley moved forward and cupped his hands around Frank's. Frank was shocked at how cold his gnarled hands were when they touched his own.

The librarian took a deep breath, the cigarette bursting into flame before he blew out a cloud of white smoke. "Thank you boy... ahhh, I needed that. Been a busy day... what's that?" Stanley gestured with the hand holding his cigarette, smoke swirling from the end as he waved it towards Frank's hand.

Frank glanced down as he extinguished the lighter... he'd almost forgotten why he came. "Oh, Fleming asked me to return it to you." Frank pocketed his lighter and reached under his arm to grab the obscure book. As he pulled it out, he noticed a frisson of fear flicker across Stanley's face.

"Where did you find it?" Stanley asked, eyes widening.

Frank shrugged. "The warden asked me to give it to you."

"But before that, where did it come from?"

"It was in a prisoner's cell; the one that committed suicide last night, Jasper Legg. Why?"

"Oh... nothing." The wave of fear seemed to pass. "Just not seen it for a good while. Did you read it?"

Frank wondered if Stanley were more than a little senile these days. "No, I just took it to the warden."

Stanley nodded. "He read it?"

"He flicked through it I think? Is it any good?" Frank turned the book over and was about to start thumbing through it, but just as he flexed the book open, Stanley's hand shot out and snatched it away from him.

"Oh, it's a good book. One to be... savoured. It's been around the block..." Stanley opened the book and glanced at the stamps on the inside. He thumbed through the book, his eyes dancing across the pages, as one would look when flicking through a photo album; memories seemed to play across his face. Frank craned his neck to take a peek, but Stanley noticed his motion and closed the book. "It's been one of the most read books at the many institutions I've worked in. Had it shipped here when I moved to Juniper. Before that, it followed me all the days of my life. Seemed to call out to me wherever I end up."

Frank was intrigued. "What's it about?"

"Oh, you know... good versus evil." Stanley took another deep drag off his cigarette.

"Right. So, is it any good?"

"Such a fabulous little tale." Stanley clutched the book to his chest, almost hugging the life out of it. He reached forward and stubbed his smoke out in the ashtray. "Was there anything else?"

Frank was taken aback by the sudden brush off. "Err... no."

"Then you'd best be off. I've got to start my rounds..."

"See you soon, Stanley. And don't you let Fleming catch you smoking in here. He's been looking for an excuse to fire your ass!" Frank turned and walked towards the door. As he left, he glanced over his shoulder one last time to see Stanley muttering to himself. In that instant, he looked so weak, so old and fragile. It was only a matter of time before he left this place for good, most likely in a coffin.

Frank closed the door and headed back to the guard station.

CHAPTER 5

Fleming sat at the wheel of his car, engine idling like his mind. A lit cigarette was gripped between two fingers, the smoke rising and drifting up the windshield, creating a vaporous cycle with the rain outside that poured like a river over the window. After the day he'd had, Fleming was desperate to be lost in time and space, and leaving the wipers off made it feel as if he was hidden. Cars would pass by, their headlights glinting like growing stars until at last the light blazed and he was blinded for just a second. Then they disappeared from view and his car was bathed in a red glow from the fading tail lights. The alternation of colour had an almost hypnotic effect upon him. As the vehicles passed, it would rock his car from side to side, giving him a sensation like being in a cradle. He'd watch in the rear view until the cars were gone and his car was washed with blackness again, allowing him to disappear into his own world.

He raised the smoke to his lips and inhaled, listening to the deafening cacophony of the rain. The cigarette licked at his fingers as it burned down to its filter. He removed it and stubbed it out in the car's ashtray. His fingers instinctively reached into the pack in the dashboard cubby and pulled out another, placing it to his lips with a steady hand, which surprised him considering the fury inside that was raging like a tempest. He threw the pack onto the passenger seat, and pressed the car lighter button. His mind flew back to the phone call mere hours ago.

The click of the opposing receiver as the caller had hung up. The all-encompassing rage at the announcement that the United States Federal Fucking Marshals would be descending upon his prison for an "Investigation into the safety and well-being of the incarcerated men within Juniper Correctional." It was the biggest load of goddamn fucking *horseshit* that he had ever faced in his thirty five years of fucking service.

After taking a deep inhale, he slowly blew out the grey air left in his lungs, where it joined the ever-growing cloud above his head. The latest cigarette was shoved into the ashtray, which was smouldering like a volcano about to erupt. On the seat next to his discarded pack of smokes sat the letter. He had almost left it on his desk as he had gathered his coat from the 7-foot mounted alligator gar that served as a coatrack, a gift from his hunting buddy Brandenburg. He stuffed in his briefcase the remaining bottle of scotch. Annoyance at his near fatal mistake had further spurned his ire and he had cursed, loudly and without restraint, as he stomped back to the oaken pedestal and crammed the letter in his pocket. The stuffed line of squirrels watched him curiously as he had opened the office door and froze. All the lights in the prison had been turned off. Clearly, he had been on the phone far longer than he thought.

The lighter popped out, the clicking noise telling him it was ready.

Fleming removed it and watched as the coil inside burned bright orange. He caught sight of his face in the mirror, the glow highlighting his swollen, pockmarked face. He thought for a fleeting moment about how the coil would feel on his flesh. His mind was muddied after the day's events, and pain might bring sudden clarity. His hand wobbled, bringing the lighter towards his cheek. It was as if his thoughts were suddenly out of his control. But as his skin felt the heat from the coil in his hand, the thought skittered out of his head and he lit his cigarette instead before placing the car lighter back into its holster.

The smoke drew his gaze upward as it rose in wispy tendrils and Fleming reflected on seeing Frank in the window near the library as he had rushed to his car. It had been odd, noting him standing there. Usually Frank was very prompt to follow orders, but if he had just been getting to the library... Fleming sighed and more smoke joined the Olympian cloud above his head; whatever had kept Frank from turning in the book could wait until the next day.

Passing lights illuminated the passenger seat. The letter from the dead prisoner sat waiting. Even in this light, Fleming could see the blood-stained fingerprints and smears. He reached over, scooped the letter up, and slipped it from its bloody sleeve. The paper rustled as he unfolded it, muffled by the rain that continued to hammer down on the roof of the car. He squinted, trying to read in the dark. "Gawd*fucking*dammit," he muttered as he reached to the interior light button. The yellow ball filled the car just enough to read the last words of Jasper Legg.

Jasper Legg (IN-17634)
Juniper Correctional Facility

My dearest Sally,
If you are reading this, then it is clear I am no longer. This is the

letter I wrote to ensure that my voice was heard. Strange that for it to be audible I had to commit it to silence, but I hope you can forgive me and remember my voice. I have done many a bad thing, but I do not regret them. I am who I am due to them, and I take my punishment fairly. I don't regret shooting that spot-stealing Nelson in the face, I don't regret slicing up those peoples' faces, I don't regret burning and decapitating those people I purged in the fire – because I don't remember them. Even now, all this time later, I still don't remember them... but they remember me, that much is sure.

They haunt me each night. Cut up ragged faces lurch at me from the shadows. Little bodies laugh at me within my cell, but when I peer into the darkness that houses them, I wonder how they can laugh, as they have no heads. Only a bloody bubbling crevice, where the severed throat gargles and laughter pours forth in icy torrents that chill my bones.

People don't believe me. That's fine. People don't even see me; they don't see the man you once knew, and once loved. But I'm tired of preaching to the blind, tired of talking to ears that don't hear. I'm tired of everything.

I must have done the things they say I have. I get recollections every now and again, small glimpses of me acting out and doing those things, but it's foggy, as if it wasn't me. I sound crazy, I know. I guess that's why I'm in here and you, my love, are out there.

Do you still think of me? It's lonely in here. I've been keeping to myself. Not many of the inmates want to speak with me. I've hurt quite a few since being in here, and my reputation has marked me something wicked. They avoid me like I am the plague. But they might be right- I do have a sickness, don't I? That's what everyone has been telling me- the doctors, the warden, the priest. A deep-rooted sickness that has taken me over, consumed everything I used to be.

But having mentioned all of this, I wouldn't change a thing.

I.
Regret.
Nothing.

I'm broken, It tells me through gnashing teeth. I'm a mess, It whispers in my ear. I'm an abomination, It screams at me. Time and time and time again. It repeats these truths like a stuttering record. It visits me. Cleaves itself to me.

I don't know how much longer I can keep going, Sally. I don't have much strength left. It is very persuading. I feel that I've used up all of my usefulness. I'm like a spent battery, just removed and thrown aside, a husk of the man or monster I used to be. I think It knows I'm spent.

Do you still think of me?

I'm sorry if I'm repeating myself, my mind is muddled. I'm sad. Not for what I've done but that I will never see your face again, I'll never get to mark it with my fists, never get to bruise you, break you, make you see. See...

It's talking to me again and I can't stop Its babbling. It speaks to me, though I can't recall what It looks like. Odd, isn't it? All this time, all these conversations, and It's no more than a ghost to me. I'd think I was imagining It, but it can't be my imagination. It hurts me, you see, cuts me when I don't do what It wants. I sometimes glimpse It sitting with me in the dark, but It stays hidden, changing with each passing visit, concealed within a veil, a membrane of deep darkness. It comes each night, tempting and whispering Its desires –

I don't know how much longer I can last...

You must think me crazy? Who doesn't?

I must go. It comes again.

Yours, truly,

Jasper

. . .

The shadowy streaks of rain danced across the paper, giving the words an ominous living quality as the ink seemed to fidget on the page. He glanced over the words once again, then cast the letter aside with a derisive snort. A mad letter from an even madder man who never was able to stop the madness from bleeding out.

Fleming rubbed his face. He was exhausted. With a sigh, he picked up the letter again and folded it. He pulled a new envelope from his briefcase and slid in the sheet of scribblings. His cigarette was pinched between two fingers as he licked the gum on the envelope opening. A frown crossed his face as he dug a pen out of his shirt pocket and began scribbling the address on the unstained container, copying it from the bloodied envelope.

He frowned at the road in front of him. Another car was approaching in the distance, the headlights sparkling like tiny jewels as it crested the hill. But this time a void of light, as though someone had cut a hole out of the scene, stood in the middle of the road.

He looked down as he tapped the letter on the steering wheel. There was a choice to make. One path would cast him as gracious, benevolent even to those less clear-eyed. The other path would save him trouble with the board and ensure no further suspicion about the cause of death; it would prevent the things in the letter from being used against him. The second path was an already familiar one. What with limited budgets and calls for closure, he'd done all he could to protect everything he'd built. He'd worked too hard, for too long, on dragging Juniper Correctional up from the gutter. But the prison, or perhaps Juniper itself, had an odd way of corrupting all that was good.

Fleming glanced up as the car continued to approach, the light burning bright through the rain that was flowing over the glass. The void had grown bigger, and seemed to have moved closer to his car. *A hitchhiker?* They were a common enough sight, folks trying to get to the places and towns outside of the city limits. But a body'd have to be deranged to be trying for a ride in this weather.

The car continued, overtaking the shape in the road so it was lost to the darkness again. As it sped past, Fleming felt his own car rock more sharply than before. He glanced into his rear view, his face bathed in red from the tail lights.

"Fuck!"

Fleming scrambled, desperate to turn around in his seat. The tail lights of the passing car had highlighted a shape in his back seat, directly behind him, its silhouette outlined in red. It was a person, he was sure of it.

He smacked the horn with an elbow as he wrestled with his girth in the small confines of his car. His smoke had fallen from his mouth with his sudden outburst, and burned somewhere on his lap. "Shitshitshitshit!" Fleming desperately began scanning the back seat of his car, whilst his hands frantically tried to tap out the cigarette. The visual search turned up nothing. What the hell?? He knew there had been something there, but...

Nothing.

He breathed a strangled sigh of relief. "Pull yo'self together, Hezekiah..." He finally found the smoke tucked into a fold of cloth and pressed it into the ashtray. Fleming faced forward and closed his eyes, trying to slow his haggard breathing. "*What* in the fucking hell!"

A new set of headlights lined his eyelids in red. The rain continued its unrelenting assault, but louder, heavier, the sheer force of it causing the car to lurch as if the weight of the downpour was shoving the nose down into the mud. He felt the car tip forward and his eyes flew open. Fleming squinted through the torrents of water. He reached for the wipers. He watched as the lights of the oncoming car lowered gradually as the car crested the hill.

"Holy shit!"

The lights revealed the void of light crawling across the hood of his car. Something huge and black, staring in at him through the veil of water. Fleming slammed the wipers into the highest speed. As they whipped up from their slumber, the rain was brushed away, as was the monstrous apparition. He sat there, looking out the semi-clear windshield, as the oncoming car sped past. Long after the lights had faded he kept scanning the darkness, frantically in search of the void. It was gone.

Fleming reached over and clicked the button to lock the doors. "What the fuck... where the *hell* did you go??" His head twitched back and forth as he scanned his mirrors, so fast he wasn't really taking in all that he was seeing. He'd had enough idling. Fleming turned his lights on as he moved the car into drive. He crept onto the road and reached for the letter. The wipers were still beating at the rain. But everything was much clearer in the light. Fleming pressed the accelerator slowly and the car lurched forwards.

In the distance, a post box appeared like a beacon as he crawled along the empty road. The line passed unnoticed as he crossed over to the left side of the street. As he bumped the car fully onto the curb, his body rocked from side to side, and he continued along until he had pulled up alongside the blue metal beast.

Fleming glanced around briefly, leaning forward to check the blind spots in his mirrors, then pressed the button to lower his window. With the window down, the rain spilled in like a busted dam, and Fleming's pants were immediately soaked to the bone. He grabbed the letter, desperate to rid himself of it before he changed his mind. He thrust his hand out through the gap and dropped it into the dark mouth of the mailbox. His exhausted mind imagined some deranged clown appearing within the slit, staring blankly back at him. He quickly snatched his hand back, fearful that something would grab it. The window rose at an excessively slow pace and he wished for a hand crank to make it faster.

Safely tucked inside the car, Fleming slammed his foot down and leapt off the curb to speed into the night. He glanced in the rearview out of habit. The red glow from his tail lights picked at the edges of something. The void was lurking by the mailbox. He pressed down the accelerator and tried to put as much distance between him and the thing as he could.

The entire drive home, he thought he saw it again and again. Standing by the side of the road. Appearing from the woods. Sitting at the abandoned gas station. It was everywhere he looked, a wild beast prowling around in his peripheral vision. Whenever he tried to pinpoint it, it would vanish like an eye-floater. But when he least expected it, it would come into view again. Only when he had safely pulled into his garage did he allow himself to relax. He groaned and leaned against the headrest.

God... he needed a drink.

CHAPTER 6

T he rain thundered on the building in the steady beat of a marching army, amplified by the steel ceiling covering the catacomb cell blocks in Juniper Correctional. Stanley shuffled along the hall before the cellblock, thin bony hands clutched around the handle of the cart he pushed. The *thudder-thudder* of the front wheel usually signalled his arrival long before he had made his way onto a wing so there was never a need to announce his arrival. But between the rain and the nightly heckling, he might need to cough up a call.

Prisoners shouted to be heard over the noise as they slung insults from their pens, baiting each other with curses and threats. 'Fishing' the guards called it, the idea of reeling someone in for taunting throughout the long nights. It was a barbaric game that could turn a man crazy. But in the prison, they just thought of it as entertainment, a kind of despicable theatre. The Latinos would gang up on the Blacks, the Blacks would gang up on the Neo-nazis, and the ungrouped whites sided with whomever wouldn't kill them; but everyone would gang up on those with a penchant for children. The midnight callings would turn into the next day's gladiatorial battles within the yard. Blood was guaranteed to always be spilt.

Stanley didn't much care, so long as the books weren't harmed. His goal was simply to meet the needs of those he served be it through books, comics, newspapers, or even porn mags, though some of those stayed in the library and did not reside on the cart for his evening rounds. Literature was literature to him, and even in Playboy the articles were good, though Stanley was very sure most weren't looking at the words. But he figured would get them all to read something, someday; after all, the prisoners had all the time in the world.

As he turned the corner, two officers approached him with a clipboard. He ducked his head and tried to walk by.

"Evening rounds?" one of the guards asked.

"Like cancer- always delivering!" Stanley offered with a little laugh, before his cough took over.

"If you'd just sign here, Stan." The other officer held out the clipboard. "Anything good in the pickings today?"

Stanley took the pen from his breast pocket and scribbled his name. "For it to be good, Officer Phillips, you'd need to be able to read."

"Funny one, Stan," Officer Phillips said dryly. "Well, you better get a move on!" He turned around to his colleague and screwed up his face in exasperation.

Stanley caught a glimpse of the officer's mocking expression. He ignored the slight as they usually ignored him. "I will, Officer Phillips. You take care now, y'hear!" With that, he shuffled off down the rows of cells.

The cart was filled with an array of books, everything from science fiction to romance to the classics; he had something for every taste. There was even a stack of contraband hidden under some of the hardbacks no one ever picked. The prisoners rewarded him greatly for this small misdemeanour. He could get a few packs of smokes, or some crumpled dollars, and more often than not, a Snickers or Twix.

The most "top-shelf" products that Stanley delivered were the horror books, closely followed by old issues of Playboy. The Warden had banned any horror books being allowed into the prison, citing the idea of purifying the minds of the convicted, rather than polluting them further. But, of course, as soon as something becomes prohibited, people only want it more. Eventually he relented, but kept restrictions on the number of books available at any given time, often hiding many titles within the rows of books in the library where they'd never be found. It wasn't as if it were heroin or crack. Addictions always seemed to find a way to thrive in this prison anyway, so what harm could a little Stephen King, Michael Clark or Gemma Amor do?

After all, they were only words and words never really hurt anyone.

Stanley moved toward the first cell. It was strange how at ease he felt. He had no qualms wandering right up to the cells of hardened felons. He glanced down at the faded and flaking yellow line which designated the safe perimeter for those walking the cell block. It was the same line inmates had to stand on when their cells were being flipped or when they were being moved from the pens to lunch or the yard. Not even the guards got as close. Stanley was on the wrong side of that line, but it didn't trouble him at all. In fact, it made him feel alive. There were rules; and then there was Stanley. Even with his liver-spotted hands and fingers twisted by arthritis, he still managed to give the rules the finger.

"Books?" Stanley croaked into the darkness of the cell. He could hear movement within but couldn't make any object out. The darkness was impenetrable. He pulled the cart to a stop and continued staring into the darkness, seeking out whatever beast was locked behind those bars. No answer came, so he started off down the concourse.

"Books?" he proffered at the next cell.

"Yeah, I'll take one." The voice was so deep it rattled Stanley's fillings. Stanley picked up his clipboard, turned to the cell and waited. He heard the bed springs squeak under the weight of the person within, heard two heavy feet hit the floor. Stanley bent his hunched back into an angle as he craned his neck up to look at the figure emerging from the darkness. The dim light bathed his face as he approached the bars of his cell. He was a giant of a man, six foot seven, Stanley would have surmised. His leathered face was marked by several scars, the deepest creeping out from each corner of his mouth, causing his face to resemble the jaws of a creature that lurked the ocean depths.

Stanley blinked.

The prisoner stared.

"Name?" Stanley finally asked.

"Christopher."

Stanley began jotting it down on his form.

"You got anything good?" the giant asked.

Stanley finished writing and then placed the clipboard down. He turned to the cart. "Everything you see, my friend." He moved his hand across the books, letting his twisted fingers rise and fall over the different spines as he revealed them to Christopher, like a magician working a trick. "What type of book are you after?"

He grunted. "Something... good?"

"As I said-"

"That one. That one there!" Christopher pointed, his arm barely squeezing through the bars.

Stanley took a small step back. It was important that he show he wasn't intimidated, but he'd have to be insane not to be intimidated by this man. Stanley's gaze followed Christopher's arm down to a waffle iron of a hand, which lead to bratwurst thick fingers pointing at one of the books. There was another deep dark scar on the prisoner's wrist, a long cut which raggedly snaked up the inside of his forearm.

"Ahhh... H.G. Wells. *War of the Worlds.* That's a classic." Stanley picked up the hardback and turned the book over in his hands, his fingers rubbing at the cover and the gilded edges. Christopher watched him intently, his fingers snapping in the air like a crab, his desire to hold the book evident. Stanley placed the book on top of the others and added the title to his clipboard under Christopher's name. He turned and handed the book over.

As Christopher took it, his other hand shot out from the darkness, grabbing hold of Stanley's outstretched wrist. "Please... don't shout..." Christopher's strong grip easily trapped Stanley's frail old arm, "... could you pass this onto the cell two over?" He nodded in the direction Stanley's cart was facing. "Please?" Christopher's eyes had grown wide and pleading. Pools of brown stared at Stanley in desperation.

"Please remove your hand..." Stanley mumbled, low and without panic. Christopher immediately withdrew and Stanley rubbed the parchment thick skin of his forearm. It smarted. He was little more than a bag of bones, and that had hurt to his marrow. Glancing down, he could see that Christopher had rested a small piece of paper on the horizontal bar of his cell "... two smokes!" Stanley barked under his breath.

Christopher disappeared from view, then re-emerged with the required two sticks, placing them next to the paper. Stanley glanced over his shoulder at the guard station. They were busy chatting. He picked up the note and placed it under the sheet on the clipboard, then deposited the cigarettes into his pocket. He nodded and moved on.

After passing the note, and gaining a full pack for safe delivery, Stanley continued on his rounds. The inmates depleted his cart until it resembled an eviscerated tree corpse. He was happy though, as it meant all those books, all those words, were being read.

He smiled to himself as he continued walking the floor. He was almost finished for the night. Three more cells remained. "Books?" he offered to the darkness. Silence. He began to move on to the next cell.

"No... wait, please... come back!" The voice sounded sad, the voice of a broken man who'd been sobbing. Stanley figured the man had been caught by someone fishing.

"Hey! What about me?" a voice issued from the next cell over. A face squeezed against the bars, trying to peer around them and set his sights on Stanley.

"I'll get to you in a moment... you'll just have to wait your turn," Stanley spoke softly.

"Wait my fucking turn? You were just here! Don't worry about that fat tub of shit. Now c'mon!"

"Wait." Stanley replied, puncturing the air with surprising authority.

"Man, you wanna get your ass over here now!"

Stanley paused for a moment. "Excuse me?"

"You heard me! Don't be wasting your time with no kiddy fiddler. Dumb motherfucker's gonna get his soon enough. Come on... you got Playboy? I got some money man, lots of green, or smokes, whatever you need, man." His voice was desperate. Stanley thought he sounded like a junky needing their next hit.

Stanley was distracted. "Look, I said-" He stopped as he felt something clammy touch his arm. He glanced down to see a fat hand on his exposed flesh. It was damp and warm. He shook it off as if it were some type of bug and stumbled back into his cart, knocking some of the books off as it rocked back and forth.

"Ah shit! Now look what you gone an' done. Fuck you, old man!" The inmate suddenly spat at Stanley, the mossy coloured globule of phlegm landed on the floor in front of him before the inmate disappeared back into the darkness of his cell.

A flashlight beam swung over the rows of cells. "Hey, Stan. Everything alright?" The guards were shining lights towards him from their seat at the entrance to the cell block.

Stanley lifted his hands, trying to block out the light that was in his eyes as much as anything, but also to say that he was ok. "Yeah. All ok, the wheel got jammed and some of the books fell off... Don't worry, I'll get them. You guys get back to your discussion."

"You sure?"

"Yeah... yeah. All okay here."

The guards clicked off the flashlight and turned back to their conversations.

The fat hand that had grabbed him was now reaching out and pawing at the books on the floor. Stanley shifted to his knees and watched it grope at the stories. The hand was attached to an even bigger arm, swollen and indented at the wrist as if some hidden band were segmenting it, cutting off the circulation, but it was just two rolls of fat converging. While Christopher's arm had spoken of power and control, this arm spoke of softness and gluttony. The hand pulled two books into the cell as Stanley stretched to pick up the ones which were out of reach. As he stood again, he peered into the cell and was repulsed by what he saw.

It was a rotund man made of mounds of fat that hung down like the pendulum weights in a grandfather clock, jiggling with his subtle movements. The inmate appeared to be naked, but Stanley noticed a small band of white disappearing beneath the folds, his stomach so low it was resting on his knees as he stood at the cell door. It appeared that his body had been abused so much, swollen to such a gargantuan mass, that gravity had become his enemy. *His body's pulling him all the way to the grave,* Stanley thought with some degree of pity amidst the horror.

Numerous rolls of neck fat trickled down over one another like a melting ice cream. The rolls on his arms that dribbled down over his elbows and forearms were pushed further up his arm like a bunched-up sleeve as the prisoner stuck his hand through the bars. "Here you go." His voice was soft, like a child's. He handed the two books back through the gaps in the cell bars. The fingers clutching them had no form, no indications of knuckles, just slabs of white, anaemic and swollen.

Stanley reached forward and took the books from his hand, placing them back on the cart. "Thank you."

He reorganised the books with a swift sleight of hand and turned back to the cell. The inmate was pressed right up against his bars, his flesh seeming to ooze between them. Stanley stifled a snicker at the mental image of a waffle imprint that would be left on the man once he stepped away from the bars. The inmate stared at him, bloated cheeks squeezing his eyes, making them look tiny and ferret-like. Fatty jowls swung loosely, pulling his lips into a drooping mess, as though he had suffered a stroke. But a mouth did lurk in there, a small pouty wet thing, like a hidden beak with which he uttered his soft words.

"Do you have anything I might like?"

Stanley blinked in surprise at the question. "Wha... what are you interested in?"

The question was met with silence. The prisoner's beady eyes strained within their sockets, glancing left and right to see if anyone was listening. He pressed his face harder between the bars, as if trying to get closer to Stanley; it made his wet mouth pout even more. "I like..." His voice was wavering, straining against the sound of the rain which continued to thunder down, "... books about children... have anything like that?" He licked his lips, wetting them, then sucking on his lower lip as if savouring something.

Stanley shook his head. "Nothing of the sort. I already gave away Peter Pan."

"Oh..." The prisoner turned his face slightly away, a little string of drool caught in the light, connecting the cell bars to his mouth like a spiderweb.

"But... I do have this." Stanley moved over to the trolley and lifted up some copies of Playboy. He reached underneath the magazines and pulled out a book which had been concealed the whole time he'd been doing rounds. He replaced the Playboys, much to the prisoner's confusion, and then turned back to the fat man.

"What's that?" The prisoner licked his lips again, severing the saliva conduit.

"Just something I think you'll enjoy... a real page turner, or so I'm told. Just came back into my possession today." Stanley held out the book. A fat, damp hand relinquished its hold on the bars and reached for it.

"Tut, tut, tut." Stanley pulled the book away just before he was able to grab it, "Forgive me. Where is my mind today... what's your name?"

"Antonio. Antonio Frustaglio..." the soft voice answered. "What is it? What's it about??"

Stanley scribbled the inmates name down and handed the battered book over. "It's a classic tale of good versus evil... and in this place, I guess that's why it's so popular!" Stanley chuckled to himself.

Antonio pulled the book into his cell and began turning the

pages instantly. Stanley thought he might have been looking for pictures, and waited for Antonio's face to look up in disappointment. But Antonio never glanced up from the book.

Stanley watched as the last parts of Antonio freed themselves from the bars as he turned and shambled away into his cell, his gigantic frame waddling off to his bed. As Antonio turned his back completely on Stanley, the librarian observed that he was even more hideous from behind. His small head seemed to pop out above a huge slab of dimpled and creased leather, red and swollen where sweat had fermented within his flabby folds. It was like he was watching a fleshy boulder rolling off into the darkness of his cell. He soon heard Antonio collapse and the bed groaning under his weight. Antonio started muttering to himself.

Stanley hobbled over to his trolley and began pushing it past the final two cells. He didn't bother saying anything to the first one he passed. The inmate was new, and with the attitude that had been exhibited, he wouldn't last long enough for Stanley to even learn his name. Besides, spitting at the librarian was cause for an immediate revoking of book privileges.

He approached the last cell. "Books?"

CHAPTER 7

Fleming sat in his armchair, a bottle of scotch nestled in his lap. It was half empty. He'd needed something to settle his nerves, to drown out the doubting voices surfacing in his head. He felt like a struggling swimmer; each time his doubts started to kick and fight for the surface, he turned for something to pull them down again. It had been going on like this for some time, but the more he drank, the more tired that swimmer got. He stayed under the water longer, struggled less to surface; so he kept drinking.

After he had stumbled through the door resembling a drowned rat, Fleming had grabbed himself a microwaved meal and stomped around the house while the incident in the car preyed on his addled mind. He'd checked that nothing was lurking outside, across the street, or huddled under his porch. He didn't know what to do and so he'd started drinking. The liquor cabinet in the dining room held an unopened bottle of his preferred poison. He'd cracked the seal and took a long gulp. As he moved back into the hallway, he'd noticed the incessantly flashing red light on his answering machine. He'd tossed the lid of the bottle off into the distance and hit play as he sucked greedily at the bottle like a baby at a mother's breast. The voice of the smug bitch made him choke on his drink.

"Hello, Warden Fleming. This is a message in case I miss you at Juniper Correctional. I am calling to inform you that we are pressing forwards with our investigation due to the recent spike in inmate fatality at this particular facility. It has been reported by various individuals, who are protected under the whistle-blower policy, that this could be due to negligence at the facility from those whose duty it is to keep these convicts safe. My team and I will be arriving tomorrow to carry out a thorough examination into inmate safety at Juniper Correctional and will be staying in town for as long as it takes to rectify these issues and implement substantial improvements to the safe running of this penitentiary. We do not take the abandonment of the rules by those in charge lightly and look forward to helping correct whatever has caused this unfortunate catastrophe. You have a good day now, and I'll try you at the office." The machine beeped off.

"'Y'have a good day now!'" he'd mocked. Fleming had torn the answering machine from the table, yanking the wire from the wall. It flailed around his head like a whip before he'd hurled the whole infernal contraption at the front door, where it shattered into plastic shards.

After that mess, Fleming had hastily scoffed his dinner in front of the television. There had been a story on the local news about a fatal accident out at Betty's farm. A reporter stood in frame with her while the local PD roved in and out of the barn in the background. The reporter had stated there had been one male fatality. Fleming had wondered if he should try to call Betty. He'd known her and her husband forever, whenever he'd drive up to their house they'd greet him on the porch a real-life vision of Grant Wood's American Gothic. Fleming had got on well with Betty's husband, who'd often looked out for Fleming, even brought meals 'round from time-to-time; the man had been a good cook and an even better ear to listen to Fleming's growing concerns about Juniper Correctional. But as Fleming had started to rise from his seat, he'd glanced over at the door where the entire phone had been smashed to smithereens. A grunt had left his lips. He'd pass by Betty's in the morning, that way he could drop in before work, or depending on what happened tomorrow, he'd call on Betty in the evening. She didn't really have any family anymore, and now, here, in this moment, she was a widow.

He'd wallowed in the armchair for a good few hours, a true pig in shit, suckling the bottle. The taunting swimmer of doubt was slowly drowning, rolling over and over in the powerful currents of scotch which coursed through his veins and muddied his mind. The empty dinner plate sat next to him, piled on top of the previous night's detritus. He stretched his legs out, knocking over an empty bottle, which whirled and came to rest near the coffee table.

Fleming idly mused on cleaning over the upcoming weekend. The place had gone to shit since Martha had left. He thought about her wistfully, why she'd left. Undoubtedly, it was the pressures of the job and his obstinate desire to change the very fabric of the prison from the ground up, pouring himself into the duties so Juniper Correctional could become a beacon of light in a much-troubled system rather than just another casualty. She'd left when his job had become all-consuming, when he spent more time tending to the prisons needs than her own. But when he really thought about Martha, he'd never actually loved her; she had just been a port in a storm. There had been another woman that had won his heart... but it hadn't really worked out. In a way, Fleming had despised Martha ever since the day he succumbed to his carnal yearnings for another's flesh, because he wanted more of it, and she couldn't give him what he truly craved.

Fleming didn't miss the charade of a connection that had existed between the two of them. He missed coming home to a place that was clean; where food was on the table and where someone tidied up after him. As he thought on it, he realised he didn't actually need Martha back. What he needed was a cleaner. He pondered hiring one of the Mexican cleaners he'd let go from the prison a few months ago, but thought better of it. They would have a field day ransacking the house of the man that had sent them packing. A bunch of thieving, tax dodging, sojourners in his house? No, better the three that had escaped deportation were left standing in line at the town square, waiting to be picked up and used for cash in hand jobs that the Juniper townsfolk couldn't be bothered to do themselves. The town had been built on the back of slaves, not citizens, and any work that could be passed off, his fellow Junipereans would send it on.

His head was heavy, weighed down with the mornings meeting and a barrel-full of scotch, a stew fermenting in his body. Fleming languidly reached for a cigarette, lit it, and reclined back into his seat, his mind still swimming, his equilibrium rocking like a ship out at sea. He took a deep intake of sweet nicotine and became light headed almost instantly. A sigh escaped as he closed his eyes. The words from that book, the one Frank had brought to him, seemed to appear before him. He was reading them on the back of his eyelids. How true they were. He lifted the smoke to his mouth, took another deep inhale, and felt his body relax, the tension releasing across his skull. He was drunk. He was tired. And he was apathetic about everything.

Fleming felt something rub up against his leg. It wasn't uncommon for one of the towns stray cats to wander in and feast on his leftovers; or at least, that was the logic his brain applied. In his altered state, he shook a limb out to fling it off. His leg connected, and he felt it topple over. Almost immediately, Fleming felt another brush against his leg. This time something was pawing at him. He shook his leg harder. He dazedly mused that it probably looked as if he were having a fit.

"Fuck off!" he grumped. Fleming flicked whatever it was away with the foot of his other leg. But it was insistent. It came back again, and this time he felt two heavy paws on his thighs. The thing was attempting to get onto his lap.

"What the *fuck* do you want?" Fleming batted his hand forwards as if to wipe away whatever was climbing onto him, half opening his eyes to try and find the annoying feline. "Just get off!"

His hand connected with something hard and he felt it shrink away. But then it returned with more pressure. Whatever it was, it was heavy and now quite aggrieved. His vision was a fishbowl of distorted colour. The combined relaxants had made him near blind.

"Ah said get off!" Fleming batted with his other hand, but this time it was caught by something. Fleming fully opened his eyes. He followed his arm down to where he could see his hand - in the grip of necrotic fingers.

He froze, now fully aware of his surroundings. For all his desire to stand, to get away, he was pinned down by some unknown force. The lights in the house were off, as though in closing his eyes, it had dimmed the whole house. Only the moonlight shone, streaking in through the rain spattered window, splashing patterns that looked like VHS static across the room. But there was something dark in front of him, something silhouetted by the moonlight. It bobbed in front of him, before slinking up his body.

"*Relaxsssssss...*" the thing hissed from unseen lips on a silhouetted head.

Fleming tried to remove his hand from its grip, but the power of the thing was unshakable. It squeezed his wrist. Fleming could feel claws digging into his fleshy wrist and he let out a pained whimper.

"I don't want to hurt you..." The figure in front of Fleming said, its breath smelling of soured milk and rotten flesh, warm and damp on his skin. "I want... to *use you, mould* you. Do you *acccccc-cept...* my request?" The figure released Fleming's arm, and it fell lifelessly over the arm of the chair. He could not command his own arm to move, not with any amount of effort or will. He wanted to snatch it back and cradle it with his other arm, but before he could, the thing was fully on him, sitting on his lap and breathing heavily, anticipating an answer to its request. Hands pinned him to the chair. Fleming could feel the barbs of its claws penetrating the skin of his flabby chest. "Sssssoo, what *do you ssssssay...* Fleming?"

Fleming couldn't shift, couldn't move; he was a passenger on this ride. The thing drew closer, the stench swelling, heavy and suffocating.

"What do you want from me?" mewled Fleming.

The thing pressed forwards. Fleming felt its breath intensify as if it had puckered its mouth and was purposefully blowing on him. Something wet touched his cheek, snaking up to his eye. It flicked off near his eyebrow, a cold trail of saliva left on his skin.

"I want... what's *in here...*" The hidden thing tapped the side of his head, near his temple, "... and what's *innnn...* here!" Another tap, small pins punctured the skin that housed his heart.

"Ah... Ah don... Ah don't understand?" Fleming found words increasingly hard to put together.

"That's becaussse... you don't see... let *me help...* you sssssee!" The terror reached forward in the gloom and placed what Fleming assumed were hands on either side of his head. Pressure built and he felt fingers creeping through what remained of his hair, gaining purchase on his scalp. Fleming was paralysed as he felt something hot jolt his body, an electric shock of searing pain. In the misery of that moment, an epiphany of light burned the darkness away.

He awoke with a start. "Fuck... Fuck! wh... what was that?!"

He looked to his hand, still in pain from the grip of... the cigarette? It had singed his fingers while he dreamt. Fleming dropped the cigarette. It fell and smouldered on the carpet. He shot out of the chair, whirling his arms around like windmill sails. There was no other living thing there. The room was as it had been moments previously: the television droning, lamps lighting the corners, and the wind and rain still hammering at the window. Fleming walked over to his vacated seat and stamped out the cigarette that was smoking on the floor. He glanced into the corners of the room, still trying to locate his nightly visitor despite how preposterous that was.

Was it a dream? An apparition, warning of the impending investigation? What had his visitor wanted; what did it want to show him? What did it want him to see? Fleming rubbished the premonition as a drunken dream, but still turned once more, peering around the room, investigating the deep shadows.

Nothing.

He lifted his hand to his head and rubbed at his temples. Fleming surmised it was time to go to bed, and sleep – if that could come after what had just happened. He walked out to the hallway, stepping over the broken plastic bodies of the telephone and answering machine. He peered upstairs, swearing into the den of the night, and flicked the light on. The darkness scattered into the other vacant unlit rooms.

As he groggily reached out for the bannister, he saw a trail of blood snaking down his forearm. He lifted his arm and inspected it, seeing wounds there as if from a deathly grip, wincing as he probed them with his other hand. His head swam with realisation and the swimmer that had gone down and fought with the dragging currents for so long had surfaced at last.

His visitor was real.

CHAPTER 8

The grey morning found Frank walking the yard, though calling it a yard would suggest some sort of green space and in Juniper Correctional the grass had gone years ago, so he walked on muddy concrete instead. It was a bleak wasteland, badly in need of work. Frank headed toward the bleachers on the far side of the open space, the only neutral place sheltered from the rain.

As he walked, he noted the stakeouts of the day. The Blacks had commandeered the tarp-covered area near the weight station. The Latinx inmates had taken over the best area, a mini shelter near the basketball hoops. White supremacists and rapists had taken over the outdoor picnic area; the flimsy tin had holes scattered in it so a tarpaulin had been stretched to catch the water. Swollen and undrained, it hung low above their heads as the rain continued to fill it up. Frank observed that every couple of minutes a side would bulge like a tumor and rain gushed off in a steady stream that splashed those closest to it.

To Frank, the divisions and racial stand points were all a bit

ROSS JEFFERY

| ROSS JEFFERY

clichéd, but it seemed to keep the peace. And Juniper Correctional, right now, could do with a bit of that.

Frank continued toward the plastic seating. The bleachers were considered a safe zone, a place for those who hadn't been, or would never be, picked up by the gangs, or ones who just hadn't yet been convinced to pick a side. Some had no choice in the matter; they were easy pickings, intimidated into being slaves of gang leaders or made a "prison bitch." Others were more like soldiers for a cause they were indoctrinated into but didn't believe in. They were hostages that couldn't leave without a bloody, and probably deadly, confrontation. Protection in this place made the strongest of wills bend like a stalk of wheat in a storm. Frank had seen it first hand: Juniper Correctional made monsters of men, willing to fight at the literal blink of an eye.

Out of the rain and beneath the awkward shelter over the bleachers, Frank stood listening to the water continuously pounding like someone hammering on the door to get in a church. Or, perhaps more pertinently, to get out of some unholy place. There was a strange hum in the air. Was it the power cables overhead, humming with the energy flowing through their inner cabling? Frank had returned to JC after only a few hours of sleep; perhaps it was that. He hated pulling a double shift, but he was always there to help others.

As he stood there, looking out at the assembled gangs huddled under their various covers, he longed to be home, to see his wife again. He missed her as if a part of him had been torn away and left open a festering wound. When he had woken that morning, she wasn't there. Exactly as the day before. Rainy days made him want to be with her, under the sheets, connecting with her in ways they hadn't explored.

His thoughts turned to another married person left alone. Frank mused about the accident at Betty's farm. The woman was abruptly a widow; how quickly things could change. When he had gone downstairs, expecting to find Cynthia like he always did, hip checked against the counter and smelling the scent drifting from her mug of rich coffee, all he had found was an empty house. Maybe she had gone to see how Betty was coping. It was the kind of thing she would do. Frank loved how compassionate Cynthia was, how she cared for others in an unwavering commitment. She saw the good in everyone. She'd not had it easy. Being a black woman in Juniper was like living with the bubonic plague. A body was automatically shunned, dismissed, and insulted. But his wife always showed love towards her haters, in a way that had gotten to them more than any harsh words ever would.

Frank returned from his reverie as thunder rumbled across the sky. He scanned the yard. The gangs ebbed and flowed in their own tension filled sea. The guards on the towers looked eager to fire warning shots. Lightning wasn't the only thing crackling in the prison.

The crowd on the bleachers were a sorry lot of misfits. They were the ones that didn't quite fit in with any mould. What the society of Juniper would label 'freaks of nature'. Mainly consisting of paedophiles, which were not welcome in any of the gangs, there was also a smattering of homosexuals - a fate worse than death in this place. If they hadn't been picked up by the Sisterhood, they soon would be. A nighttime call or a secluded spot in the prison would be their initiation to a gang who denied their true selves and inflicted a toxic rhetoric on the dangers of sodomy while simultaneously getting a blow job by the favoured pet of the week.

Frank turned and began walking the length of the polyethylene boards, relieved to be out of the downpour. Every now and then the thunder would rumble and a flash of lightning would soon follow. Pools of water splashed under his footfall, and with each heavy plod, his keys and baton jingled at his side. He passed several inmates who nodded or grunted as he walked by, content to minimally acknowledge his presence. Antonio Frustaglio was seated at the end of the rows, his huge frame melted over the bench he resided on.

As Frank drew closer, he noticed that Antonio had his face buried in a book. His skin was covered in a thin layer of moisture which Frank assumed was rainwater. With a start, Frank realised that he recognised the book clutched in Antonio's hands. It was the one that he'd dropped off at the library yesterday, the one from Jasper's cell, Frank couldn't believe how quickly it had been recirculated back into the populous.

"Good book, Antonio?" Frank asked.

Antonio was so enraptured he didn't seem to even hear the question. Frank watched as he turned each page with gusto, almost tearing it with the speed of flipping over the page. Antonio's blood-shot eyes flicked back and forth across the page as if he were watching some thrilling tennis rally; he read at an insatiable speed.

"Antonio...?" Frank waved his hand in the man's face. Antonio glanced up from the book, a vacant expression in his eyes. "Good book?" Frank nodded towards the book, which remained tightly gripped in Antonio's sausage fingers.

"Errrr... yeah... it's good." Antonio seemed confused.

"What's it about? I've seen it around a lot lately."

"Well, I don't know... it's difficult to say... don't really know yet, but it's speaking to me in ways I never expected. It's opening my eyes..." Antonio slowly returned his gaze to the book. He lifted a finger, wet it like someone licking a popsicle, then he flipped the page over and continued absorbing the words through his wide watery eyes.

"Can I take a look?" Frank asked. Antonio didn't move. Frank wondered if his words were lost in the thunder or the thrumming noise of the rain. He was about to ask again when he heard the bell ringing from the observation tower. He turned and peered up at the guard; it was difficult to see through the rain but he was sure it was Samantha, judging by the cut of the figure: short and with a shaved head, and an axe to grind against the establishment. He couldn't help but like the queer prison guard. She was like him in a way, an outcast and a victim of common gossip from the bigoted, backward Juniper locals.

Frank knew what the bell signalled. He lifted the collar of his jacket and stepped out from the bleachers and into the downpour. As he glanced back, he noticed that Antonio was still glued to his book, which was strange. The bell meant fresh meat, and with Antonio's... tastes, Frank had figured he'd want to be first in line for some young-looking bit of ass, grim though that was. Frank guessed he was judging Antonio just as many of the Junipereans judged him. It just went to show, you couldn't judge a book by its cover.

As Frank trotted across the quadrant, he could feel the buzz of excitement in the air. The separated groups all began whooping and hollering obscenities, gesticulations flying like flaming arrows between the triangle of gangs. It reminded Frank of the fire triangle he'd learnt in school – each element feeding into the next, a cocktail of bad intensions. When they all converged at once, it made for a bad day indeed.

The gangs stayed put under their awnings, not wanting to venture out into the sopping courtyard, but they vied with each other for the best vantage point to see the delivery of takeout that was soon to be arriving. Frank reached the other side of the courtyard. Reaching out, he placed his key in the lock, turned it, and walked through the chain linked fence. He then repeated the process to lock the gate behind him. Other officers wandered into the yard, like ants from a flooded hill. Recreation time was almost over, but they wouldn't be moving anyone until the prisoner transport bus was in and the new inmates were given the baptism of fire they deserved as they stepped off the bus, more often than not sweating with fear.

Frank walked the length of the honeycombed chain linked fence, toward the drop-off zone for the Juniper Correctional transport. As he stood there, waiting for the huge gates in the outer wall to open, he wondered when on earth it was going to stop raining.

CHAPTER 9

"You guys better not give me any shit. Y'all don't wanna start your stay at Juniper Correctional in the hole," the guard shouted over the noise of the bus growling into life outside the court house. He was a short and scraggly man, barely more than a wafer of flesh, the bird's nest of hair atop his head unkempt and greasy looking. The guard turned to the driver and laughed at his own statement. He twisted back to facing the inmates and readjusted the shotgun nestled securely in his arms, the stock resting on his spindly legs.

As he laughed, Klein Lehey sat two rows away, shackled and manacled, watching as the guard's mouth opened wide, revealing teeth like a burnt fence; black, stubby shards poked out amid red and irritated gums. Klein just sat there silently judging his ferrymen. The shotgun guard was clearly the runt of this outfit.

There were three officers in total: the guard facing the prisoners, the driver, and another officer riding in the passenger seat with the window opened just a crack, allowing in the sound of the heavy rain, like a constant backdrop of static. A fine misty spray crept in and enveloped the whole bus. Klein enjoyed the cooling effect on his face. The passenger-seat guard was smoking, blowing his sweet-smelling tar into the bus, filling the space in a haze, and filling the lungs of the shackled prisoners, torturing them before they'd even set foot in Juniper Correctional.

"Close the fucking window, Larry. It's like a cat's spraying my fucking neck here!" shotgun guard yelled, followed by another caterwaul of a laugh. Everything he said seemed to be followed by an intense cackle, as though he thought himself quite a comedian.

"Keep your fucking drawers on, Davy," Larry retorted. He nudged the driver and said softly, "Wearin' his mother's today, innit he?" They shared a snicker at Davy's expense as he sat oblivious to all but his own importance. Larry began to wind the window up. Instantly the sound of the rain on the roof seemed to intensify in its relentless hammering.

The bus pulled up at a stoplight. As it sat idling, the tension mounted. Inmates shuffled in their seats, their shackles jangling as they tried to shift their feet, eyes darting from Davy to their comrades in chains, sizing each other up. Klein was annoyed with it all.

The light changed to green and the bus moved forward slowly, the wipers slashing at the rain-covered window, headlights on full beam. The soon-to-be-inmates observed how heavy the rain was falling, and some of them began praying that their short ride would end in a traffic accident. Their minds filled with visions from a Hollywood movie set: the bus spinning out of control, crashing into a tree-lined street or down a canyon gorge. It was the desperate hope of being spared their incarceration. Many of them would rather try their luck with surviving the accident and spending their life on the run than the shame of prison life.

None wished more for a chance to escape than Klein. Though still a young man, he was all too familiar with the horrors that waited for him in Juniper Correctional. He was a local boy, had grown up going out into the hills that surrounded the prison and hurling rocks over the walls; he and his friends made a game of trying to hit those on the inside. He'd even seen the chain-gangs working the roads when he was little, seen the long rows of black men swinging hammers and crushing stones. One man's skin had split along whiplashes he'd received from the overseer. Klein had never gotten over the fear he'd one day be made to work the same chain.

But the real reason Klein wanted the bus to crash, why he wanted to escape, was due to some... unfinished business. He'd been arrested for assaulting his wife, Janet. The problem was, he hadn't been aiming to leave a bloody mess of a woman, he'd been planning to leave a bloody corpse of one. He'd gone to town on her, a beating followed by a bludgeoning with a steel poker. But it was his bravado that had gotten him tossed on the bus. After he'd done the deed, beating Janet to within an inch of her petrified life, Klein had gone and run his mouth off in the local watering hole, boasting about it as though he'd just broken some kind of record.

When the Sheriff had found Janet crawling down the 701, he'd thought she'd been run over by a car. The lacerations marking her head had been so deep, like the split skin of a rotten watermelon, the Sheriff wasn't sure how she was still alive. Juniper was backward in many ways, and while wife-beating wasn't exactly uncommon, the Sheriff had been shocked by what he saw. He'd wasted no time going straight to Klein's favoured bar, and found him bragging about his exploits. Klein had been arrested on the spot.

Klein leaned toward the window, the chains connecting linked wrists to linked ankles clinking as he shuffled over the cracked leather seat. His body was stretched in an awkward position but he managed to rest his head against the cold glass. He watched the rivulets of water work their way down, joining with other droplets of water, growing fat until they were blown off the window.

They passed the town square. The Dead Mexican bar, where he'd enjoyed his last taste of freedom, stood tucked into a row of closed shopfronts, the ugly neon sign throwing gaudy light into the street. Then, like the rain on the window, it was gone.

The sky was dark. It was mid-morning but a perpetual darkness had swept in with the storm, choking out any light before it could get a hold of the day. The storm continued to rage like Klein's thoughts in his head, growing with intensity, the unfinished business with his wife and what was awaiting him at Juniper Correctional revolving like a twister. Each mistake he'd made replayed in his mind with blinding clarity. He should have just killed the dumb bitch.

The bus hydroplaned sharply and Klein's head came away from the window with the momentum. For a brief moment, they were out of control, weightless and in a kind of horizontal free-fall. An electric crackle of hope pulsed through the bus as the prisoners looked to get their chance to escape. Then the bus corrected itself.

Klein's head swung back and ricocheted against the window. "Fuck!" Others echoed his cry, but only Klein's was about the loss of finishing the job he'd left behind.

"Watch your fucking tongue, you piece of shit!" Davy barked. He glanced over his shoulder, checking that the bus wasn't about to nosedive into a ditch.

"Fucking hypocrite," said the inmate in front of Klein, a brooding guy covered in tattoos. The ink formed a spider's web which seemed to wrap itself around the inmate's throat, a tarantula disappearing down his neck, beneath his collar, and deep into his olive-green jumpsuit. He glared at Davy, who sat directly across from him.

Davy turned back, a wry smirk on his face, eyes alive with

some type of evil intent. His hands gripped the shotgun in his lap so tightly that his knuckles turned white. Klein knew what was coming before the inmate did.

The butt of the shotgun flashed out, ramming the spider-tattoo inmate in the mouth. The inmate's head rocked back and then slumped forwards. Klein could hear him spitting clotted, wet lumps, and saw him struggling within his restraints trying to stem the blood pouring out of his shattered mouth.

"Something funny, motherfucker?" Davy snarled. The inmate was coughing and moaning in pain. Davy leaned forward, resting on his gun. He cupped one of his hands around his ear. "I'm sorry. Did you say something?" The inmate shook his head. His chin hung against his chest, rocking side to side as the bus continued its fateful journey.

"What the hell, Davy?!" Larry had turned around and was staring at the man from behind the mesh that separated the inmates from the front cab.

"Sonofabitch insulted me." Davy leaned back and cocked his head to the side, "Need to get these pieces of shit in line before we drop them off, don't we?"

"Yeah, but they need to be able to walk off the fucking bus."

"Walk, drag, gurney... fuckers still got a cell at the end of the day – food and fucking board, the whole shebang."

Larry turned back and picked up his clipboard, scribbling something down. Klein was now eye level with Davy since the inmate in front was doubled over. Their stares locked. Klein didn't blink.

"What're you looking at?" Davy spat, through a thin-lipped snarl.

Klein shrugged his shoulders nonchalantly, then slowly turned his gaze away from Davy.

"Thought so. Alright beating on a woman, but ain't got no balls when it comes to a man, huh?"

Klein's hands gripped his knees. The whirlwind was still raging within him, threatening to break free. He glanced back at Davy. "Says the man with the shotgun."

"What'd you say?" Davy rose out of his seat slightly.

"Did I stutter?" Klein deadpanned, his eyes narrowing into slits.

"What?"

"Did I stutter? I said, 'Says the man with the shotgun,'" Klein replied slowly.

"Why you son of a bitch..." Davy began to unclip his seatbelt.

"Sit the fuck down, Davy!" Larry hollered over his shoulder.

Klein observed in that instant that everyone served someone, and Larry was Davy's superior.

Davy's jaw clenched, making his face look even more skeletal than it already was. His muscles twitched under his skin, as if he had tiny creatures burrowing in his flesh. He clipped his seatbelt back on. The bus slowly came to a stop. A smile broke across his tight, cracked grey lips. Davy stifled a laugh. The rain continued to thunder down on the roof again, like a marching band.

"Something funny?" Klein mimicked Davy's earlier taunt.

"Actually, yes." Davy wiped some white spittle from the corner of his mouth with the back of his hand. "Y'see, out there, you think beating on a woman makes you in charge, makes you a big man. But in there?" Davy flipped a thumb over his shoulder in the direction the bus was pointing. "In there, beating on a woman, all that will get you is one thing. Do you know what that is?" Davy didn't let Klein answer before cutting back in. "Being made someone else's bitch. You'll be lucky to see out the week once those guys find out you mangled your wife." Davy doubled over with laughter again, unable to contain his joy at Klein's expense, his blackened teeth flashing in the light. 'Only one thing worse than a woman beater, you know what that is? Kiddy fiddlers. They get chewed up and spat out of Juniper Correctional as quickly as they arrive. But guys like you who beat women... well they get made someone's bitch. You'll become that in here, mark my fucking words, asshole. Beatings. Raping. Abuse. It's all coming to you. You'll get to feel what it's like, you dumb sonofabitch!" Davy rocked back into his chair, pleased with his diatribe.

Klein shrugged his shoulders again, his bravado his shield; he'd always had that way about him. People in Juniper assumed it was due to him being shorter than average. His expression remained steadfast and unmoving. Any worries he had about life on the inside remained concealed. He glanced to his left and noticed that they were almost there. A sign by the road read;

JUNIPER CORRECTIONAL NEXT EXIT

DO NOT PICK UP HITCHHIKERS

As the bus waited to be let into the double-walled perimeter, Davy kept trying to goad Klein to look at him, to give him another excuse to start another onslaught, but Klein looked right through him; through the mesh, through the windscreen, and out into his immediate future looming on the horizon. The caged doors of Juniper Correctional loomed before the bus. They stood unmoving, nestled within the stone walls that made up the outer perimeter.

He heard a distant *thunk* break through the noises of the bus. The doors began to swing open slowly. The bus started up again, rumbling into life and rolling forward, inching towards the gaping and hungry maw of Juniper Correctional.

As the bus moved through the outer wall, Klein noticed chain linked fences between the walls, dividing the internal space like the intestine of the prison. The other convicts on the bus were peering out through the now steamed-up windows, getting a first glimpse of the life that awaited them. Klein could hear someone weeping in the back of the bus, mumbling incoherently to himself.

The bus shuddered to a stop near one of the guard towers that stood like monoliths at various points within the prison grounds. The engine turned off and the doors opened with a hiss. Rain immediately began to slash through the opening.

"Welcome to the church of JC!" Davy jeered.

The inmates were soon unshackled from the floor rings. They shuffled forward and began stepping off the bus in their olive-green jumpsuits. The huge **J.C.** printed on the back of the jumpsuit in front of him amused Klein; there was no way some holy Son of God was going to save them from what awaited.

They lined up in the driving rain, where a man wearing a prison uniform moved down the line with militaristic precision, ticking each inmate off his checklist. "All present and correct. What happened to him?" The guard pointed at the inmate with the spider tattoo, still bleeding from a ruined jaw.

"It was Davy," Larry muttered, almost a whisper "sorry, Frank, he's a bit of a loose cannon."

"If I have another prisoner that comes in here needing medical assistance, I'll personally see to it that he gets a week suspension, no pay!" Frank glared at Davy, who was off beneath the shelter, having a smoke, cradling his shotgun in the crook of his elbow, looking like a vagabond from a wild west film. Klein wondered what this Frank would have thought of Davy's taunting.

He turned back to Larry as the officer said, "Sorry, Frank. It won't happen again."

"It better not," Frank said sharply, before turning to address the prisoners.

Klein watched as Frank cleared his throat and began shouting over the wind and rain. "Welcome to Juniper Correctional, inmates. You will be processed shortly. You'll each be showered, deloused, and given your prison-issue clothing. Then we'll show you to your cells. Follow me!" The guard turned and headed towards the tower.

There were whoops and cheers from the inmates on the other side of the fence, wolf whistles and insults slung like shit at the newbies, trying to see what would stick. The inmates from the bus slowly followed Frank, and Klein took his last breaths of free air before he disappeared into the bowels of the prison.

CHAPTER 10

The bank of monitors in Fleming's office flicked between the various cameras around Juniper Correctional. The eyes of the anxious Warden flicked around the screens, trying to spot anything out of the ordinary. Fleming's lips were moving, as if he were uttering some incantation that his mind was unaware of, trying to fix the day that had started so poorly.

He'd woken in a cold sweat, as if he were lying on a waterbed that had sprung a leak in the night. Resigned to changing, he'd slid out of his wet sheets and begun walking across the room. His feet had splashed in puddles. It had dredged up a time he'd tried his best to keep buried, drowned with whiskey and work, but its head was breaking the surface again. Everything had come flooding back to him: the dark, the damp, the well... and *her*.

The alarm had woken him from the dream. He'd flailed around, feeling like the sheet lying across him was a ghost suffocating him. He hadn't been able to breathe, his lungs seemingly filled with water, but as his consciousness grew, he'd tasted the sweet influx of oxygen. Fleming had coughed and spluttered as he'd fallen from the bed, landing on his outstretched hands and crashing down on his knees. To his surprise, the puddles were gone, but his mind was still latched onto the dream logic – he'd awoken and there had been a leak in the house, the rainwater had pooled...

Fleming had stood groggily, his knees letting out their protestations in creaks and groans. But in the din he'd made out a dripping sound. He'd glanced up at the ceiling, checking for leaks. Perhaps there had been some truth in his dream after all. The rain hadn't let up and was hitting the roof, clinking like tiny needles peppering metal. He had moved towards the bathroom, naked and still groggy. His hanging gut had jiggled with each heavy, slapping footfall. He'd pushed the door open to see the tap dripping. And he'd thought of her again.

The black, lifeless face. The afro floating around her head like a ghastly halo, a sea sponge that had soaked up dirty drain water. A shudder had run down his body.

He walked in and twisted the faucet, but it didn't shut off... so he wrapped his fat fingers around it and strangled it closed. He felt strong, like he had all those years ago.

Glancing up at the mirror, he'd taken in his reflection. Grey and clammy skin surrounded bloodshot eyes rimmed by dark circles. Lines had riddled his face. He'd aged, almost overnight.

He had looked at his naked body, fatty rolls like a child's stacking toy, his blue and pink veins the coloured plastic rings. He had been disgusted by what he saw.

The grey, naked skin of the new inmates drew Fleming from his reverie and his lips paused their soundless muttering to quirk into a smirk as he watched them shuffle awkwardly into their cells. Many changes had been implemented when he'd taken power, but the one thing he had insisted on keeping, however wrong it may have been, was bringing inmates into the prison stark naked. It gave the guards the upper hand from the start. Intimidation ruled supreme in correctional facilities. Shame broke the inmates' spirits, and the vulnerability they felt robbed them of the last drops of pride they had – all of these things Fleming believed made the prisoners more malleable in those first few hours, and so he had continued degrading them further than they already were. Many Fleming had heard crying for their mothers once they were packed away in their cells.

He watched as the guards moved the prisoners along as they carried rolled mattresses and clothes. Most tried to use them to protect what was left of their dignity, considering their asses were hanging out for all the world to see. He couldn't hear it, but he knew there were whistles and jeering, other prisoners shouting sweet terms of endearments at every ass they watched stumble along the gangway. Each inmate was slowly ushered into a vacant cell, where they disappeared from view. Then the screen cycled onto the next image. Four people were quickly approaching his office. He barely registered the encroachers before there was a dainty rapping on his door. Fleming grabbed the tumbler from his table and swiftly stowed it in his desk drawer, checked the rest of his table, and adjusted his tie. He never wore a tie, and just having it around his neck felt like a hangman's noose. He could feel it constricting his throat with each movement. But today was different.

The knock came again, this time harder and more persistent.

"Yes?" Fleming put on an air of importance.

The door creaked open. Three unrecognisable people flowed into the office, as though a floodgate opened. The last of the three turned and said something inaudible to Nevaeh and then closed the door in her face before the office manager could say anything in reply. Fleming made to stand, but his pant leg caught under his chair and he almost lost balance.

The first woman thrust out a hand to him. "Warden Fleming? Nice to make your acquaintance. I'm Dolores Fink from the Correctional Investigation team of the U.S. Marshal office."

Fleming reached out and took her smooth hand in his chubby paw. He didn't know if it was her hand that was moist or his, and he cursed inwardly that he hadn't wiped his hand first. The smell of coconut oil began to fill the office.

"Do you understand why we are here?" Dolores removed her hand from Fleming's. As she sat down, Fleming noticed that she absentmindedly wiped it on her black trousers. She crossed her legs and relaxed into the chair.

"As Ah understand things, some-one feels these suicides are not as they seem."

"You could say that... how many is that now?" She flipped open a file and offhandedly scanned it. Fleming watched the corner of her mouth tick into a smirk. He took a moment to process her before answering. Clearly, she was a black bitch with a chip on her shoulder. A tailored suit, the scent of expensive perfume and superiority. She reminded him of someone he'd used to know, someone he thought he'd shared a connection with; but she had gotten married and it was a lifetime ago at this point.

Fleming became aware of a feeling that Dolores was judging him because he was from a small town that had quite the coloured past. Well, he'd punish her for underestimating him. "Ah believe it's-"

"Four," interjected the man sitting level with Dolores. Fleming turned to look at the person. He was another African American, a hulking mass of muscle bulging under a tight suit and shirt; it was as if his clothes had been painted on. Fleming briefly thought of finding a way for this man and the colossal inmate Christopher to have a fight, just for shits and giggles.

"Correct. Oh. Sorry, Mr. Fleming, before I carry on, perhaps I should make some introductions. This is Alex Rose, my second in command. He'll be conducting interviews of staff and inmates, and reviewing your policies at Juniper Correctional. And this," Dolores waved absentmindedly over her shoulder, to a bespectacled wraith of a mousy woman, plain in every way, "is Sophie Collins. She's only here as a stenographer."

"Right..." Fleming's voice almost quivered with laughter, and he unknowingly raised his eyebrows.

"Everything okay, Mr. Fleming?"

"It is *War-den* Fleming, and you'd do well to remember that." Fleming's tone conveyed only authority and betrayed none of the disgust he felt. Inwardly, he was seething, railing against her obvious contempt for him; it seemed to ooze from her like pus from a festering wound. It made him reflect on the indoctrination of his parents, one drilled into him from childhood, about the uppity ideals of those damn darkies. But he had not risen so high for nothing. For more than thirty years, he had faced-off with some of the worst, most pompous-assed human beings imaginable. This paper-pusher of an investigator would not get the better of him.

"My apologies if I offended you, Warden Fleming; it was not meant to be a slight. We understand you have done a great many things to... rectify the issues at Juniper Correctional." Dolores uttered her words with contempt at having to address this privileged white man, sitting there on his crumbling throne.

He nodded in acquiescence. "Where would you like to start?" Fleming offered, Southern voice mollifying. He turned his gaze back to the monitors out of habit. The screens flipped over to the next camera. Fleming felt his heart beat faster, felt a hand grip him around the throat.

It was the well.

It was there on the camera. But... how could it be? He leaned towards the monitor and as he did, the camera seemed to zoom in.

Now leaning over the edge of the well, he could see his own hands on the bricks, peering deeper into the abyss below. Two blank eyes, white with a pinprick of black, stared back at him, piercing and malevolent. His skin ran cold. Things wriggled over his flesh; he looked down at his hands and saw maggots crawling over them. He jumped back.

"Warden Fleming, is everything ok?" Dolores was reaching over the table, genuine concern etched onto her face.

Fleming saw her hand, with a perfect French manicure, resting on his. How familiar; how strange. It reminded him of that night - the car, the rejection, the blood. He recoiled from her touch.

Dolores' expression soured. She withdrew into her seat.

It wasn't you, Fleming thought, desperately, *it's her!* He cleared his throat. "Ah'm sorry, Ah... ahem. Ah did not sleep well last night."

"Worried?" Alex sneered.

"Not a'tall, simply bad dreams. Why? Is there something Ah *should* be worried about?" Fleming stared at Alex a long moment before glancing down at his hands again. He could still see things wriggling over his flesh, but realised it was from the shadows cast by the rain on his window.

"Well, it is quite a serious charge, Warden Fleming, otherwise we wouldn't be here. The ramifications of our findings could have widespread consequences-" she paused and tilted her head. "-but if you work with us, we are sure everything will work out just fine."

Fleming knew Dolores was loving this, sticking it to the white man. *What a fucking liar.* He smoothed away invisible dust on his desktop as if he were wiping her disdainful face off. "Well, why don't you three g'on about your business and let me get back to running this prison, *without* your incessant distractions." He dismissed them with a condescending wave of his hand.

"Certainly. Shall we speak with the young woman outside about getting set up somewhere in the prison?"

"Oh Ah'm *sure* there's a cell available."

"I think we'd need something bigger, but thank you." Dolores thrust her hand out over the desk again. Fleming looked at it, hanging across the table like some United Colors of Benetton advert waiting to happen. He ignored it and wrestled himself out of his chair, heading for the door. The others got to their feet and followed him. As he opened the door, he avoided any attempt at eye contact. Sophie left, scurrying away like a rat fleeing a sinking ship. Alex stalked out, sneering at Fleming again. But as Dolores breezed past Fleming, he could smell that sweet coconut again. Was it in her hair, her lotion, or was it just her natural smell... he couldn't be sure. But it was intoxicating and repellent in equal measure. It reminded him of *her*.

"Pleasure, Warden Fleming," Dolores offered on her way out.

"Was it?" And with that, Fleming closed the door on them.

He leaned back against the door, lifted his hand to his face and rubbed at his eyes. When he opened them again, he was staring out at the rain hammering against his window. Always hammering. The floor had come alive with rain worms. He felt a chill run down him, his mind flitting back and forth over the previous events: the maggots, the well, the nightmare, his night visitor, and the note. The suicide. He muttered under his breath, something he'd been repeating all morning, though he hadn't even been aware of it. Only now had it risen above the din outside.

He walked back to his desk and grabbed a bottle of scotch, cracked the lid open, and poured himself a large glass. He moved over to the window and stood looking out at Juniper. The mantra returned again and he spoke the words firmly, hoping in doing so they would fall into place.

"'The only thing necessary for the triumph of evil, is that good men and women do nothing.'"

Through sheets of rain, and the swinging pendulum of the pulley rope Fleming's eyes returned to the hill near the woods, and the standing sentinel of the well.

CHAPTER 11

Lunchtime at Juniper Correctional was like feeding time at the zoo. The plethora of options available to the inmates included everything from basic quarrels to stealing cutlery for making shivs. Though there were always an abundance of guards on duty who should have been paying attention, mistakes were often made, because catching up on the latest ball game or the latest gossip mattered more than the safety of the inmates

Klein's first day at Juniper Corrections was no exception. He noted that the guards had a few extra things on their minds. He'd heard rumblings about some woman called Betty and her now dead husband. Davy had sworn it was foul play. Even Petty speculated it was Betty herself that had whacked the old dodger, but he'd been quickly clipped on the ear by Larry. But that was all there really was to know: she was now a widow, stuck out on the outskirts of town with only her thoughts for company.

He also noticed three suits walking around, eyeing the guards and the prisoners as if they were meat before a hawk. One was observing the lunch routine from up on the gangway, a mousy looking woman clearly scared of her own shadow, let alone brave enough to venture down with the depraved and deplorable. She wasn't a looker, but Klein knew there were men who'd take her nonetheless. Her head bobbed as she followed a swarthy man talking to the Blacks, leveraging their shared skin colour to get details out of them – and some of them were actually falling for it. The third person was snooping around near the guard station. From what the guards and Klein had witnessed so far, she was the one in charge: a slender athletic black woman, clipboard in hand, and an axe to grind.

Klein sat at the table closest to the corner, where he could easily watch the rest of the room. The only things behind him were the wall, a trashcan, and three guards speculating on whatever was to come after the Marshals finished their investigation.

"You know, if they shut this place down, the town's gonna go with it," Davy said, chewing the inside of his own mouth with his broken teeth.

"You reckon?" Petty asked, wide-eyed.

"What are you blabbering about, Davy?" Larry grunted, irritated. Perhaps it was the latest suicide, perhaps the presence of the Marshals, but Klein noted the tensions seemed extremely high.

"Ain't no other place can take a workforce the size of ours. Ain't another job going in thirty mile!" Davy said. "And definitely ain't a job this enjoyable." He grinned his black-toothed leer as he saw the spider-tattooed inmate take a seat, his mouth a lacework of puckered skin and stitches.

"Then we gotta stop these marshals," Petty murmured. "We gotta make sure they don't find any dirt on us."

Larry snorted. "If it's gonna happen, it's gonna happen. Ain't nothing we can do about it."

"That's mighty pessimistic," Petty said.

"Shut up, kid," Davy said, but it was half-hearted. Klein reckoned it was more related to Petty being such a wet blanket. After the incident on the bus, he could tell that Davy preferred angry tornado types.

A brief pause filled the space behind Klein, then Larry said, "What about Frank?"

"What d'ya mean?" Davy sounded sour at the mention of his name.

"Well, him being Mr. Goody Two Shoes, maybe he'll get to keep his job? Hell, maybe he'll keep this place standing."

Davy muttered a string of swear words under his breath. "You might just be right, Larry, but not in the way you think. I reckon he'll end up banging the black bitch to get us a pass on the inspection. You know he likes a little bit of black puddin'!"

Their laughter rolled over the inmates, harsh and cruel. Klein didn't blink.

———

Frank knew what they were saying. He wasn't an idiot, and had seen Davy looking from him to Dolores, but he paid it no mind. He was there to perform a job, and at that moment, he was the only guard doing it. There'd been a rumour that some of the newbies like Officer Petty thought he was putting on airs and graces for the Marshals, but the guards who'd been there longer knew better and had laughed when they'd told Frank. Eventually everybody learned that was just the way Frank was - couldn't miss a beat.

He stayed moving. "An idle mind was the devil's workshop," he recalled his wife saying one time; she'd caught him drinking on the porch instead of cutting down a fallen tree that had partially blocked their driveway. *She has a way with words,* Frank mused as he kept circling the hall, taking in the inmates before him. He knew some of these men would sell their grandmother for a fix, because some of them had. Frank watched as the male Marshal exchanged fist bumps with a group of the inmates. He puzzled over the man's name for a moment, trying to decide if it was Andre or Antony... Alex, maybe? Frank settled on that for the time being.

The other guards were now pointing in Alex's direction, watching the fist bumps and handshakes. He couldn't make it out, but he was sure they were saying something racist. Their scowls gave them away.

The Marshal with the clipboard was heading over to the lunch line. She walked past the serving hatch and peered into the kitchen. Frank observed that the chefs all had their hairnets on, wore clean aprons, and none of them were smoking in the kitchen. He guessed they all got the memo about the investigation.

Marshal Fink began talking with the inmates that were still waiting for their tray of food. Officer Petty, who had moved away from Larry and Davy and was managing the line, seemed to visibly tense at her arrival, his hand instinctively reaching down to his baton. Women were a rare commodity in this prison, especially one so attractive. Frank absently wondered how long it had been since he'd had sex, and how good Dolores might taste.

The thought brought him up cold.

He could never cheat on his wife! He huffed and rubbed his chin. Shit, working in this place was a sickness. If his wife had heard his thoughts, she would have flayed him alive. He shook his head. This place had a thing with corrupting all that was good. No one entered that didn't leave as a stripped down, chewed up husk, and that included the guards.

He watched as Petty stepped forward and asked, "Could you step back from the inmates, ma'm?"

There was an instant hush around the room. Larry and Davy

ceased chatting, turned and stared at the young man, clearly thinking he had more hair on his balls than they'd initially thought.

The Marshal blinked slowly at him and then complied. "Yes, of course... so sorry." She swirled a pen around in the air as if she were trying to perform an incantation, her face questioning. "What's your name?"

He coughed on his words. "Petty. Officer Bill Petty."

"Thank you, Officer Petty. Your concern is much appreciated." She stepped back from the prisoners, and began scribbling notes.

Petty looked as though he was about to pass out, the colour draining from his face. He glanced about looking for Davy's approval but Davy averted his gaze. Petty stood there like a lost boy, then he seemed to shake loose the fear. "Next!" he bellowed, his chest puffed up again as he shoved the nearest inmate toward the servery.

Frank had come around the end of the tables and was heading down another aisle. He could see one of the new inmates, a short little fellow that went by the name of Klein, sitting by himself near the corner where Larry and Davy lounged. His tray of food sat in front of him untouched. Frank observed him taking in his surroundings. It was always a difficult pill to swallow. These new fish always stuck out at first, fearful of making alliances and what they might cost in the long run.

Considering Klein's rap, Frank was intrigued by his choice of seat. Those convicted of sex crimes would normally sit near the guard station when they were first processed, thinking they'd be protected. But the guards hated them as much as the other inmates; if Juniper still had the death penalty, they'd have been hanging in the yard. But the penalty had been repealed, so the guards would simply turn a blind eye, or leave a few doors unlocked in the evening, forget they'd seen someone slip a knife off a table or tray. Some went further, changing a shift when given the nod by an inmate. Frank was not like these guards. While he despised the kiddy fiddlers, it was his job to keep those in the prison as protected as possible. It was his job, but he didn't have to like it.

Frank started walking towards Klein. He always tried to check in on the new inmates when they arrived as part of his working practice to start the dialogue and begin the long process to rehabilitation. His mother had instilled in him the idea that a personal touch went a long way and his buddies at the AA meetings used to have a saying, "If you can't love anyone today, at least try not to hurt anybody." The other guards treated the inmates as numbers, but Frank liked to treat them as people, and in doing so, it meant he rarely had any issues with the inmates. They seemed to like him and listen to him, to be more open to his leading.

As Frank approached, Antonio barrelled down the aisle opposite him, and stood in front of Klein with the book gripped underneath his tray of food. Klein lifted his eyes to greet Antonio with a soured glance, clearly irked that he'd been interrupted from his time by this large abomination that stood before him. Frank knew in that moment that Klein was trouble. It seemed to simmer in his eyes, a deep-seated, slow burning hatred.

Antonio dropped his tray down and swung his gargantuan behind over the metal stool. The inmate's body seemed to envelop the seat, flabby sides rippling down like wax from a candle. He was oblivious to his surroundings, his face once again buried in the book he'd been reading in the yard. As Frank passed, he could hear incoherent babbling. Turning away from Antonio, he glanced up to see Klein eyeballing him. His eyes were dead, but in a very non-corpse way.

A while back, Frank had noted that Antonio's eyes were burnt out, as though his brain was a lightbulb that had exploded. Klein's, however, were pure cold; serial-killer eyes. Frank felt his body strain to shutter, but he didn't want to give the prisoner the upper hand so early in their "relationship..." if it could be called that.

Klein's eyes flicked away when he heard laughter coming from the corner of the lunch hall.

Frank followed his gaze down the aisle, where someone was cackling. Frank noticed that Officer Davy had moved across the lunch room and was in discussion with The Sisters. The group was Neo-Nazi, racist scum that blighted his prison like locusts on crops. The irony of a homosexual cult following Nazi ideology was not lost on Frank.

The Sisters dominated one corner of the room, some flouting protocol by sitting on the actual table tops, others standing around them, guarding the inner circle, like a royal court willing to do the bidding of the depraved queen at the drop of a hat. And that queen was Henry Crumb, sitting at the centre of it all, his shaved head entirely tattooed, a scar running from his missing ear down to his chin in a ragged pink mess.

Frank watched as Davy manoeuvred his way into the inner sanctum, saw something change hands. He turned to see if the Marshals were watching, but they were too busy being busy.

Henry, the self-proclaimed president of the group, placed whatever it was into his pocket and then moved his hands back onto the head of the man sitting between his legs on a stool. Henry ran his fingers over the man's shaven head, stroking his fingers down the side of his face. Davy was pointing across the hall, mouthing something. Henry leant down and licked the man's head, whilst staring across the hall in Klein's direction. Frank turned to see if Klein was watching but he was now busy eating his food.

Davy slunk off like Judas, furtively eyeing left and right. He'd betrayed his duty right there; everyone could have seen it if they'd wanted to, but they didn't care to pay attention. Frank noticed a look of triumph on Davy's face as he walked out of the hall, and it made him sick.

Frank moved to the end of the row and leaned against the wall, observing the goings on in the hall, now on high alert. He watched as a few inmates got up to clear their plates, walking past Antonio and dropping off their deserts. The room was a hive of activity. Frank noticed the Marshal in charge, scribbling furiously onto her pad. She turned, searching for one of her companions, and the light shone off her molasses skin. He thought she was pretty, but there was something about her that was quite frightening at the same time.

He noticed her make eye contact with her partner who was still talking with the crowd of Black inmates in the corner opposite the Sisters. The male investigator walked over to the woman. They exchanged some words and then looked into the rafters to find their mousy friend, still scurrying around up there and flinching at every dropped piece of cutlery. After gesturing to the doors, all three left the lunch hall. *Off to discuss their findings,* Frank thought to himself.

No sooner had the visitors left Henry stood up from his seat, stepping over his pet and sauntering into the middle of the room. Frank casually reached for his baton, keeping the balance between being ready and not provoking more issues. He fired a quick glance at the group of Blacks, who were also straightening, as though they knew what was about to unfold and wanted to watch. Their bodies were masses of muscle from hours in the weight room and if a fight went down, they always wanted in.

Henry slinked through the throngs of inmates, some shrinking away as he passed, as though his madness was catching. He made his way towards Klein's table. Five of his Sisterhood followed like a wedding train: his pet and four other enforcers, all ready to defend their queen with their lives. Henry arrived at Klein's table and sat down next to the new guy, who seemed to be oblivious to their approach, but Frank surmised he was playing dumb, more than aware of the room he was sitting in, and the danger. Frank began to straighten from the wall slowly, to hear what was being discussed, without looking as though he was imposing.

"So. What's your name?" Henry purred.

Klein kept his eyes down, pushing a half-eaten roll around his tray.

"Ah asked what your name was, sweet cheeks." Henry reached out and touched his arm. Klein slapped his hand away. Henry's goons shuffled forward, about to intervene, but Henry stilled them with a wave of his bony hand. "Touch the merchandise, petal, y'better pay. First one's free, next one will costcha!"

"I ain't no queer, so you're barking up the wrong fucking tree,'" Klein said.

"Oh hush.... y'got me all wrong. Think Ah wanna fuck you? Boy, don't go flattering y'self." Henry clicked his fingers and his pet crawled next to him, kneeling before his master, arms wrapped around his waist, head in his lap. "This here is *my* bitch. Look at him; ain't he just the prettiest little thang?" He drawled, reclining like a cat.

"Nice pet," Klein spat. He reached out with his fork to skewer his sausage on his plate, but before his cutlery descended, Henry snatched it out from under him. Henry held it up in the air, between his thumb and forefinger. He took a bite out of it, then placed the remains of it phallically into his bitch's mouth, moving it back and forth.

Klein sighed. "What do you want?"

"Hunny, Ah don't have to want for *anything*. Ah *know* people. People tell me things, they trust me. Can you believe that? In here, in this place just full of criminals and the deranged, trust is still sought after – and Ah? Well... Ah'm someone to trust."

"I fucking doubt that."

"Y'question me, do ya... Klein?"

"How the fuck do you-"

"Ah know more'n your name, Klein." Henry smirked and said in a singsong tone, "Ah know whatcha did..."

"Bullshit!"

"Ah *know* what you did to... Janet, was it?"

Klein twisted towards Henry, inadvertently turning his back on the slowly advancing Frank. Henry's goons closed in around Klein, creating a wall around him, obscuring their conversation from view of the security cameras and the eyes of the guards.

Klein's voice burst out of the circle, sharp with rage. "You say her name again and I swear to god I'll... I'll..."

"*You* will do nothing."

Frank edged around the circle toward the break in the line of tables. He could just about see Henry and Klein in conversation.

Henry rubbed the head in his lap as if it was a cat in some James Bond film, a villain hatching his dastardly plan, "Y'see, Klein, people in this place despise me for what Ah represent, for what Ah do to get by. But we aren't homo*sexuals*, y'really must know that. We're simply men; men with urges. In here, things are... different. Everything can be made difficult from our circum-stances. The needs of each one of us must be met in... more creative ways. Obedience, for example. The people serve me by doing minor requests to ensure they are safe or belong. They serve their master. We've got urges, all of us men, and in return for protection, we simply ask thatcha help us meet those urges." Henry picked up his lover's hand, splayed his fingers, and started to suck on one of them. "Y'see those people over there?" He flicked the wrist attached to the fingers in his mouth towards the guard station, where a group of frightened looking inmates sat. Klein's eyes followed. "They, my friend, are the true sexual deviants. They are despised more'n little ol' me. Coon, spic, nat-zee– we all hate those sick bastards. But d'you know what else all of us despise?"

"*Do* enlighten me."

Henry leaned forward and growled, "We hate motherfuckers who beat up on weak little girls, even if they *are* old enough to bleed." He leered at Klein. "Ah hear you did a good number on-"

Klein tensed. "You shut your-"

"Shhhhh... that's our little secret, innit? Ah won't tell anyone aboutcha dirty li'l secret, if you don't want me to, but... well now, that all depends. On. You."

"I couldn't give a fuck."

"Ahh, but'ya do, Klein, don't you?" Henry's smile was salacious. "You asked me what Ah wanted, remember? Ah want for *nothing*. Ah just take; and you'd do well to remember that. Ah take what Ah want and you," Henry reached out and walked his fingers up Klein's arm, "will give... it... freely!"

Klein jumped to his feet, "I said don't fucking touch me!"

Frank was on the scene in a flash. The other guards were less responsive, until they remembered that Federal Marshals were in the building, and then they began to make their way towards the confrontation, albeit still slowly.

Frank had his baton out and waded through the wall of Sisters, who reluctantly let him slip through. "Back off; move away from the table now!" Frank bellowed. He cast his eyes around, trying to locate Klein, half expecting to find him on the floor in a pool of crimson soup, but then he noticed him. Tiny dwarf of a man though he was, Klein was squaring up to the Queen of the Sisters, conceding a good foot in height to Henry. "You! I said back away, now!"

The goons started to back off in the presence of Frank's commanding aura, and with the realisation that more reinforcements were on their way. As they did, Frank noticed that the confrontation had brought the Marshals back, as they peered into the lunchroom from the far side.

Movement against the guard rail above him caught his eye, and he glanced up to see Warden Fleming standing there, partially obscured within the shadows. *What did I do?* Frank thought, and then, *Wait. What the hell has brought him all the way out here?* Fleming never voluntarily left his office.

Frank felt himself wobble, legs momentarily shaky. But he quickly turned back to the prisoners. "Henry. Step back."

"Nothin' t'see, Frank... no foul." Henry held up his hands in a submissive gesture, his eyes boring a hole in Klein's face. He moved one of his hands to his lips and licked it, saliva coating his entire palm. As he moved to walk past Klein, away from the confrontation and Frank's baton, he slapped the wet hand on Klein's face and rubbed it into his cheek. Henry leant forward. His lips inches from Klein's ear as he muttered just loud enough for Frank to hear, "Struggle all you *want*; Ah *love* when they play hard t'get. And get'ya Ah will. Ah'll be seein' y'round!" Henry sashayed back through the crowd towards his waiting cheerleaders, who welcomed him back with hugs and whoops.

Klein sat down. His body was rigid with anger. Frank noticed that he looked like someone who was perpetually close to the edge, and there was nothing deadlier, or more troubling, than a man with nothing left to lose, especially in the powder-keg that was Juniper Correctional. The guards started to disperse to their various corners of the lunch hall, bored from the lack of action.

When Frank looked around the hall, the Marshals had gone. He checked the rafters and the Warden had disappeared, too. The man's presence had an ominous air. As he mused on why Fleming had been watching, he looked back down at the tables surrounding Klein's, and saw several chocolate pudding cups uneaten on the table and an entire tray of food untouched, but no Antonio. It was extremely peculiar, and he made a note to check on it later, but Frank had bigger fish to fry at that moment.

The Warden had actually been amongst the prisoners? Ever since he'd been promoted to the position, he never left his desk unless he was leaving for the day. Frank wished he could talk to his wife right about now, he needed her wisdom, but most of all her comfort. Fleming making an appearance in any form outside his office was never good news.

CHAPTER 12

S tanley sat staring at the three stooges that had blindsided him just as he was going to get his lunch. The late afternoons were usually his to do with as he wished, because after recreation time in the yard and the shitstorm that was lunch, prisoners were escorted back to their cells for a few hours, to enable the staff time to clean, change shifts and do whatever else was needed, which usually just meant fucking around as they wanted.

For Stanley it was getting his lunch, coming back to the library and enjoying it in peace and quiet as he smoked and read a book. Any chance of that happening now was like getting a vigorous blowjob. Completely out of the question. Especially with this woman shovelling questions down his throat.

"Are there any concerns about your safety, Stan? You don't mind if I call you Stan, do you, sir?"

The crumbling old man made a proud face. "No problem whatsoever, Miss... ah..."

She smiled politely. "Please call me Dolores."

"Like the book?"

"Sorry?"

"*Dolores Claiborne*, the book by Stephen King." Stanley rose to his feet, his ancient body never fully upright. His feet shuffled on the floor and a hand reached to his lower back, where the kidneys were, as if in support. "I think I've got a copy of it just over here."

"Please, Stan, there is no need. We're here to discuss your safety, not books."

"Hey, it's no bother. Been sitting too long now anyway, that's why my back's giving me gip..." Stanley tottered towards Alex, who had his head cocked to one side, reading some of the titles on the shelf. Stanley stopped just behind the imposing figure. "You wouldn't mind doing an old man a favour, would you, boy?"

The giant smiled politely. "What do you need, sir?"

"Ahh... manners and in a darkie like you; I never would have guessed such things were possible... but I guess education is changing things. About time in my book. I've always thought it possible, that education can bridge the gap, and you're a shining example!"

Alex looked up at Dolores, annoyance etched across his face, as if imploring her to intervene. She lifted her hand, silently urging tolerance, before leaning over to Sophie, who was taking notes of the interview. "Strike that from the record, Sophie," she said softly. Sophie nodded and Dolores turned back to her other companion. "Alex, would you mind helping Stan with whatever it is he wants so we can get on with the interview?"

"Of course. What is it you're after, old man?" Alex struggled to conceal the irritation in his voice.

"Third shelf from the top... *Dolores Claiborne*; brown-looking spine, red writing..."

Alex reached up, towering over the hunchbacked old man who

had to crookedly twist his neck to see the top shelf, let alone be able to grab something from it. Stanley eyed Alex's fingers as they danced across the spines until he found the requested item. He pulled it from the shelf, a faint noise of cover scraping against cover.

"Ahh... I love the sound of books. Thank you, Alex, much obliged." Stanley took the book and began to hobble back over to the seated women. He placed the book on the desk and slid it over to Dolores. "Dolores... meet *Dolores*. I think you'll like her."

"Thank you, Stan; now can we get on with the interview? Have you any-"

"Where are you staying? In town?" Stanley interrupted.

"I don't think that's pertinent to this interview, Stan."

"No harm meant, I was just going to say if you were staying at the Western Motel, they have a nice library there, perfect for reading in, if you can't sleep at night, 'cos of the rain and all..."

She nodded politely, but Stanley could tell by the tightness of her lips he was testing her patience. "So, Stan... shall we continue? I know we have taken up far too much of your time already, but these next few questions are rather important and then we can get out of your hair and let you get back to what it is you do here..." Dolores' eyes drifted across the pile of yellowed cigarette butts scattered amongst mini towers of books. "Do you have any concerns over your safety here at Juniper Correctional?"

"Can't say I do, Dolores. I've been here an age, and the inmates, they know me. They like this place." Stanley waved his arms around as he spoke, as if showing them sights they'd never seen before. "In here, they can escape; they can get away from their lives and become explorers, astronauts, heroes of their own stories; they become free men. In those cells, they are caged like animals. Many for a good reason, mind you; but in here, no problems at all. When it's recreation time, I have two guards in here with me at all times and then this here," he gestured to a button on the corner of the desk, "this here is my little panic alarm. Anything goes off in here, I hit this switch like I'm swatting a mosquito in the hot June sunshine. Bang! Guards come a'running."

"It sounds like you've had experience pressing that button, Stan." Alex offered, as he meandered across the library back to the group.

"Nope. That's just what they tell me will happen. I've never had to use it... want me to test it for you?" He raised gnarled fingers as if to push the alarm.

"That won't be necessary, Stan." Dolores shuffled some of her notes and leaned over to Sophie who handed her another sheet of paper. Dolores scanned the document. Stanley watched her eyes flit back and forth across the page. A smirk began to crack her face, as if she'd found something of value known only to her. "Are you aware of the high suicide rate here in Juniper Correctional, Stan?"

Stanley adjusted his posture in the chair. He reached for a stack of books, and began leafing through them, stamping the books in red with "Property of Juniper Correctional." He mashed the stamp into the inkwell and then pressed it firmly into the title page of the book. Dolores was the one watching now. As he pulled the stamp away, the page was pulled momentarily by the ink before falling free. Stanley could feel her eyes on his hand, watching it shake. The process was repeated a few extra times as he let the silence stretch between them.

He laid the stamp on the desk, lifted the last book to his mouth, and started to blow across the pages, the tremors even more prevalent. "Yes, I'm aware, Dolores." Stanley returned the book to the pile on his desk, shuffled through his pockets for a tissue, and then dabbed it on the ink. He grumbled, "A bloody murder."

"Did you say 'murder?'" Dolores leaned in closer, as did the other Marshal and even the typist. All three simultaneously seemed to stop breathing.

"Eh? Oh. Bloody murder, this ink. If you don't make sure it's dry... the number of books I've ruined by being too enthusiastic. You see, I gotta keep things going, but at my pace, not the pace of the world. The pace dictated to me by the books."

"Right... so... you are aware? Of the suicides?"

"Yes, I just said that," he replied curtly.

"My apologies for repeating myself. I understand we've been asking you a lot of questions but I am just trying to gain some clarification on some troubling issues. Is it ok if we continue? Not much longer, I promise."

"I just don't know what an old man like me can offer to your investigations. I rarely leave this room when I'm here. The only times I shuffle out of those doors is when I get my lunch and do my rounds in the evening with the cart." Stanley tapped the wooden cart next to the desk. He waved to a door in the far corner of the room, "I've even got my own toilet in here, too, so I don't even have to bother no one. When I need to, I just shamble over there and take a leak."

The Marshal nodded thoughtfully. "I see. Did you know any of the suicide victims?"

"Are they victims, Dolores?"

"I'm sorry? I don't follow."

"'Victim: a person harmed, injured, or killed as a result of a crime, accident, or action.' It would assume they were targeted. You think there's some sort of crime going on here?"

"We don't know anything for sure, Stan. That's why we are conducting these interviews."

"Well, you might want to choose your words more wisely, missy. Insinuations in a place like this can be like gonorrhoea. You don't want the guards to get wind of your assumptions, 'cos they're also supposed to be here to protect you, right?"

"Is that a threat?" Alex stepped forward, casting a shadow over Stanley.

As the shadow hit him, Stanley noticed his hands looked visibly weaker, his pallor becoming jaundiced. He waved the frail twigs of fingers in surrender. "No, no threat. You're getting me all muddled. Yes, I know about the suicides, but they weren't no victims, I can tell you that. Things I heard they've gone and done to themselves, they were fully committed to ending their sorry lives - one way or another." He looked from Alex, to Dolores, to Sophie, his face pensive. "Is that a crime, to end your own life?"

"What drew you to this line of work, Stan?" Dolores switched tactics to try and get the conversation back on track but Stanley wasn't thrown.

He blinked at her. "What's that got to do with anything?"

"Humour me, if you would?"

"Well, I'm getting pretty tired..."

"This will be one of the last questions." Dolores reached across the desk, touched his bony hand. He could feel her warm blood flowing over his hand and thawing his joints. Her hand Stanley noted was full of life.

Stanley placed his other hand on top, sandwiching her hand in his cold paws.

"Ah... how. Ahem. How long have you worked in the library?" she forced herself to say, pulling her hand back from the cold embrace. Stanley watched her fingers twitch, as if she were waiting for him to look away so she could wipe her palm against her pants.

"I've been doing this since '45, just after the war."

"And I hope you don't mind me asking, but how old are you, Stan?"

"You in on the bets?" he chuckled.

"What bets?"

"The guards've all been trying to guess my age ever since I started working here. Word has it that the pot is pretty big now... so, you entering?"

"No, Stan, I'm not interested in the wagers amongst the staff. We just couldn't find your date of birth on your paperwork and-"

"Let's just say I've seen a lot of summers."

"How many?" Dolores pressed, an edge to her voice, determined not to be run around the houses again.

"A lot."

"That's fine if you don't want to tell me, Stan. I'll have Sophie check your transfer papers, not just for here, but Shady Mountain Mental Hospital, Oswald Federal Mens Penitentiary... I'm sure one of these places will have something to share with us, considering they all have two things in common."

"What's that, my dear?"

"Well, each of them are on our records for having a high rate of suicide; and each of them has your name in their employment history."

There would have been complete silence, were it not for the relentless rain.

Stanley's face flickered with what seemed to be a thousand tiny emotions. "I don't think I like what you're insinuating, Dolores..." Though his voice was weak, the depths of cold it carried made it ring around the large, dusty space. "Taking advantage of an old, rambling man the way you are. You were all sweetness and light when you came in here. I should have known, really; *you people* are all the same..." Stanley looked between Alex and Dolores, leaving no doubt to what *he* was implying. "You want to talk to me again, Dolores, I'll make sure I have some representation."

"It's been a pleasure, Stan." Dolores stood up to leave, brushed down her pantsuit, and then held out her hand across the desk. It hung there for a while in the space between them before Stanley moved towards her. He saw the muscles in her arm tense as she braced herself for the chill of his fingers, but then he placed the book in her hand.

"Enjoy the story." Stanley avoided her eyes. "It's one of his best. And don't let the door hit you in the ass on the way out!"

Before Dolores could reply, Stanley turned his back on them, shunning their presence in his library. He busied himself picking up books and shifting them from the desk onto his cart.

He heard her heels click toward the door and pause. He heard the strained breath through her parted lips that betrayed how annoyed she was. And then he heard the door groan open, and more footsteps as Alex and Sophie followed in her wake. When the door didn't groan close, he looked up. Dolores held the door open, her veil of brashness and contempt lifted, replaced by levity. "Thank you, Stan. You've been of great help."

His shoulders drooped as he turned away from her. "I'm just a tired old fool, Dolores... sorry if I came across... odd... I need this job, you see. I've got nothing, got no one... it's all I have."

"I'm truly sorry to say this... but you're a person of interest, Stan, so don't try to take off."

"Does it look like I'll be skipping town, Dolores?" he called. He fumbled with the lip of the desk, using it to support his wasted frame, hobbling to his waiting chair. Exhaustion swept through him like a monsoon.

"Thank you for the book!" Dolores finally offered.

"Not a problem, my dear... I'm just going to rest a while here. Please close the door and turn the sign over. You've worn me out with all your questions... I just need a little time to recharge the old batteries before rounds..."

"Do you want me to get someone for you, Stan?"

"No, it's fine, I'll be okay. Just let me be!"

She finally closed the door, leaving him alone in the library at last.

Stanley closed his eyes as he slumped into the chair. When he heard the scratching of the sign on the door being flipped, he reached into his pocket and pulled out a packet of cigarettes. He tapped one out and stuck it between his teeth before throwing the packet to the side. Then he reached into his other pocket and removed a lighter. His finger rolled over the wheel, and the flame was instantaneous. It flickered, but it wasn't from the flickering dance of flame, but his shaking hand. He bent towards the fire and sucked the flame to his cigarette. The tip was a burning ember as he reclined back into his chair and clicked the lighter closed. Stanley took in a deep lungful of smoke. The cigarette sizzled with the intake, paper receding with a crackle and a thin line of orange fire.

A ragged cough made his whole body heave as he tried to clear his lungs. His head grew weary, his vision blurred; a roaring noise flooded his skull. When it finally passed, he fell further back into his seat, letting his chin rise to the ceiling, his neck taut. If it was hard for him to swallow, it would make it harder to cough.

The rain was coming down in sheets, the sounds deafening against the roof and the clattering on the windows. But through all the noise, or perhaps in the middle of it, Stanley could hear something. Like the prelude to a storm, or the electricity on the tracks of an approaching train.

"*You... did well,*" a voice uttered from one of the rows of bookcases.

Stanley choked. He retched in the chair, like a cat coughing up a fur-ball.

"*I'm proud... of you...*" The voice was louder now, clear above the din of the outside storm.

"It is... time..."

It was the last thing Stanley heard before his body gave up, his mind slumped into blackness, and his jaw hung open. He remained unaware as tendrils, like fingers, began to crawl from his mouth.

CHAPTER 13

Antonio sat hunched on the edge of his bed near the door. It had been lights out for a while now, but there was still the familiar discordance that greeted every evening: inmates chatting; a volley of insults and threats; the constant *swish swish* of notes and contraband being flung between cells. But Antonio was oblivious.

His elbows rested on his knees as he squished himself up to the bars of his cell so he could continue reading in the light from the apex of the cell block. Hung high up in the rafters, it provided continuous light to the block, but only to a point just inside the barred door. It was the only light in the desolate place after the sun had set. The clouds and rain shielded any moonlight from entering the cells.

Antonio felt something touch his arm. It was soft and delicate, and something of such love felt out of place in Juniper Correctional. He lifted his free hand, and reached across his large body to thwack away at the intrusion he presumed to be a moth drawn to the light like himself. He felt the soft brushing again, this time by his ankle. It fluttered up against his leg and tickled his inner thigh. He reached a hand down past the fleshy veil of stomach that covered his groin. The sensation abruptly stopped as his fingers brushed the area. He'd touched whatever it was, but it had vanished.

He absentmindedly scratched at the itchy sites of his persistent pest. His eyes never left the pages of his book, and between his scratches he'd lick his fingers and turn another page, all the while muttering to himself.

There was another tickle, this time at his back. He swung at it, slapping the space between his shoulder-blades. The pool of his skin slapped like his palm had belly-flopped onto it, leaving ripples dancing across his body, his entire flesh jiggling. The tickle returned.

He stood and placed the book on the foot of his bed. He turned away from the light and peered into the darkness of his cell, trying to locate the little grey sliver of wings.

Nothing.

He inspected his sheets, half expecting to see a spider there instead, and then looked at the hand he'd used to splat his back, thinking he might see a crushed bugs green pus smear splayed out on his palm.

Nothing.

Antonio stepped away from the door and dismissed the phantom. A gurgle rumbled in his lower body and he began working his way over to his toilet in the corner. It was a tiny metal box, so close to the wall that he had to almost stand in the space to enable himself to shit directly into the pan. Even then, most of it ended up on the seat. He crept into the darkness, pulled open the cord to his shorts and dropped them. He reached under his gut and began pulling down the underwear lodged within the further creases of his flesh. His hands splayed against the wall and he tried to lean backward over the toilet. It was an effort. He lowered his body against the brickwork, sliding down the wall. Antonio thought he should have one of those disability handles put into his cell, but the Warden had turned his request down three times already. The Warden had said he was already in the *handicrap* cell and he should "Figure it the fuck out."

Antonio's arms were spread wide, his palms towards the brick on either wall. An image of some insectoid superhero one of his pretties had liked appeared in his head, except instead of scaling skyscrapers, he was trying to hug the wall to ensure he didn't slip down and get his shit all over himself, in places that he'd never be able to reach again.

The coolness of the walls was soothing against his incessantly sweaty skin. His shit tumbled from his guts into the water that splashed up and soaked his ass.

Something tickled his ankle again. The wretched invisible moth made his skin crawl, but he couldn't move. He was delicately balanced; one false move and he'd topple over, or get wedged in between the box and wall, and have to call out to the guards. The last time he'd fallen, they'd warned him that if it happened again, they'd leave him there until morning, when more men were on the staff to help pull his fat ass out.

The fluttering sensation worked up his legs. It seemed to move in a tumbling motion, rising upwards only to drift down a little, before repeating the process. It progressed slowly over the sagging skin dribbling over his knees, circling patches on his thighs, rising higher still to the veiny bags of grape-sized blubber near his scrotum. The touch was so soft, and he was naked in the dark; he began to feel aroused. He basked in the darkness, relief at being so fat none of the guards could see it.

He finished dropping his load in the toilet. Quickly, he reached down for his toilet stick, feeling his way to it in the darkness, finding it leaning against the wall opposite the toilet. He moved closer towards the wall, to ensure his body didn't slip down into the mess between his legs. Picking up the stick, he lifted it and made out the end covered in an unwashed rag. He leant forwards further still, putting the stick behind him, and began moving the ragged end up and down, the stick finding its way between his gelatinous cheeks. He rubbed until he thought he was sufficiently clean. Dropping the stick on the floor with a clatter, Antonio braced himself for the most strenuous part of his daily ablutions, pushing his gigantic frame back upright.

His breathing grew wheezy and asthmatic. Composing himself for the final push, his gaze landed on the book; he needed to get back to it. That was enough motivation for him to fully stand.

He felt the tickling sensation again. He looked down, hoping to catch a glimpse of whatever was brushing against him, to snuff out this invisible tormentor, but his gigantic belly obscured his view. He waited. His entire body was rigid. Antonio felt the fluttering move higher now, at the underside of his gut, following the path of stretch-marks turned silver by the dim light of the cell block. This time, he was sure he'd get it.

He steadied himself again, waiting as his breathing continued to be laboured. Suddenly, he thrust his hand down, his chubby mitt open, and laid hold of his unseen tormentor.

It was thick, which he didn't expect, and cold. He felt it tug away. His already troubled heart began beating faster in his chest. He glanced down at his empty hand. Where did it go? What was it? He tried to step away from the wall but his body failed to adjust to the sudden movement. His equilibrium kept trying to overcompensate and balance out his weight. But his knee slipped to the side and he heard a crunch as his weight bore down on the isolated joint. A searing pain shot up through his body and sent him crumpling to the floor.

He seemed to splat against it, his flesh pooling out around his prone body as if someone had just thrown a spoonful of jelly on the ground. His head cracked off the concrete, and he passed out.

A searing poker of pain inside his knee brought him back to a state of awareness. The discomfort ran deep, radiating up into his groin and then into his back. He tried to move but couldn't get enough purchase as his hands scrabbled against the smooth floor. He'd never be able to lift his own weight anyway. Irritation flared through him. He'd fallen in the dark, so no one would see him floundering here until lights up in the morning. On top of that, he was naked, his pants tangled around his elephantine ankles. The guards would have a field day if they came and found him like this now. His only hope was to wait it out until morning when Frank was doing rounds. He'd at least treat him with some dignity, maybe even throw a sheet over him.

So Antonio stayed silent and dozed in the shadows.

A shuffling noise alerted him to another being in the darkness and he blinked in confusion. The cell block was deathly quiet. How long had he been out? Hours, most probably. He turned his head as best he could. Then he remembered what he'd felt, that thick, cylindrical, cold thing that had tugged itself away from his grasp. He realised what it reminded him of.

A child's wrist.

It wasn't possible, of course; he was still in a prison facility. Maybe it was his desires creeping back in, creating some degree of hallucination. Hopes and unspoken wishes were powerful things.

Antonio continued scanning the darkness, a shark smelling blood in water. Memories surfaced, thick and fast: leading a child away from their family, abducting another in plain sight, walking off hand in hand with one from a celebration.

A wrist. He'd held enough of them. Squeezed his fat fingers

around them, sometimes they'd bruised like a peach, sometimes they'd snapped like twigs.

Antonio was brought out of his reverie by the noise of little feet slapping wetly on the cold floor, moving through the dark. He followed the sound across the room, from the toilet to the opposite corner, where the blackness was deepest. There was a short, stifled giggle, like the sound of a trickling brook. He strained his eyes in the darkness, but whatever lay there was hidden.

"Wh... who's there?" Antonio croaked. He tried to turn his body, to even lift his head from the ground, but the slightest of movement sent pain coursing through his entire fame, striking the back of his head in bright white bursts.

The small voice began to giggle again. Antonio assumed it laughed at his pain. Rage filled his thoughts. If he could only tempt this thing into the light... he might be injured, but he could drag this little thing down, overpower it, have his way.

"Come out into the light... I'm hurt... I need help... please..." Antonio pleaded, his voice quiet and friendly, exaggerating his pain to draw his prey closer in.

"You've gotten fat," a voice whispered from over his shoulder. He started to roll his head, but as he turned he heard feet once more slapping on the floor behind him, the creature evading his gaze. The little feet scampered off into the corner to join the first shadow. Giggling started to pour into the room from the dark corner. It grew into a small chorus.

"*Fatter*, I'd say..." a voice mocked from near the toilet. A young boy's voice.

He racked his brain, thinking of the voice, pondering where he'd heard it, who it belonged to. There'd been so many voices. A wave of recognition washed over Antonio.

It was his first.

"Matthew? Is that you?" Antonio questioned the darkness, his breath quickening. How could it be? He must be dreaming, he'd wake soon. His pulse kept time with his rapid breaths. How delicious Matthew's cries for mercy had tasted. But in the end, he gave up his ghost, as they all did eventually. Antonio had admired how long he had fought.

"Matty? It's me..." Antonio frantically scanned the darkness, ignoring the pain in his head, trying to locate the boy. He could hear the footsteps more clearly; he was sure he knew where the boy was- crouched low in the corner of the room.

"Shut up, you... you... fat man!"

Something small and flat struck Antonio. He felt it rake down his face, but before he could move his hand to clutch the thing striking him, it disappeared back into the darkness. Antonio investigated his face with his podgy fingers. When he pulled away, his hand was slick with blood, black and oily in the muted light.

In a flash, he saw Matthew's bloodied body. He saw himself looking down at the little bruised and contorted boy. His first. It was as if Matthew were a mosquito trapped in the amber of his mind, a perfect specimen, suspended forever.

"Matty, you've hurt me... why don't you come over here, help me up? I know you didn't mean it... it was an accident, right?"

His words were met with silence. The rain battered against the window as the moments stretched.

Two voices started giggling. "We're all here, Antonio," a young girl said.

The room exploded with the sound of running feet, smacking on the concrete. Antonio heard them clambering on the walls, scuttling around like rats, almost too numerous to count. They were close to him. He flailed his arms, attempting to grab an ankle, but as he tried, he felt the air move, as if he were pushing bubbles just out of reach. His whole cell was alive with the sounds of rushing children, laughter and chatter hanging thickly in the air.

Fear began to outweigh desire. "What do you want?" Antonio cried into the abyss of lost souls, where everything and nothing resided. The room felt suddenly colder, as if their presence had lowered the temperature, bringing with them the frost of the graves from which they'd crawled out.

"We've come to say hello, Antonio..."

Antonio sought the darkest corner of his cell where the blackness seemed to be ebbing and swelling from. The laughing intensified, becoming deafening. Then suddenly it stopped.

Slap.

Slow, wet steps worked towards him from the corner of the cell.

Slap.

Slap.

Straining his eyes, Antonio could see two stick-thin silhouettes of legs. He'd recognise those sweet dainty legs anywhere. It *was* Matty. He was clinging to the darkness, there and not there, all at the same time, as if he were fighting with reality.

"Matty... what is it you want from me? Please... help me up..." Antonio reached out a hand to the shadows, shaking, the fat of his arms jiggling. The pain from his leg burned all the way up to his shoulders. His large hand dropped from the exertion of holding it aloft and the pains pricking him. He was so weak. He began to sob.

They were crocodile tears.

He'd done it before to lure in his prey, and now he was desperate.

Something struck him in the face.

"Stop it!" Antonio cried. "Owww... what the hell?!" he spat through gritted teeth.

"Does it hurt, Antonio?" Matty's voice came as a whisper.

"Yes... why are you doing this to me?"

"He's s-s-sso fat... like a hog wait-t-ting t-t-to be s-s-sl-slaughtered!" sneered a tiny voice. There'd been only one who stuttered. "Dana... is that you?" His eyes stayed locked to the deepest void in the room.

"*Shhhhh-*" the voice answered.

"Dana..."

"Sh-sh-shut up... you... you fat...p...p...pig!"

Another blow rained down on Antonio's face. Antonio tried to shield himself with his hands.

"It's t-t-t-time!" Dana said.

"Time for what?" Antonio spluttered.

The sounds of bare feet again filled the cell, a cacophony of soldiers marching on stone. The abyss grew in size, encroaching on the dim light in the cell, and finally vanquishing it.

"Time for what?? Antonio cried again, peeking through his hands.

The darkness swelled around him. "Time for you to pay for your crimes." Matty spat.

Antonio's lips quivered endlessly over his teeth. "Please... no... I don't know... what do you want?" Antonio sobbed, this time for real, flopping around on the floor like the beached whale he was. "What can I give you? Do you want me to say I'm sorry?"

"Th-th-tha... that's n*ot going to cut it, Antonio!*" Dana screamed as other voices meshed with hers.

"We're here to claim what's ours," Matty said calmly.

"Then take it!" Antonio shrieked into the void, trying to wake himself up, sure that this nightmare would end soon, willing it to cease.

"We've each... come *to see you one*... last time, *Antonio...*" It was too many voices, too cacophonous for him to tell what child was speaking. The din of those little feet racing all across the cell were like firecrackers detonating across a black sky. The dark swarmed over Antonio's prone body, enveloping him in its embrace.

Antonio felt something crouch close to him, hands reaching out and holding him down. He tried to fight against it, tried to lift his hands in defence, but there were so many cold bodies now weighing him down, pinning him to the floor. Icy breath grazed his neck. It moved up to his ear. A shiver ran down his body and his skin broke out in goosebumps. Antonio tried to raise his head, to try and see, but a hand slammed into his face, twisting his head to the side and pinning him to the concrete. The breath was against his cheek, the breathing short and sharp. Then a whisper. It was Matty.

"We've each come to claim something from you, to get what we're owed, so we're each going to take it from you; a payment for what you did. To each and every one of us."

"But I've got nothing... what can I give you?"

"*You've more than enough to offer us...*" Laughter broke out amongst the group, and more hands seemed to reach out from the darkness.

"What... what do I have?" Antonio blubbered.

"*We're going to claim our pound of flesh...*"

A hand dug into Antonio's shoulder. He felt the heat of the incision and tried to throw off his aggressor, bucking like a bull at a rodeo show, but the hand was latched on, fingers deep clawing at him.

Matty's breath tickled against his ear "...each of us Antonio; each of us *is going to... take our pound of flesh...*"

Icy hands descended into his body as others reached for his mouth and smothered his cries. Feet slapped. Voices gigged. Skin ripped.

Then nothing.

CHAPTER 14

Fleming stood at his window, a cigarette in one hand and a bottle of scotch in the other. He tried to drink from the bottle, but dribbled more than he swallowed down his chin. He used the back of his cigarette hand to wipe away the liquid and peered out into the rain. The cancer that was the Marshals was rushing to their car, umbrellas up, battling with the wind.

"Good *fucking* riddance." Fleming turned from the window and pulled out his chair. On his table lay a thick pile of notes, the hand scrawled interviews and observational findings from the first day of investigations. He crumpled into the chair and placed the bottle down on the table. He inhaled the remainder of his nicotine cuisine and then stubbed the butt out on the burgeoning ashtray. The pile sat malevolently in front of him, and his right hand cautiously stroked the many post-it tabs which hung from the side of the document in some luminous fringe. Greens, oranges and reds. The irony of the multi-coloured brightness contrasting with the dreary walls of the correctional facility was not lost on him.

There were more reds than anything else. Fleming took that as a bad sign.

He began to flip through, stopping every now and again to read.

It is our recommendation that...

We found the services offered to inmates to be wanting.

... gross misconduct...

Requires improvement...

It was too much. After the day he'd had, and the mess of his inbox from actual incidents and things that needed his attention, it was all he could do not to take the still-glowing butt from the ashtray and burn the documentation. *This bullshit investigation can wait until tomorrow,* he thought. His parents used to say that things always looked better in the cold light of day; not that they'd seen daylight for a while in Juniper.

Fleming moved the mound of papers to the side of his desk, briefly contemplating just tipping them off the edge and into his trashcan. But he squelched the urge. There was no point fighting the inevitable. Shit was going to happen, things were going to be implemented, and he just needed to hang on and pray that he wouldn't be let go before he retired with a full pension. Being discharged in disgrace would not only be a nasty blot on his exemplary record, but could end up as cause for the Powers That Be to forfeit his pension.

His attention turned to his bank of monitors. He watched his guards scurry around the prison like ants over a forgotten popsicle, a hive mind working for the common goal of continuing operation of Juniper Correctional for however long they could. He reached for another cigarette as he mused, lighting it in an automatic manner. Although there were issues within the prison, he knew his guards were supportive of his overarching vision. They would never bite the hand that fed them, never turn on him like a rabid dog. Fleming thought it was out of fear of him, but he also hoped it was a little down to loyalty as well.

If the correctional facility closed, it would be an even bigger stain on the already soiled sheet of a town. The townsfolk who relied on the steady jobs and income that Juniper Correctional offered would face a strain unlike any they'd ever seen. They'd be on the breadline, and that line was all too close already.

It was too much for him to bear. He had enough on his plate, he couldn't worry about them as well. He had to look after Number One. Fleming lifted the bottle to his mouth, and pondered for a moment; then he wrapped his lips around the top and took a deep swig. There was one option... and if it meant that one of his ants had to take the fall to preserve his reign, then that's what he'd do.

He reached into his drawer, pulled out the large ring-bound file that said **PERSONNEL**. The folder *fwumped* as it dropped on his desk. Idly, he started thumbing through the pages, flipping over the profiles of employees within. He took in the photographs of every guard and staff member on his team. Dull faces stared out from the page at him, as though they knew what he was about to do. If they'd known at the time of taking these photos that he'd be using these as a tool for deciding their worthiness, maybe some of them might have fucking smiled or even ironed their goddamn uniforms, any small gesture to try and swing the axe away from them and onto the neck of one of their colleagues.

If he'd employed a more diverse workforce, he might have had an easier time with his judgement, but African Americans were in short demand in Juniper. Unless, of course, it was within these walls, behind bars. Then Juniper Correctional offered hospitality to them in spades. The *come and stay for life* kind.

Having already gotten rid of the immigrant cleaning crew, Fleming was left with the privileged white faces that made up most of the employed townsfolk of Juniper, and all of the correctional employees. He exhaled smoke through his nose, a demon about to extinguish a life with one flick of his finger.

Fleming fingered the edge of one profile, deliberating. He turned the page and Officer Davy stared up at him, a glassy, vacant expression on his face. Fleming tapped the page, ruminating over his worth. Davy was a hick sonofabitch, but he was also a pawn. He'd go into battle for Fleming, no questions asked. Anything that needed doing, no matter how dirty, Davy would do it. He was a grunt. A piece of wet clay that could be moulded to suit Fleming's needs. If an inmate needed a very specific form of persuading... Fleming knew he could count on Davy. No. The man was too valuable. He needed another scapegoat, so he continued to flick through the pages, scanning through more faces that stared pleadingly out of the page, willing him to keep on turning.

Fleming paused on another, lifting his bottle to his mouth. His watch rattled on his wrist, like a set of toy teeth, and he realised he was shaking. He took in another drag of his cigarette and then crushed it in the ashtray. Smoke billowed out and drifted across the table, tendrils curling like evidence of some dark ritual about to be performed. The greyish blue smoke ebbed across his desk, obscuring the image before him. When it cleared, he let out a hoarse yell as he violently stood from his chair, shoving it back so hard it thundered across the room until it hit the window.

He didn't know how or when it had been altered, but the face in the photo was not a guard. It was the face from his vision. Her eyes were dead and milky, her hair like a wet sponge around her head. Fleming stretched horrified fingers toward the image. What the hell was going on? Who had put that photo in his *personnel* folder?!

He pulled the chair back from the window and sat down, but when he looked again at the folder, the image was gone.

He sat still for several long moments, thumbing the page. A chill filled the office. He grabbed the bottle again, drained the remaining amber liquid and chucked the empty glass into the trashcan. The page before him was not her, but Frank. Fleming tapped his fingers on the page, weighing his thoughts.

Frank was a do-gooder, a stickler for the rules; he'd be the first one to sell Fleming up the river if he caught wind of some of the stuff that had happened behind closed doors. He was loyal though; loyal to the cause, loyal to Juniper Correctional. He served with an aptitude rarely matched by his co-workers. An unblemished record. But was he loyal to Fleming or just the establishment? He'd given his all to this place, struggled through despite his personal difficulties. In a weird way, Fleming had helped mould him, transforming Frank from what he had been into the person that served so dedicatedly now. But Fleming still didn't know if he was loyal to the job and the badge, or the man that kept him housed and fed.

Had Frank outlived his usefulness? Fleming had kept him around as it meant he could forever be close to her. When he'd see Frank it would remind him of that night, of the time they had shared together, before it had all turned to shit. Fleming needed to keep his friends close and his enemies closer; he wanted to be as close to Frank as white on rice. If Frank ever got wind of what he'd done, Fleming could be ahead of it before the shit hit the fan. He'd already made sure *she* wouldn't talk about it, but when did that ever stop things from raising their ugly heads...

Frank would be the ideal patsy. No one would think of him as the cause of all the rot, and that's what made it so perfect. A spotless sacrificial lamb, primed for the slaughter.

Fleming reached for a pad of sticky notes and grabbed a pen. *Possible*, he scribbled. He was still wrestling with the decision, because if he got rid of Frank, in a way, he'd also drive the memories of that day away for good, too.

As he underlined his scrawl, the door burst open.

"*What* in the hell??" Fleming sputtered. He quickly pulled the note from the pack and stuck it over the photo in the file, snapping the folder shut. He glared up at the intruder. "Well?"

"Sir... Warden... you better come quickly... there's been another..." The guard was out of breath and could barely get the words out.

Fleming stuffed the binder in the top of his drawer, slamming it shut. A tinkling of glass bottles knocking against one another emanated from within the desk. Fleming wondered if the officer had heard, but seeing the guards panicked face, he realised the coast was clear. He was soon standing and barrelling towards the panting officer. "Another *what*, officer?"

"A... suicide."

"Fucking *hell*," Fleming growled as he followed the officer out of his office.

As the guard led him down the hallway towards the main cell-block, Fleming remained a few yards behind. The Warden could feel apprehension rising in his throat the closer he got to what he and the inmates called "the pen." There was nothing he hated more than walking through the cellblock, surrounded by the varying degrees of scumbag. His usual observations of the cell block were from the rafters high up in the prison apex, where prisoners could not gain access. He always feared for his life, even with the inmates behind bars; it would only take one error for him to be at the end of a knife, his freedom bartered for their release, and errors were commonplace here.

Fleming could taste the sharp tang of acid reflux from his whiskey. He desperately longed for a smoke to rid his mouth of the bile rising in his throat, the constriction in his chest. The metal grating rang out under their footfalls as they stepped from the private corridor into the open gangway. He could hear hushed whispers. The shocked utterance of his name. They moved past numerous cells, hands reaching out through the bars and making lewd gestures, some even trying to grab Fleming, like something from a zombie movie. Fleming took a step to his right, pressing up against the rail, removing himself from the possible grasp of their hard fingers.

Ahead of him, a group of officers stood outside the cell near the end of the block. Some of the officers were leaning on the railing, heads resting on arms. One was bent over with his hands on his knees. As Warden Fleming approached, the officer threw up inches from the Wardens feet. A hot lumpy mess splattered onto the grated flooring, before dropping in congealed lumps to the level below.

Fleming stared down at his puke-speckled shoes. He stood rigid for a moment, working out the anger and disbelief. He lifted one foot and rubbed it on the back of his trouser leg. Placed it back down. On inspection it was clean, so he did the same with the other shoe.

"Get this man *out* of here!" he ordered in a barely restrained tone. Two other officers came to wrap arms around the kneeling guard's waist, and began to shuffle him past the warden and down the corridor to get some fresh air.

The guard who had brought Fleming from his office turned. "He's a bit spooked, Warden. We all are."

"*What* are you talking about?"

"Take a look, sir, it's... it's...' The officer glanced into the cell and stifled a gag. "...well, take a look for yourself."

"Well then, get out of my way." Fleming brushed the officer to the side, stepping around the leftovers of steaming stomach contents still dripping through the floor. As he made his way into the open cell, he grumbled, "What the *hell* is wrong with you all, have you ne'vah seen a...?"

The sight of wet strips hanging between the bars of the cells distracted him and he trailed off. It glistened in the light like creamy, frayed streamers. He stepped further forward and disappeared inside the cell.

Fleming's eyes took a while to adjust to the dimmed light. His shoes seemed stuck to the floor. He lifted each one, fearing to venture in much further. He could hear the squelching noise his feet made as they parted contact with the floor. As he glanced down, the floor had a slight sheen to it, like it was wet with a black liquid.

Black like the water in the well.

Fleming felt unease ripple up his back, as though her fingers skimmed his spine. His heart seemed to skip a beat and he felt light headed.

"Are you okay, sir?"

Rain created a white noise background.

"... Warden?"

The words startled Fleming forcefully out of his musing. "Yes. Everything's fine, officer."

The officer leaned inside the cells entrance after him, keys jangling on his belt. The officer's shadow moved behind him, which was odd, though Fleming had to take a second to figure out why. The position of the overhead lights was similar to a noon sun; it normally cancelled shadows.

Fleming shivered. He could feel the officer watching him. He cleared his throat and asked, "D'you have a flashlight?"

"Yes, sir. Here."

He waited for the officer's approach. None was forthcoming. The officer was standing at the threshold of the cell, arm outstretched, flashlight in hand. He was frozen to the spot, and Fleming noted that his pallor was bleached like a ghost, as if he'd been drained of all his blood.

Fleming rolled his eyes but moved to the door, his feet slipping as he retraced his steps. He took the flashlight from the officer's outstretched, shaking hand and snapped the beam of light on. It shone brightly into the guard's face, making him look more bleached than before. "Jesus. Go on an' get some air, officer. You look like shit."

"Sir...I'm... it's okay. I can stay and make sure-"

"Ah *said*, get some air!"

"Yes, Warden Fleming... sorry."

Fleming stood in the doorway of the cell and watched the officer shuffle off down the gangway, his hand clutching the railing like a lifeline. It was as if he were to let go, he'd slip through the grating like the puke. When he was out of sight, Fleming turned back into the cell. He kept the flashlight aimed low, and the yellow light soon turned red as it reflected off the oily carpet of blood that covered the floor. He inched his way into the dark, toward the deepening red. He knew that soon, the horrors hidden in the dark would be forced into the light.

Fleming shuffled forward gingerly, his feet sliding on the slick floor. He noticed a shoe. It was empty except for a thick clot of blood. He stepped forward again and a strip of bloody, tattered fabric hanging from the broken ceiling light almost brushed his face. Fleming shone the light on it. The fabric was odd; he wondered if it was a sleeve or maybe a pant leg. It was covered in minute lines that crisscrossed the bumpy, pink texture. The lines were imbedded within it, with darker lumps, as though these imperfections had been sewn into the very fabric of the garment. He reached out a hand into the beam of the flashlight. It trembled ever so slightly, like it did when he needed a drink, and god*damn* did he need a drink. He was scared of what he'd discover once he touched it.

Inch by inch he came closer to first contact. Then his fingers graced its glossy surface. He withdrew his hand immediately, shocked by the coldness of it, and the rigidity. Fleming grew emboldened by the fact that nothing sinister happened, and after inspecting his fingers for signs of smears, he reached out again and gripped the fabric. He tugged it, testing its structural complexity. It stretched under the pressure, the puddle in his fist morphing to fit his hand; but when he released it, the fabric returned to its original shape. Shining the flashlight higher up the strip of fabric, desiring to get to the bottom of the mystery, Fleming's foot suddenly slid backwards and he landed on the sticky floor.

Fleming kept the flashlight aimed in the direction of the fabric. He slowly moved it, following the lines of the fabric, trying to find the source. His free hand, which he'd thrown out to stop him falling completely over, slid out from underneath him, leaving a smeared handprint in the clots of blood on the floor. As he fell sideways, the light jerked up and illuminated the garment connected to the sleeve. The fabric that Fleming had been touching, the silky garment, was not a garment at all.

It was the skin of the prisoner.

He dropped the flashlight in horror as a wave of nausea swept him. It illuminated a hard white object on the ground across from him. It looked like an ankle. He scrabbled for the flashlight and lifted the light back to the skin to find other bones. Fleming could see more white surfaces, directly below the garment of flesh hanging from the ceiling. There was no muscle left, just the bright white of a shin, then higher the gleaming slab of femur, leading up to a gutted-out corner of a hip joint. He moved the light across the corpse, vanquishing the darkness. It revealed the full extent of what was left of the body.

Each extremity was peeled back like a banana. Still, each fleshy garment was attached at either the wrist or ankle. The prisoner had been "opened" in such a way that each limb was spread to every corner of his cell, like some ghastly reimagining of The Vitruvian Man. The last item his flashlight alighted on was with the prisoner's bright white skull beaming out at him from the darkness.

Fleming managed to stand up from the squalor of the floor. The blood and entrails were like a thick soup in which he was the roll of bread to scoop it out. He could not resist checking the entranceway to the cell, wondering if anyone was watching him grope around in the gore. No guards stood there and he found some relief in that. But as his flashlight shone towards the illuminated side of the cell, he could see the pinkish ribbons still hanging on the cell bars, turned almost translucent in the light. It was then he made out the tiny veins, and the thin, wiry hair. They were slivers of flesh. And these parts of the prisoner had been hung up to dry. But how the *hell* had it happened? There was no way he'd have been able to do such a thing to himself. The guard had said suicide... but that was madness.

He spun back to the corpse, the light surrounding it in a harsh spotlight. The flashlight shook in Fleming's hand. Its beam exposed crude chunks of missing torso, ribs cracked open like some prehistoric dinosaur's ivory teeth in a gaping maw. The body had been hollowed out.

The thing before him was half the man it had been previously. Antonio was gone, and so was his huge gut of sagging flesh. He'd been reduced to bare bones. Every internal organ was missing. Just the ivory remained in the darkened cavity, covered with the most persistent of sinews, tiny pieces of muscle. His face was a cream mask, sockets deep and empty and a mouth stuck open in a death cry.

Fleming lifted the flashlight from the body, shining it into the darkest parts of the cell. In the far corner, he noted a pile of deep purple-red fleshy bags. They were large and mirrored each other.

He assumed they were Antonio's lungs. He panned the torch to the other corner and noted another similar bloody pile; perhaps the kidneys? Across from that, the corner held a brain and, judging by the massive size, the stomach. He checked the corner near the entrance to the cell. A heart, and a string of what he assumed were intestines. Two whitish pink orbs stared out of a gelatinous mass of flesh. Eyes.

He felt his stomach turning, the sting of vomit rising in his throat again. He'd done his fair share of bad things, but this... this was an abomination. It sickened him. He was starting to feel light headed. The room spun around him, the corners of his vision drew in like curtains. He scanned the room one last time. Near the edges of the room, where the blood hadn't pooled as much, he made out *footprints.*

He edged toward them, stepping over what remained of the prisoner. As he got closer to the footprints, he began to see that there were many pairs, all moving in different directions. They were small, childlike. But... how?

The prints were from bare-feet. He followed one track that seemed to come from the wall, towards the victim, and then back again. He noticed that they walked right up to the wall, and then on to it, as if whatever was responsible for leaving the prints had walked *vertically* up the wall. He followed the prints with his flashlight. They snaked higher and higher. Fleming pointed the light at the ceiling of the cell. His jaw fell open, his face a mirror of Antonio's gaping skull. He saw hundreds of footprints and tiny hand prints crisscrossing the ceiling, like a trail left by rats.

"Warden Fleming?"

He spun around, the flashlight held out in front of him, the room descending back into darkness. He was shining it in the face of a scraggly, stick thin officer at the entrance to the cell. Fleming blinked as if awakening from a nightmare. "... Day-vy?"

"Yes, Warden. Do you need me to do anything?"

Fleming moved through the cell towards Davy. He lowered the flashlight and turned it off before holding it out to Davy. "Ah need you to take care of this, Day-vy. If this gets out... Ah do not have to explain that, do Ah?"

Davy took the flashlight. "No, sir. I'll get it sorted. I know a few guards who share my view on things in here. I'll get them to help with the... er... cleaning."

"Good boy. Ah trust you, Day-vy." Fleming leaned over the railing. His hand automatically pulled a smoke from his pocket. He barely registered lighting it and inhaling deeply. Fuck the rules that said smokes were contraband.

Davy had moved into the cell, Fleming heard the click of the flashlight. "What do you want me to do with his personal effects, Warden?"

Begrudgingly, Fleming turned back to see what Davy was talking about. The flashlight was trained on a watch and some pictures on a little shelf bolted to the wall. On the bed was a book. A few bottles of soap sat atop a washcloth that hung over the edge of the shelf. Fleming took another deep breath, the smoke pluming around his head. He turned and leaned against the rail again. "Do what you must, Day-vy. Ah trust you, remember that. Make sure it is not misplaced... d'you understand?"

Davy wandered out from the cell with the book in his hands. Fleming saw the guard's eyes widen as he flipped through the pages. There was no way Davy had read a book since he'd gotten out of high school some 20 years earlier, but this one seemed to spark an interest in him. Fleming rolled his eyes but said nothing. He began to walk away.

Offhandedly, Davy asked, "Do you want me to make it like he never existed, Warden?"

Fleming ignored him.

The sound of the book being snapped shut echoed in the block. "Warden?"

"Just get *rid* of it," Fleming called back from down the hall. Davy would take care of the cell, and he would take care of the scotch in his desk.

CHAPTER 15

Two weeks passed, and the Marshals remained at Juniper Correctional. They buzzed around the prison like flies looking for the next scraps to feed on. And within that small time period there had been more than enough to keep their appetites sated.

Antonio had, for all his size, simply been the appetiser. Although Davy had done his best to clean up the mess and make it look more like a suicide than a slaughter, it didn't placate the Marshals. The death of Antonio hung over everything like a putrid gas explosion. The Marshals kept sniffing around like a hound dog, constantly trying to dig deeper, to unearth the things that both Davy and the Warden had been concealing from them. It boiled down to Antonio being yet another death under the supposedly watchful eye of Warden Fleming, and that was enough to keep the Marshals interested.

There had been a few incidents that had provided more mental entrees. A fight which had led to one of the Sisterhood being killed. Two more suicides, one a hanging and a burning. And then, the dessert that hit too close to home: the disappearance.

The hanging was Odi Cathcart, a forty seven year old African American. He had been an old timer, in and out of jail for numerous misdemeanours, serving time all over the States. His last crime had escalated to a kidnapping in Juniper, yet the sorry sono-fabitch hadn't even known he had committed it. When he'd hitch-hiked to Juniper after fleeing an armed robbery gone wrong, he'd found an idling Cadillac by the town square. He'd been trying to get across state lines, and without thinking, he'd jumped in and drove off. When he'd heard the sirens behind him, he'd figured it was simply in relation to the gas station clerk he'd stabbed before making off with the bag of cigarettes and liquor, and pockets of crumpled bills. It was only when he looked for the lights in the rearview that he'd seen the sleeping boy in the backseat. Odi had gunned the Cadillac down the highway in sheer panic.

The young boy was Teddy Barnes, son of Edward Barnes, the officer in the driving seat of the cruiser directly behind Odi. There was a car chase, which had led to Eddie having to use aggressive force to subdue Odi. No one had batted an eye. The report had officially read "Resisted arrest." Odi had just been another crook, and a black one at that, who'd deserved a beating in the eyes of the police. But Odi never walked right after that day. The town still hailed Eddie Barnes as a hero. He was just another deadbeat getting locked up, so no one cared. Odi was left in the racist swamp of Juniper Correctional.

The morning shift had discovered Odi hung in his cell. The shoe laces that he'd used to hang himself had to be peeled from his neck. They'd imbedded themselves deep within his skin, becoming part of his flesh. The odd thing, a little thing dismissed by the guards, were the little crescent marks around the ligature site, as if he'd been pulling at the laces. The guards had reasoned that everyone struggled, even if they wanted to die. It was the body's natural instincts, wasn't it? He was just another sorry soul who'd chosen the coward's way out.

But the Marshals saw things differently. He was a black man who'd died under the blatantly-turned-away eye of Warden Fleming. Dolores had her assumptions about Fleming's true racist nature. She kept thinking about the way he had looked at her with disdain, as if he were somehow superior to her. How he'd wiped his hands when he'd had to shake hers. How he always evaded eye contact. She knew that he found it difficult to answer to her, a woman, and a black one at that. But she loved to see that racist dick squirm.

So as soon as Odi turned up dead, Dolores had enough ammunition to pursue a probable case of racial abuse against Juniper Correctional and Warden Fleming, and she launched that bullet straight to her supervisors. She cited the neglect her team had unburied as being due to an inherent racial hatred that was spoiling the town like a piece of rotten fruit in a bowl. Dolores focused on presenting her report as a statement that institutional racism was the main reason Odi took his own life by suicide, but she had her team working on a murder angle, believing it was a guard who had actually killed Odi. It would be another nail hammered into the coffin of both Fleming and Juniper Correctional. And then an explosion rocked the town.

The fire had taken place in Juniper Correctional's very own parking lot, so fierce the flames had stretched ten feet tall. The rain had fallen unabated while the blaze had raged, fizzing and hissing off the hot metal of the car before evaporating into a haze which mixed with the plumes of smoke. The raging inferno had continued as the flames had licked out of the shattered windows like devils' tongues, the ground covered in broken glass glistening in the fire's light. The firefighters had struggled to subdue the possessed fire; it had raged with a thirst and a hunger they'd not witnessed before. But still they had continued to spray water on what remained.

They'd only been able to watch as the body within the vehicle had been consumed within the dancing glow. Those that had witnessed the pyre claimed they saw someone moving around *inside* the car with the body, holding it in place – but their claims were deemed rubbish. No one would have been able to survive such an inferno and only one carbon mannequin had remained to be found.

When the flames had eventually been extinguished, the body had been discovered, fingers moulded to the steering wheel. The two skeletons of human body and driver's seat had been welded together by the metal springs, forever fused into one.

The charred body had smouldered in the flashing lights of the emergency vehicles. Tiny embers had glowed within the joints, where remainders of fat still bubbled away. What remained of the car had been unrecognisable. The heat of the blaze and the coolness of the water had caused the metal to constrict and buckle. It was nothing more than a twisted metal coffin.

When they had removed the body, cutting it free from the springs, they had carried it reverently. The corpse's arms had stretched in front of it as if for balance, like a crash test dummy. The body had been placed within a hastily erected tent, the rain had pooled on the roof. It had been a feeble attempt at trying to preserve what had been identified as a crime scene. They'd realised that the corpse had no hands; they had snapped off when the body had been peeled away from the car. Tension and horror had mounted in the gathered crowd when they'd realised the hands had been fused to the steering wheel by handcuffs.

The body in the car was eventually identified as Officer Davy. It shocked Petty and Larry, who had viewed the old bastard as invincible. Both suspected foul play, although Larry wondered if the job had gotten to him in the end. Davy had always been a loose cannon.

Others uttered that it was the Sickness prevalent in Juniper. The town was a place where bad things seemed to manifest and take hold for no apparent reason. The monolithic prison, that had stood for generations like a colossus protecting the town from the beasts that lurked within its walls, was cracked and bleeding. It was only a matter of time before the poisonous members of society inside would find the cracks and begin to ooze out.

To Dolores, it was another reason to stick around and see the investigation through. Sick though it was, she saw this development as interesting. As far as she was aware, Davy and Fleming had been thick as thieves. Had something happened to change that? Did Fleming finally use that man up and decide to dispose of him? The accusation was wild, but Dolores had good instincts for detecting corruption.

Everything was falling apart, and she wanted nothing more than to drive that final nail home, true and firm into the chest of Warden Fleming and his failed attempt at trying to drag the prison up from the gutter. But at times, she questioned herself. She felt awful that the town's main employer would soon be defunct, that there would be numerous families on unemployment... but getting one over on this racist backwater town would be a jewel in her crown. Though her main responsibility was for the prisoners and their safety, she couldn't help but enjoy the pain she was putting Fleming through.

So when Dolores walked toward Warden Fleming's office the week after Davy's body had been found smouldering, she was buoyed by the fact that she was closing in on him. The death of Davy had rocked him, perhaps for more reasons than simply their apparent closeness. She was sure of it; his crown was slowly slipping down his head into a choker on his neck. Fleming was a wounded animal now, his closest confidant a pile of ash, perhaps even by his own hand, but Dolores knew there was nothing more unrestrained than a wounded animal.

Fleming had never willingly held a meeting with her. He was clearly appalled at her wandering so freely around Juniper Correctional. So inviting her to his office on a gloomy Wednesday afternoon was quite out of the ordinary. She wondered if she was finally getting to him in a major way, whether he might crack and confess all, but a deeper part of her smelled a very dangerous trap.

Dolores knocked at the door.

"Do-lores, do come in!"

She was surprised at the jovial sound of the Warden's voice. Dolores opened the door and moved into the office. There was a cloud of smoke hovering at the ceiling about a foot thick. As she walked into the room, Fleming extinguished his cigarette and stood up behind his desk.

"Warden Fleming, I-" she began.

"Please; how long *have* we been doing this? Call me Warden." He said it through a smile which seemed to be etched deeply into his fat cheeks. Dolores *definitely* knew something was up.

"Come on in and sit down!" Fleming waved a paw to the vacant chairs opposite his desk.

She took one of the seats opposite Fleming. "To what do I owe the pleasure, Warden?"

Fleming waited for Dolores to be seated before he slumped back into his chair. He couldn't help but think that with each passing day, with each encounter with Dolores, she was becoming more like his forbidden fruit. He despised her for it. He wanted to ruin her for looking so similar to the woman who'd won and then dashed his heart. Was she doing it on purpose? Did she know about that night? Was she rubbing it in his face? He didn't care, because nothing could wipe the grin from his face.

He rested his elbows on the arms of his chair, his hands forming a steeple near his mouth. The smile stayed etched on his face. "Well, Marshal, Ah wanted to in-form you personally. Ah've come across some information, and well... Ah don't really know how to tell you, but Ah thought that honesty to be the best policy; that's what they say anyway."

"Yes, Warden, I believe that is the saying... what information?"

"Well..." Fleming lowered his hands and began thrumming his fingers on the table, "... there's been a dis-appearance."

He watched Dolores duck her head to hide a sly smile at yet another possible disclosure. Fleming was sure she thought this would be another tool for her to finish her job at Juniper Correctional, shutting this place down, and getting the fuck out. "Is that right?" Dolores offered.

"It is with a very *heavy* heart that Ah must in-form you that Alex, that is to say Marshal Rose, is... missing."

"Missing?" Delores snorted at the idea. "That's impossible. I just saw him last night."

"Oh... you *were* the last one to see him were you, Marshal Fink? Ah'm sure Juniper PD will be keen to know that, as it would greatly aid in their in-vest-i-gations."

"Look, Warden, I don't know what you are trying to get at, bu-"

"Oh please, Do-lores... Ah'm just tryin' to help the police follow their line of duty. And if you were the last person to see Marshal Rose, then it makes *sense* that they follow up with you directly, does it not? You are an investigator; you must know the lay of the land...?" He paused before staring her directly in the eyes. "The way this must look?"

Dolores' white knuckles gripping the arm of the chair revealed her barely concealed rage. "How is someone declared 'missing' after less than twenty-four hours? For Christ's sake, he's not a child. How do you know he's missing?"

"They found his car out by the Lehey farm, just sitting there with no-one in it. Around here, that is a *bad* sign. This ain't the city, ma'am. This is rural America. We look out for one another round here. *We* notice when someone doesn't turn up for work, or wher*ever* they're supposed to be at any given time. A curious place, too, for his car to be, don't you agree? What *was* he doing out there? Some background checks on my inmates, perhaps?"

"I've no idea what he was doing out there. We had not discussed looking into inmates' families, it just doesn't seem-"

"It's fine, Marshal Fink, you can tell it to the police. Ah've taken the liberty of having them come in to talk to you." Fleming placed a cigarette in his mouth, flicked his lighter to life, and took a deep breath. He exhaled, blowing smoke across the desk towards Dolores, who waved a hand in front of her as if she were swatting away a mosquito. Fleming continued, "If you'd like, Ah can arrange a room... or a cell, for you to talk in?" The smile on his face had become wry and harlequin-like, a subtle irony creasing the corners of his eyes.

"You sonofabitch," Dolores hissed. Fleming enjoyed watching her unravel before his eyes, the lie of her professional demeanour too much to keep in check any longer. "What have you done?"

"Now, now, Miss Do-lores. Ah do *not* appreciate what you are insinuating. Ah've no i-*dea* what you're talking about... Ah think it's best we leave this conversation." Fleming turned his head to the monitors and noticed a police cruiser arriving in the parking lot.

Delores stood slowly, coiled in anger and righteousness. "You think this conversation is over? It isn't. Not by a long shot."

"It is for today though, isn't it, Miss Do-lores? Ah see the police have arrived, so why don't you scuttle off and talk to them about Marshal Rose. Ah am sure they will have lots of questions to ask the last person to have seen him alive. You might be tied up for some time, Ah expect." Fleming turned his chair around to look out of the window, shunning Dolores, as if the rain streaking down the glass were the most interesting thing he'd ever seen. He sat there smoking, unflinching, until he heard the door open and close and Dolores' heels click away in anger.

CHAPTER 16

F rank was deep in thought while on his way to the infirmary. He had dealt with yet another night without his wife's company, and the call of alcohol pulled at him something strong. There was a minor possibility of making an AA meeting after work. God knew he needed to unload, and there was nothing better than venting to a group of recovering addicts that shared the same bond of teetering on the edge of the abyss.

"Hay th're."

The voice was familiar and jerked Frank out of his internal dialogue. He blinked at the officer in the hall. "Oh... hey, Eddie. What're you doing here?"

"Got called in t'speak with Marshal Fink 'bout a missing person. Tell you the truth, we should just set up an office in this place, we've been spending so much time here already. What with the suicides, and... Davy. Now this."

"Missing? Not one of the inmates?"

"Huh? Nah. Found an abandoned car out by Lehey's farm."

The name instantly rang a bell for Frank. "What, Klein's place?"

"Yeah, you know 'em?"

"No, not personally. I'm just on my way to see him. He's in the infirmary since the incident with the Sisterhood. You know, the self-defence case?" Frank paused and scratched his chin. "Wait. Is Janet okay?"

"Yeah, ain't nothing t'do with the Lehey's... well, as far as I'm aware. It's that big black 'un of the Marshals." Eddie's mouth puckered like the word was sour. His attitude gave the impression that just mentioning a black person might cause him to turn into one. Frank flashed back to the last time he'd heard Eddie go off on black people. The two of them had prior dealings with each other, black folks, and police records. When they were younger and struggling to decide what they would do with their lives, they'd gotten into a bar fight. Eddie had been slinging shit in Frank's direction about him being a "coon lovin' gawddamn race traitor." Eddie had said Frank was a fucking sympathiser, with emphasis on the fucking.

The news wasn't news, but Eddie had acted like it had just started. Frank and Cynthia had been courting for years. He'd never quite fallen in line with Juniper's racist history, or the way the town still had slaves by way of paying them pennies on the hour to pass any legal inquiry. And when Cynthia had shown up, outspoken and fighting for equality, with a wild, gypsy look to match her personality, it had really only been a matter of time before Frank had become smitten. Not long after making their relationship public, they had become the talk of the town; not because they were young love's dream, but because the town decried them as an abomination, something to be scoffed at and snuffed out. Despite all the anger, all the resentment, Frank and Cynthia's relationship had swelled, their love only growing like a balloon, the poison the townsfolk spat, all that hot air filling it up. But, as with most balloons, sometimes people try to pop them.

It had been a winter where the cold was of the kind that would seize the muscles and crack the skin on freshly balmed lips. Eddie had been in the town's only bar, trying to put off the inevitability of joining the local law enforcement. He was a Barnes, and that's what they did. Ever since the founding of the sorry town, there had been a Barnes somewhere in the local law enforcement. He was planning on having one last summer off before resigning himself to his lot in life in the god-forsaken hole that was Juniper.

Frank had walked into "The Dead Mexican" for one last drink before heading home, a bunch of flowers tucked under his arm. It had taken him a few moments to realise all the other patrons had fallen silent. He hadn't truly known he was seen as an outsider, even though he had been born and raised in Juniper. But his money was the same green as theirs and for that reason, and that reason alone, the barman let him drink. Nothing was more important in Juniper than money.

Eddie had taken an exception to Frank's appearance in the bar. Emboldened by hours of drinking, his belligerence had grown until he could no longer contain it. He'd walked over and brushed Frank's glass onto the floor, where it had shattered and exploded into a foamy mess.

Even a young Frank hadn't been naïve. He'd known who Eddie was and the people connected to him. If anything happened, it would have been the darkie lover to get tossed in a cell, not the racist streak of piss that stood before him.

Eddie had tried throwing insults for a while before eventually throwing punches. But Frank had never hit back. Some caught his face, but most had landed on his body. He'd tried to protect himself, but mostly had just accepted Eddie's beating.

When Juniper PD had finally turned up, Eddie had been

reprimanded by his father in front of the entire bar. Frank had felt a sneaking suspicion that Eddie's father had been proud of the beating his son had dished out, and had only been disappointed that his son had done it with so many witnesses. There was a time and place for a beating and there were more than enough dark places in Juniper to get away with such things. Frank had been asked if he wanted to press charges, but he'd just picked up his flowers and headed off.

Frank hadn't seen Eddie for some time afterwards, and when he finally did, Eddie was part of the law enforcement of Juniper. It was a perfect match– he'd found his lot in life and was thriving.

"... signs of a struggle but–"

"Sorry, Eddie; I must have phased out. What'd you say?"

"Just that Mr. Rose's rental was found with the door open, out by the fields near the Lehey's farm. Didn't look like no real struggle but... what with him being... black..." Eddie winced with the utterance again. "Don't think it'll be long a'fore he turns up, if you catch my drift."

Frank wondered if Alex would be in a ditch or body bag.

Eddie rubbed his neck. "How's Klein, by the by?"

"He's a bit worse for wear, but he'll be okay. Got roughed up by some inmates, but he's... well. You know Klein... he's not making it easy on himself in here."

"Damn trouble, that guy. What he gone and did t' his wife? Unforgivable."

"Well, hopefully he'll get what he needs in here and return to the world a reformed man."

"You always could see th'good in people, even if they ain't deserve it."

Frank knew that this was a cheap shot about his wife, but he let it slide. "We can hope!"

"'Bout all we can do, ain't it?"

The conversation, unexpectedly positive, dropped into an awkward silence.

"How's your son, Teddy? Must be about sixteen now, right?" Frank offered.

"Why he's doing great. Thanks for asking, Frank. He's gettin' so damn tall…" Eddie reached into his pocket and pulled out his wallet, flipping it open to a photo of his son. Frank leaned in, peering at the photo. A young strapping boy, the spitting image of his father. He was even wearing his father's Juniper PD cap. "Gonna be followin' in his dad's footsteps. He's a Barnes, after all. It's what we do."

"He'll do you proud."

"Sure will." Eddie softly smiled as he looked at the photo once more before pocketing it. "Well, I best git. Gotta see this Dolores woman 'bout the disappearance and see what she'd like us to do about it."

"See you around, Eddie."

"Yep, you too." He paused. "Frank… I know we had our issues… but you keep your head up. I know it can't be easy, considering… well. Just keep on fightin' the good fight!" There was pity in Eddie's eyes as he walked off down the hall.

Frank puzzled on Eddie's farewell as he turned the corner and crossed the threshold into the infirmary. The walls went from the whitewashed brick to green tiles. No matter how often the grout was scrubbed, mould kept growing. He knew that couldn't be good for the inmates that were already sick. As he shook his head, he looked up at the line of beds and sucked in a breath.

Normally, the infirmary was slow and empty. He was taken aback by how many souls were in the beds. At a glance, he counted eight inmates. Each one was handcuffed to their beds by ankle or wrist, depending on their injuries. Frank scanned the many faces. It took a minute to find Klein's. Well… the half of his face not covered in a bandage. He moved forwards, shoes suctioned to the floor. The firing of the cleaners had meant the sterile environment one expected to find in a place of healing had long since given up the ghost.

Sticky floors weren't the only issue. He noticed bloodied sheets, yellowed where catheters had leaked. It was something out of a post-apocalyptic movie. He scanned the ward, looking for a nurse, but the inmates had been left to fester in their own filth, forgotten, with pain their only companions.

Frank reached Klein's bed. The prisoner's head was turned away from him slightly. Frank made his way to the vacant chair on the other side of the bed. As he walked in the gap between Klein's bed and the inmate next to him, a cry for help pierced the silence. Frank turned to see Obadiah Garside reaching out with hands covered in bandages: dirty, pus covered balls on the ends of his wrists, his fingers entombed within the mittens of gauze. He'd been in-and-out of the prison since he was seventeen. A danger to himself and others, Obadiah was a loose cannon with a predilection for arson. He'd started small, burning bins around the town. But then his destructive capabilities grew until he was caught trying to burn down the town hall, pouring gas all over the place. He was in the infirmary for trying to start a cafeteria fire.

"What do you need, Obadiah?"

"My hands..." He held them up to Frank. With the movement, a rancid smell erupted into Frank's nostrils. He stifled a gag but felt the bile creeping up his throat. Obadiah pleaded, "They hurt... I need some drugs... Can you... get me some?"

"I'll see if I can find a nurse." Frank walked back to the aisle between the rows of beds and faced the entrance to the ward. "Why'd you start a fire, anyway?"

Obadiah pulled his grubby mitts towards his body and cradled them against his chest. "I just wanted to see the world burn... it's so pretty when it burns..." He nodded to his hands, "... occupational hazard!" Giggles erupted from his mouth.

Frank sighed. "When're you going to learn, Obadiah?"

"When you sorry fucks start to see the truth!" His tone sharpened dramatically, spittle flying from his mouth. "You're all in this fucking place, day in day out, you don't see what's right in front of your faces!"

"You been taking your meds?"

"They just dull me..." Obadiah glanced to the side of his bed, nodded in the direction of the floor. Frank followed his indication and noticed a pile of blue tinted sludge on the floor. No one was around to enforce the swallowing of medication. "They give them to me, but I wait for them to leave and spit them out.... I need to be clear-headed. I need to keep the place burning, it's the only way-"

"The only way for what? You're delusional, Obadiah. That's what the meds are for, to get you thinking straight."

"I ain't no pawn, I ain't gonna let you stop the reckoning. Burning. It's the only way to rid this place of what's here, the only way to rid this town of its sickness. The evil that contaminates everything."

"Look, I'm going to get a nurse..."

Obadiah whined, "No. Please. Don't... they'll stop me." He reached for Frank, pleading. "Listen, fire, it's the only way, the only way to purge the evil that resides here. You don't see it, but it's here, I'm the only one that sees it. I'm a conduit..."

Frank pulled away. "You're talking crazy."

"Just listen to me! Fire, it's the only way to cleanse this place... like witches! They were burnt at the stake, the fire consumed them, engulfed them and scorched the evil out of existence... Fire is the only way. We gotta burn it, gotta kill it..."

Frank glanced up and felt relief sweep over him when he saw a nurse enter the ward. They shared a knowing glance and the nurse headed over to a medical cabinet.

"... you gotta listen to me, before it's too late! I'm going to burn this place to the ground, bit by bit, you mark my words! This place deserves to burn, reduced to an ash pile!" Obadiah was screaming now, his body thrashing around on the bed, as he cradled his hands to his chest. His leg trembled within the restraint. Frank stared down at the jangling handcuff, horrified by the raw chafing around Obadiah's red and inflamed ankle, the pus from the wound yellowing the sheets.

The nurse rounded the bed, syringe in hand.

"Get away from me... you don't know what's coming! Don't you stick me with that! You don't understand... fire is the only way..." Obadiah's thrashing intensified the nearer the nurse came with the needle.

"Frank, a little help, please?" The nurse nodded towards Obadiah. Frank got up and grabbed Obadiah's arms, trying not to add to the painful cruelty by touching the burned hands nestled within their crusty cocoons. But Obadiah was stronger, emboldened by his ranting. Frank laid his body across Obadiah, his head inches from Obadiah's mouth. He could smell the rankness of his breath as the prisoner continued his verbal diatribe. Frank turned away, glancing towards the nurse, who was pulling down Obadiah's trouser leg from his waistband, revealing mottled previously melted flesh. Her other hand struggled to hold the leg still, and then, with a sudden lull in thrashing, she drove the needle home and pressed the plunger down.

Frank felt the frantic thrashing diminish, like a toxin ebbing out of Obadiah's body, and he became docile and pliable. Frank could hear the prisoners breathing become laboured, then he heard Obadiah's parting utterance before he surrendered to the drugs.

"One... way or... another... by my... hand or some... else...

town... gonna burn... it's... only way... reckoning... coming!" Obadiah's body slumped. Frank stood and gazed upon the sleeping face,
seeing a smile trace the unconscious man's lips.

The nurse sighed and smoothed her skirt. "Thank you, Frank.
As you can see, we're quite understaffed in here."

"You're not kidding. This place is a literal festering wound...
How on earth is this sanitary?"

"Speak to the Warden. I guess in some strange way, we're
population control. No one bats an eye if someone dies of an infection in the infirmary. Fleming fired all the cleaning staff; you knew
that, right? We've got our hands full doing our actual jobs... well,
trying to do them at least. But adding to it? I don't get paid enough
for cleaning this shit hole!"

"But what about all that Hippocratic oath stuff? To treat the ill
to the best of your ability?"

She glared at him. "Don't go patronising me, Frank, with that
Hippocratic bullshit. Everyone's so quick to rattle that one off
when they see something they don't like about the care they're
getting but nobody wants to step up and help us. Have you spoken
to the Warden recently? He's supposedly consumed with trying to
drag this place up from the garbage, but really he's just trying to
avoid his head from being put in the noose. His corner-cutting,
"money-saving" ways are just driving us further into the mire, and
that fucking investigation isn't helping his kind nature much!" She
breathed through her nose to try and calm herself. "What are you
doing here anyway; bit out of your way isn't it?"

"I'm here to see him." Frank nodded towards Klein's bed. "Just
checking on him. Listen, next time I see the Warden I'll tell him
how bad things have gotten down here-"

"Your funeral. Don't tell him I said anything, though. He's just
looking for a reason to lay off staff, or make them a scapegoat. I'm
not going to be the one all this shit falls on. Some other shmuck can

be the chaff that's blown away!" The nurse turned and scurried away to the office at the back of the ward, closing the door behind her.

Frank turned towards Klein and patted the man gently on the shoulder. He was surprised that Obadiah's screaming had not woken him. Apparently, Klein was heavily sedated for his injuries. His head bandage was pretty clean, recently changed. Frank reached out again and rocked him. The inmate groaned and his head lolled to the side. Frank could see the other side of his face, one eye peering back at him. Klein was groggy but pulling himself back through the haze of slumber and medication. His eye seemed to flit around, working overtime at taking in the scene before him. He reached a hand up to his bandaged eye, seeming to have forgotten what had happened and why his sight was obscured.

Frank reached out to stop Klein's roving fingers. "It's alright, Klein. You were involved in... in an incident."

"What... what happened to my face?"

"You were attacked." Frank managed to subdue Klein's hand, pulling it down and laying it on the bed. "The nurses say that it's only going to be superficial. You'll be here until they take the bandages off and see how the healing is... plus..." Frank paused, thinking about what he should reveal.

"Plus what?" Klein asked crossly.

"Well, you're also here for your own protection. Do you remember what happened?"

Klein shuffled in his bed, trying to get comfortable. "It's all a bit of a haze, really. I remember being in the laundry... The Sisters... they... had me cornered. But I wasn't gonna let no fucking queer get a free ride on my ass. I remember trying to fight them off, but there were too many of them. They were gonna rape me, Frank." Klein grew agitated. He kept drawing his legs up under the sheets only to stretch them back out, as if he were suffering from a urinary infection and needed the toilet.

"It's okay, Klein... relax... you're safe here. That's why you need to stay. The Sisters can't get at you in here."

"They can get you anywhere, Frank, you know that... A guard turns a blind eye and this fucking happens." Klein lifted a hand up and touched his bandage. "I had to do it, Frank, I couldn't let them just have me, I had to defend myself, I wasn't going to take it lying down! They should have known what I'd do to them, I'm not someone you wanna fuck with, I-"

"I understand Klein. We all understand..."

Klein let out a hoarse cackle. "That's a fucking joke. You're the only one in this hole that gives a damn. And I know; I've been watching you. The rest of the guards are happy for the prisoners to run the joint. No wonder this place is going to the shit... and that fucking investigation... no smoke without fire! Frank... they're investigating *everything*. The failings of JC and the lack of protection from the guards, present company excluded. But they still let that fucking queer roam free after he did this to my eye."

Frank flinched at the remark. "Look, Klein. I know you're angry, but you're in here for your safety. You killed someone... you're lucky you-"

"Listen Frank, you know outside I was a pretty straight guy. Yeah, I liked to beat on my wife; who doesn't? She needs correcting from time to time and if I weren't there, then who'd do it? Better her beatings came from me. I loved her... well, I still do love her. But she needs to fall in line, just like everyone else. I worked hard, I paid my taxes, stayed on the right side of the law..." Klein leaned forward in his bed, his face wracked with pain. "And guess what, Frank?"

"What?"

"I had to be locked up in here to become a fucking murderer!"
A deranged grin cracked his face.

"It was self-defence. It was five on one! The beating you took,
the injuries you sustained... you're no murderer, Klein."

"But I could have been, couldn't I? If I'd just hit her again,
brought that poker down on her face one more time..."

"But you didn't, Klein; you're not a murderer... you had the
chance to be one but you didn't. For some reason you stopped... or
someone stopped you."

"Don't go spouting off your higher power shit here, Frank. The
only reason I stopped, the *only* reason that bitch survived, was that
I was tired. I couldn't beat on her any more than I had already
without collapsing myself." Klein sniggered to himself.

"I don't care what you tell yourself, Klein. I know you stopped
killing your wife for a reason. The incident with the Sisters...
goddamn it, you had no choice! They'd have killed you. You did
what you had to do, you did what anyone would do, hell what *I*
would do. That doesn't make you a killer. It makes you a survivor.
'In our weakness, we are made strong,' I firmly believe that."

"I ain't weak!"

"I didn't say you were."

"Whatever." Klein turned in the bed, so he didn't have to look
at Frank anymore.

Frank knew that was his cue to leave. He stood slowly, and
pushed the chair back to where it had been. He began to walk
away but something pulled at him. He contemplated just leaving,
not mentioning it. But he was already saying it before he could
stop himself.

"Klein? ... There was a car out near your ranch. Abandoned.
One of the Marshals is missing. And... I spoke to the police, and
they said that Janet was okay. Said she was doing well... I just

thought you might like to know." Frank continued walking to the door.

As he turned back to close the door, he gave Klein one last glance. He realised the inmate's body was rocking back and forth. Klein was sobbing quietly, holding himself tightly. He looked so small... and weak. Frank could see him for what he truly was: a scared kid.

Frank turned and almost toppled over the library cart that had appeared out of thin air. Some of the books on the cart fell to the floor. "Shit!"

"Oh, I'm sorry, Frank... did I spook you?" the croaky voice of Stanley asked.

"Sorry, Stan, I didn't hear you come in... Here, let me help you with those." Frank bent down, past the hunched figure of Stanley whose hands were darting out and grabbing the fallen books. Frank managed to pick a couple of them up and handed them back to Stanley.

"What are you doing in these parts, Frank?" Stanley asked while placing the books back on the cart. He was breathing heavily, a rattle within his chest.

"I could ask you the same thing, Stan." Frank observed Stanley's skeletal frame. He looked smaller than he had only a few weeks prior. A deathly pallor encroached on his skin like rust. Frank thought he'd not be much longer for this earth.

"Books!" Stanley said, by way of reply. He coughed, his body heaving, almost knocking himself off his feet. He reached out an arthritic bony hand, steadying himself on the cart. "You?" he spluttered.

"Klein. Just wanted to check in on him."

"That's very dutiful of you, Frank. You must be the only piece of light left in this god forsaken place... let's just hope nothing snuffs you out, eh?"

"Well, you bring your own comfort too, Stan. Don't forget the hope you offer these souls."

"You're too kind, Frank. I try to ease their passing as best I can." A smile etched itself across his papery skin. Frank could have sworn that he heard Stanley's skin crumple as it shuffled to accommodate the grin across his thin, stretched face.

"Well, I'll leave you to it. I've got to be getting on anyway." Frank turned to leave.

"I'll be seeing you around, Frank. Do stop by whenever you want. It's been a while since we had a proper conversation." Stanley shuffled into the ward with the cart, and Frank headed off to the main areas of the prison, alone, again.

CHAPTER 17

O fficer Barnes was sitting in one of the prison's interrogation rooms, staring blankly at the mould that pooled in the upper corner of the space. A window ran along the top edge of one wall, barely wide enough to let light in, but it was enough to see the rain still coming down in torrents. He sipped from a paper cup and grimaced at the contents. His fingers tapped on a notebook.

He pushed his chair onto its two back legs and caught sight of his reflection in the one-way glass. The thin patch of hair left on his head was disheveled and showed the growing bald spot on the back of his head. Barnes reached up to smooth it down, turning his head to make sure all sides looked decent. His hand paused in mid-motion and he peered into the reflective mirror as if wondering who was sitting on the other side. He grimaced again.

Easing himself back to the floor, he reached into his jacket pocket and removed a pack of cigarettes and a lighter. His side arm bothered him, and he adjusted the gun before tapping out a smoke. An orange butt poked out of the box and he lifted the pack to his mouth, bit the end of the butt, and pulled it from the box with his buck-teeth. The lighter flicked to orange. Barnes' cheeks were pulled inward as he sucked in a breath of nicotine before releasing the smoke into the air.

As the minute hand ticked around the clock, the stimulant effect of the coffee was worn down by the depressant effect of the nicotine. The officer's eyelids drooped and his blinks lasted longer each time. His head dipped forward slightly for a moment before jerking back up. The cycle of droop, blink, dip repeated a few times before his chin touched chest and remained.

Dolores decided now was a perfect time to walk in.

She quietly closed the door to the room on the other side of the glass. Her heels tapped loudly against the tile and she banged the door to the interrogation room open. Barnes jerked upright at the intrusion and blinked rapidly, clearly disoriented.

"I'm so sorry I'm late, Officer Barnes." Dolores stumbled on purpose, as if she had just been rushing and hadn't quite gotten the chance to slow down. "I had forgotten something in the car."

The cigarette in Barnes' hand had smouldered to the end, and the officer hissed as it burned the edge of his fingers. Ash covered the table, and speckled his shirt. His lips pulled tightly across his face and Dolores could hear his teeth grinding in annoyance.

"It's raining cats and dogs out there!" she continued. "Does it ever stop in this godforsaken town?"

Barnes grunted in response and then shrugged. "Been having more'n our fair share, that's f'r sure."

Dolores pulled out the chair across the table from him.

"G'on an' take a seat," he said, not noticing her movements. He had pulled the notebook towards him and opened it, scanning the contents as if to let her settle.

She pulled the chair noisily to the end of the table, letting it thump to the ground. Barnes was startled and looked further confused. Dolores smiled politely. "Do you mind? I don't like to sit opposite a fellow officer of the law when I don't have to. We're on the same side, after all, and there's no sense creating an air of interrogation or of wrongdoing. Don't you agree?"

He shrugged again. "Sit anywhere y'please."

"Thank you. One more question, sir. Where did you get that?" She gestured toward the cup. "If that's coffee, I'm in desperate need."

"There's a pot in the break room. I c'n have a guard grabya cup." He stood and walked to the door. "D'you take it black?" he called over his shoulder as he peered out the small window to see if anyone was near.

Dolores felt her shoulders tighten slightly. Was he trying to throw her off, get back on top? Juniper had clearly shown there was no liking of black people, and she could not tell if this was the officer's way of trying to put her in whatever place he thought she belonged, or if he was genuinely just asking her a question. She decided to let him know she was on to him, just in case. "And what, exactly, is that supposed to mean?"

He lazily turned around to stare at her. "Nothin'... It's just there ain't cream." He offered a smile of an apology but it didn't reach his icy eyes. Those stayed angry.

Dolores returned the smile, anger in her own eyes. "I see. Good thing I do take it that way. Black," she paused deliberately, "...is the only way to go."

If his skin grew anymore taut, it would tear. His smile fell as he nodded and looked back out the window. Dolores watched him as he spoke with a guard outside. Neither spoke again until the guard returned a few moments later and brought in her cup. The guard tried to hand it directly to Dolores, but Barnes reached between them and took it. He nodded his thanks, and turned toward her, dismissing the guard.

Dolores allowed a bemused smile across her features. "Thank you, Officer Barnes."

Barnes grunted. He sat down, scooting his chair further down the table, but not moving it to sit across from her. The only noise in the room was that of a few pages being flipped in his notebook. He pulled a pen from his breast pocket, clicked it to begin writing, and opened his mouth to speak.

She cut in, not wanting to lose her upper hand. "So, Officer Barnes. Should I be worried?"

That jaw worked side-to-side again, a bone popping. "'Bout what, Miss Dolores?"

"Marshal Fink is just fine, thank you. Should I be worried about my safety here in Juniper?"

"With all *due* respect, ma'am, we go a bit more ol' school and prefer t' call our women with... ah, more respectful terms," Barnes said as he plastered a smile on his face. "Now, to answer y'question, Miss Fink, it's pro'ly best you don't go wanderin' around, taking matters into your own hands. This is a po-lice matter now. We'll be conducting a full scale investigation into the disappearance of your colleague."

"Full scale you say? My, that is rather impressive."

"How so?"

Dolores sipped from her coffee. No wonder he had grimaced earlier; it was shit. She kept her face smooth and replied, "Well. With him being a black man."

Barnes' eyes narrowed slightly. "I don' seem t' follow..."

Sometimes Dolores loved being the cat playing with a mouse. Each of them knew exactly where she was going, but Barnes was trying to provoke her and she wasn't going to respond with anger. "Officer Barnes, you do me a disservice. I am a Federal Marshal; before I go into any situation, I do my research and dig deep. I'm not some stupid nigger cunt." She didn't blink as she said the words, but Barnes sucked in a breath and sat up straighter. "Does my use of the word make you uneasy? How terribly rude of me. I assumed someone who has been charged with racial profiling and harassment, and documented as saying those words, would be more comfortable in a setting where the language is one he's familiar with. Yes, *Mister* Barnes," she said, "I have seen your record. I know the complaints made about you from those who were entrusted to your care. Well... perhaps 'care' is a bit of the wrong word, as it implies you had their best interest at heart."

She knew it was a risk, laying out most of her cards like that, but she was also annoyed with this investigation and the town it lay in. She was annoyed with the man sitting to her left who was growing more and more red with every word. She was annoyed by all the backward, racist, inbred rednecks that crossed the street to avoid her. She was annoyed, and she wanted out. Alex was supposedly missing, and she was done playing games.

"Now look. I don't rightly know what you're aiming for, Dolores," Barnes said, trying to inject some kind of sweetness into his gruff voice. "But you might want t' be careful with what you're slinging around."

"Or what? You going to beat on me like that little black boy you arrested a few summers ago?"

"Listen-"

"No, YOU listen, Officer Barnes."

Barnes squirmed in his seat, taken aback by her authoritative tone. Though they sat in a less hostile form, he was the one being interrogated.

"I know what this town is like. I've been here for weeks now. I've spoken with the prisoners and several of the townsfolk. It would come as no surprise to you to learn that fifty four, yes, *fifty four* African Americans have come to harm in this town. With twenty three of them turning up dead, either found out there,"

Dolores pointed out the window, "or here, in this damn prison."
She breathed deeply, calming herself. "So you would forgive me
for treating your offer of a full scale investigation with the
contempt it deserves, Officer Barnes."

His hands were beneath the table but Dolores could see the
veins in his arms bulging as if he were gripping something so
tightly it was crushed lifeless. She had no doubt he was picturing
her neck clutched between his hands, squeezing so hard her chocolate eyes popped from her head. Barnes' file had mentioned his
rage, and watching the man in front of her, Dolores only questioned if the file didn't describe the anger enough.

"Listen," he said, with great effort. "I came down here to help,
show you that I would try and do my best to help find your-"

"Your 'best' Officer Barnes... Is that what you did for Jake
Hemmings?"

The utterance of the name was like a visible sledgehammer to
his chest. All the air whooshed out from him. He floundered for a
moment. "Jake Hemmin's?"

"Yes. The young man you bludgeoned to death in the back of
your cruiser."

"That warn't proved, it got overturned in court..."

"But if it were to be investigated by a proper court of law, with
a more impartial jury, would it stand up to a more *in-depth* investigation?"

He stilled completely. "Are you threatenin' me, Dolores?
Because I am very much the wrong person to be threatening..."

"Did Jake Hemmings threaten you? Is that why you caved his
head in with the butt of your rifle?"

He exploded in barely restrained anger. "I don' know where
you gotchor 'information,' but he was fleeing from sex-ual assault.
He done raped *three* young girls out back near the woods; they's
just school girls... an' he attacked me! It was self-defence, it was

him or me, and I warn't gonna let no child raping *coon* get away with any o' that bullshit." Barnes turned white and sank into the chair. He hadn't meant to say the word, but the rage inside had removed his filter. He rubbed his face with one hand.

"And now you show your true colours..." she said softly.

It was like lighting a match on an oil spill. "Listen here, missy. I coulda come in here and shown you the photos of those *niggers* tha'choo said always turn up in these parts. I coulda shown you all them mutilated bodies, hung and found in the river all bloated and ripe, but I didn't. I came t' help."

"That's so kind of you, a privileged white man, to show a nigger so much hospitality... I'm touched." Her voice was mocking, overflowing with scorn.

"It ain't hospitality," he snarled. "We're jus' puttin' up with you. Y'see, in these parts, we protect what's our'n, protect it with our lives. We don't take too kindly to your kind in these parts, an' before you g'on and get all high n' mighty, I don't mean black people. I mean y'all rich pricks. Y'come in here with your ideas an' lifestyles, thinking your shit don't stink, but it sure does, stinks just like every other mother*fucker* here! Y'come waltzin' in here with your fancy pantsuits and them heels clickin' like you're some kinda powerful being, but you ain't any different than every other bitch "*fem*-inist." Y'bring in your corruption and pollute this here town." He leaned closer, starting to almost crawl across the table, "And another thing you're a disgrace, giving the men of this town ideas about *interbreeding*. You need to keep t' your own kind! Only thing your kind ever been good for 's tendin' fields and reapin' what we make you reap."

"You need to watch yourself, Officer Barnes."

"You think I give a *damn* what you think?? I don't need t' watch *anything*! You should be the one watching out for yourself, *Miss Dolores*. People like you seem to turn up dead in this town, and I'd sure hate for you to become another one of those statistics you keep spouting off about."

She tilted her head slightly and asked, "Is that a threat, Officer Barnes?"

He sneered. "Nope. I'm jus' tellin' you straight. That boy you say I beat? I don't have t' answer t' you about that. I answer to the town and the courts of Juniper, an' they said I was innocent. So you best be sure, I will protect our little town from evil any damn way I can. Y're here today, but by god y'll be gone tomorrow. So g'on an' keep throwin' your statistics and theories around. We ain't got use for 'em. I was born and raised here; the lifeblood of this very town seeps through my veins. However tainted, or backward thinking, and racist it may seem to the likes of you, our way of life means that we protect what we have... and keep the *filth* out."

The room was thick from the outbursts. Dolores sat quietly for a moment. "I think we're done here, Officer Barnes." She scraped her chair back and started to stand.

"Sit. The *fuck*. Down!"

For the first time since she'd walked into the room, Dolores felt fear. There was something in the way his voice had changed that pricked her mind into a state of awareness she usually kept for dealing with gun-toting hostage takers. She forced her shoulders to relax and raised her hands as she slowly sank back into the chair.

His words dripped with sarcasm like gas seeping across a wheat field. "As long as you're here, you are under my protection. I've a duty t' care for you. I surely wouldn't wantcha goin' missin', so I'll make sure my boys follow you, keep eyes on you at all times. I'd just like you t' remember that before you leave here today. Anything could happen t' ya if we were to turn a blind eye. When you're outside these walls, a carjacking, a drunken assault, or even- heaven forbid- a car accident. The roads 'round here can be quite...

treacherous... but I'm sure you know that already, what with all your research?"

She tried to present an unaffected front and shrugged offhandedly. "Look, Barnes, you can threaten me all you like, but the truth is we're here on the request of someone else. You say you hate "my kind," well my kind just wants to do our job and be gone. And you spout off about us polluting your stagnant gene pool with our blackness, but what about Frank? What about him and his-"

"Them things don't concern you, woman," Barnes snapped, the nerve still raw. "It's been a blot on the town for long enough. We don't need some righteous, bee-in-her-fucking-bonnet, over-blown investigator digging into old wounds. Frank is broken goods, and everyone knows it. Let old dogs lie and get on with getting the fuck out of Juniper." Barnes manoeuvred out of his seat, stood up at the table, and began picking up his items.

"You talk about him like he's an outcast," Dolores answered, "but as far as I can see, from what the inmates have said, he's one of the only stand-up people in this godawful place."

"Good reason for that - he's served his time." Barnes said, his eyes glassy and cold. "Was that in your fucking research, Dolores? Did you know Frank has priors?" A dark chuckle left his lips. "Past few years, people been cuttin' him some slack, after... what happened... Y'might even say we moved on and forgiven him for his transgressions. We are a forgiving bunch of people, Dolores, once you earn it."

"Well, Barnes, I'm glad my colleague has earned a full-blown investigation from your precinct. Will there be anything else?"

"Oh, not today. I've learned everythin' I can from you, which is to say, nothing. Let's hope the next time I see you there's some news 'bout the whereabouts of your colleague. I might even have photos... if you're lucky." Barnes tapped his notebook on the table and stomped to the door. He pulled the door open and waited for Dolores to stand.

She stayed in the chair. "Something you forgot to say, Barnes?"

There was no attempt to hide the sinister grin he offered. "No ma'am. Just I'll be seein' you 'round, is all. Y'stay safe now!" He let the door slam shut and Dolores sat alone with her thoughts.

CHAPTER 18

The rain had left the roads slick and drains overflowing from all the branches and detritus clogging them up like clots in arteries. Water pooled in the gutters and began to spread out across the roads. It was as if the asphalt were a stovetop, boiling the bubbling liquid spreading across its surface.

The slush of a passing car woke Fleming from his sleep. He rolled toward his nightstand where the digital clock rested.

He watched until the neon green digit pixelated into the next minute. He closed his eyes again, willing sleep to take him, but it remained aloof, pulled from his body like a blanket. His mind was fully awake, so he tossed and turned, trying to get comfortable. Fleming placed a pillow over his head to drown out the incessant hammering of the rain on the roof, the sloshing of the water outside by the passing cars. *Where are people even going at this time of night?!*

He turned back to the clock. Only seven minutes had passed since he'd watched the 1 change into a 2. Shit... it felt like he'd been awake for hours. He groaned in annoyance and rubbed his face.

Fleming became aware of another sound within the slag heap of noise from the storm raging outside. It sounded like an automatic rifle, slightly muffled by the rain but ringing out in a constant rattling. *Damn rednecks.* He glanced out of the window where the moonlight revealed his late-night tormentor- a river of water was spilling from his gutter, dropping thickly down the side of his house, hitting the corrugated roof of his cellar door. He figured there must be a blockage in the gutter preventing the flow of the persistent rain. Another job he'd have to get around to at some point. *Well, if Dolores gets her way, I'll have a lot of spare time on my hands,* Fleming thought, which stirred him into a fit of giggles. There was definitely no way he was getting back to sleep now.

Fleming reached for the light on his nightstand. He took hold of the plastic cord and felt his way up the lamp body until he found the little black box. His fingers fumbled with it before clicking the switch on. The light bloomed in the room before the bulb blew, sending his room back into deep darkness. The rain continued its hammering at his window, as if someone were tapping relentlessly on the glass with long fingernails.

He was about to get out of bed when he felt the first drip. It was cold, and splattered against his chest. Another quickly followed, landing in the same place. Then a gush of water, like a glass had been emptied over him, splashing up from his chest into his face. He lifted a hand and wiped at his cheek. Another drop. Three more. Each one landing in exactly the same place.

"Y've *gotta* be fucking *kidding* me!" Fleming muttered.

In answer, the darkness allowed an uninterrupted trickle to fall onto his chin, tracing a wet line toward his hairline. Fleming rolled over to the bedside table and reached into the drawer. All the while he could hear the dripping on his vacated spot in the sheets, tapping away, like an impatient teacher drumming her finger on the table.

Taptaptap.

He rummaged around in his drawer.

Taptaptap.

Finally finding what he was looking for, he rolled again, shuddering as his back lay in the pooling water on his bedsheets. He clicked the flashlight on... but nothing happened. He turned it off and on again. Still nothing.

"C'mon... stupid... fuc..." With a hard rattle, a beam of light shone out, cutting a line through the darkness. The light severed areas of the room with each swish of his hand. Another stream of water fell on him, this time splashing his torso. He lifted the flashlight up, shining it directly above him.

Was he dreaming?? The flashlight beam revealed a hole in his ceiling, a hole which hadn't been there when he went to sleep. There was no plasterboard on his bed, no insulation lying sodden in his sheets. There was just a deep dark void, perfectly circular, hovering above his bed. It seemed to swallow the light, the yellowy beam disappearing deep within the chasm, where he could see no end. The light glinted off the deep sides, and Fleming watched as water trickled down its edges, where it collected in growing stalactites, clinging to the lip of the hole before growing fat and heavy, falling onto his prone body below.

Fleming could hear something shuffling around in the depths or was it heights, as if it were being drawn toward the light. A spongy object hovered at the edges of the circle. It was black and sparkled like gemstones, refracting the torchlight into a dense hive-like structure, feeding on the light.

It came closer, but remained at the edge of the light's reach. It was being drawn out by the glow, but seemed fearful of it at the same time. Fleming thought that at any moment, some type of rodent or bat was going to tumble out or fly into his room. He considered clicking the flashlight off to stop attracting whatever was in the hole, to ward off its hunger of the light. But then he'd have no idea what it was that was emerging from the hole and he'd be left in the darkness with the *thing*, so with a trembling hand, he kept the flashlight on, the light his last bastion of courage.

The drips continued to fall on and around his body, his sheets becoming more and more wet. The quilt grew heavy about him like a damp grave. After what felt like days, Fleming turned away from the hole to glance at his clock.

A body dropped from the hole. It landed on his chest in a crumpled heap of flesh. Water gushed as the body writhed around, fidgeting and flapping frantically. He reached a hand out, to push the writhing mass away, but his fingers kept slipping and sliding over its flesh. When he did find purchase, his nails punctured the slimy skin, causing a fetid smell to plume in his nostrils. The stench was unbearable, burning at his eyes, causing him to gag.

The figure shuffled about until it straddled his body.

Somehow he had kept ahold of the flashlight. He lifted it high and drove it down where he assumed the head was. A resounding crack filled the room. He repeated the action again and again. With each strike, a sickening crunch rang out into his room. The noisome odour intensified with the thrashing limbs of the thing on top of him. He brought the flashlight back once more.

A limb shot out from the mass. It pinned his arm to the bed. The flashlight fell to the floor and blinked out, leaving them in the darkness of the storm. Another limb shot out and gripped his throat and began to squeeze. He could feel his windpipe being crushed. His legs thrashed around as if he could dislodge the monster, but it did not let loose its hold. He began to tire, and all of his objections faded. He succumbed.

The cold, damp hand still clasped his throat. He could feel nails breaking his flesh, the strange feeling of warm blood emanating against frozen digits. Even though he was not religious, Fleming considered praying. The absurd idea made a chuckle gurgle out as he realised he had no idea how to even ask for help from a god he didn't actually believe in.

Just as he felt his life inching into death's welcoming embrace, the hand seemed to relax around his throat and his lungs began to fill again. He was suddenly breathing, drawing in ragged breaths. But the cold, damp body remained steadfast on top of him.

His eyes adjusted to the dim light, and he could see that the figure on top of him was naked, with skin the colour of rust and shadows. Its face still remained hidden within the thick sponge, water pouring from it in a never-ending stream, spilling onto his body in icy trickles. His arm was still pinned above his head. The other lay redundantly next to him, still clutching a handful of flesh torn from his assailants' arm, mushed between his fingers like mashed potato.

The hidden figure leaned forward until it was inches from Fleming's face. It hovered there for a moment, before closing the gap. A tongue lapped at his face, the cold wet organ snaking its way up his cheek to his forehead. Its head moved to hover the mouth beside his ear. Fleming could feel it breathing, could hear it sniffing him.

"*Mmmmmm...* I love the taste of fear..."

He recognised the feminine voice instantly, but he couldn't believe it to be real. *What the hell is happening?*

"Do you remember me?" she said, playfully tracing a finger

down his cheek, stroking his neck. Her hand trailed across his wet torso. He realised he was getting aroused, despite how repulsive his visitor was. He tried to stop himself, but there was something about the sensual touch, the recognition of some deep yearning. He couldn't help it.

She played with his nipple "Do you like that?" The dead fingers pinched it. He winced. The other hand continued to snake down, dipping down between the darkness of their bodies to his groin. She grabbed hold of him. "Someone's pleased to see me..."

And he was. In some strange way, he was desperate for her all over again. Fleming lay unable to move. It was pleasing and shocking.

The hand gripped hard. He could feel himself close to climax. It didn't take long. His stomach clenched and he grunted out his pleasure... and then it was over.

She pulled her hand up from the darkness, his gravy a glinting cream webbing over her fingers. She lifted it to her mouth, licked at it. "Mmmm... I love the taste of your constant failure."

Fleming began to cry. He felt abused somehow, his feelings broiling inside of him. For a fleeting moment he wondered if this had been how she felt: abused, scared, and desperate.

She leaned down and kissed him. He could taste himself on her lips.

"Can you taste them? The lives waiting to be born... *feast with me...*"

As her face pulled away from his, the moonlight caught a thin line of spittle joining them together like a silk trail from a worm. She was now fully revealed in the subtle glow of the moon. Water cascaded from her hair down her jagged, angular face. Her eyes were glowing from a haunted afterlife. He'd longed to get lost in those eyes in a time gone by, but now he couldn't look away even if he wanted to. "Cyn-thia?" he whispered.

She moved her hips against his crotch.

"Play with me won't you, Fleming? Please... I want to feel abused, I want you to treat me like you did that night..." She forced his hand to stay in place. "You can rough me up a bit..."

He lay there confused, his hand being forcibly moved against her.

She struck herself in the face with her own hand, hard enough to make her head rock back. When it fell forward, she was bleeding from the hole where a nose belonged.

He turned his face away and cried harder.

"What's wrong? Does my appearance make you sick? It didn't before... Does my new body not make you happy? Or do you only like it when you have to work for it? Ah... I get it, you're a control freak... but a word of warning, Fleming... I'm in control now!" She spat the final words into his face.

Fleming continued to blub. "Ah don't understand... It can't be you, it... Ah..."

She placed a finger over his mouth. "Sssshhhh... the time for questions is over!" She bent forwards again. The decay of her body caused him to gag, his body twitching on the bed beneath her, but unable to move out from under her impossible weight. Cynthia placed her hands on his chest, stilling his struggles.

Lightning struck outside. The room glowed with brightness, revealing more of her ragged form. Skin hung off her, puckered and blistered like spent candle wax. She was a ghastly, drowned, putrefied mess. Blood trickled from her nose to her lip. She tongued it. A maniacal laugh erupted from her mouth, her teeth covered in black blood that were anchored in even blacker gums.

"Don't you remember that night?" Her eyes fixed Fleming in a stare, the long dead eyes of a fish, glassy and in baggy, sagging sockets, surrounded with deep, bruised flesh. "I was special, wasn't I?"

It was raining, but when did it not in this hellhole town? Fleming was driving home from the prison after another late night. He almost ran her over as she burst out into the road, his headlights illuminating her shadow against the sheets of rain. A beautiful silhouette, as if her form had been cut out of the very fabric of the world. He knew it was her instantly, her sleek form that he'd studied for some time but only from a distance, unable to touch but desperately wanting. He'd fantasised about being with her, stealing her away from her husband and setting up a life together. He pressed his foot on the brake.

She ran to the window, and his heart began racing as she rapped on the glass. He stilled himself briefly before lowering it, the rain streaming in along with her scent of coconut; sweet and teasing. Then her voice followed.

"Hi, Warden, mind giving me a lift? You're heading my way, right?"

He nodded, didn't want to speak as he felt his voice would betray his nervousness. She opened the door and dropped into the passenger seat. Although it was raining, it was still quite humid, and Fleming watched as she loosened her coat, revealing her short skirt and those long brown, supple legs that Fleming had imagined wrapped around his waist. They seemed to glisten in the light.

Usually, Fleming liked paler women. It was something that had been beaten into him from a young age by his parents - anything dark skinned was corrupted, unsuitable and inferior for the likes of him. They had often warned him that he would betray his race if he ever got with one of those darkies. He'd struggled to pull away from this thinking. It had become easier when his parents died, but their racist echo remained in the quiet whispers of his mind. But in this light, with her glistening wet caramel skin, she stirred something deep within him. It felt so good.... So right. She was awakening a monster that had been better left dormant.

Cynthia was oblivious as she dabbed at the rain falling from her hair and trickling down her face. Fleming watched as the rain traced its way down her neck and over her chest. *Forbidden fruit!* His mother screamed from the depths of his mind. His father's voice boomed through the din of rain, *Don't you go getting a taste for that dark meat son, it's a poisonous trap!*

Fleming tried to ignore them, shook his head hoping to shake them loose. He checked his rearview mirror as if to adjust for the rain, but really he was adjusting for a better look, although he knew every inch of her body in his mind. But at that angle, he could see the fullness of her large breasts. The fabric had become translucent due to the downpour. He wondered if she'd noticed how the fabric was taut against her body. If she were leading him on, he wasn't going to tell her; he was enjoying this stolen moment of voyeurism. She was beautiful. He had to have her, had to tell her how he felt. He had to tell her he loved her. She might even confess to wanting him too. After all, her husband was a weak, pathetic man, a spineless piece of trash.

Fleming pressed his foot on the accelerator and the car lurched into life. The wipers worked overtime. She reclined next to him and Fleming silently imagined that this could be their life - driving home together after a busy day at the office, returning home to cook dinner, talk, and then fuck. In the car, they were alone at last and Fleming didn't want to be anywhere else.

Fleming watched her out the corner of his eye. He was sure she was flirting with him. She crossed her legs within the cramped footwell and Fleming noticed that she'd done this towards him. She was flirting. He'd taken a course on body language when he started his work in prisons and she was showing him all the signs of attraction, non-verbal cues that signalled she wanted him. Maybe she was shy, didn't know how to approach the situation with her being married. Fleming glanced from the road to her leg, her fingers tracing around her delicate knee with immaculately manicured nails. He wondered what they'd feel like raking down his back as they made love. That was, until he noticed the wedding ring and a rage burned within him. He didn't care that she was married, she wouldn't have gotten in the car with him if she didn't want him.

He'd take her. He'd show her what a real man was like.

She was making idle chit chat, of which Fleming was oblivious, as all he was thinking about was how he could have her. She had to have something of an idea in regards to the longing he had for her, all the repressed urges waiting to break the surface, of the monster that was rising up from the deep. His body quivered with excitement.

They turned onto Juniper Drive. The car thundered down the road, puddles splashing in arching waves as if they were a speed-boat carving up the water. Cynthia was mesmerised by the rain streaking the window. Her afro still glistening and wet, partly concealed her face from his own. Not seeing all of her sent him over the edge. It was now or never.

Fleming reached out his hand, past the gearshift, inches away from her leg. He felt a buzz of excitement. Finally, he would tell her how he felt; but the words stuck in his throat. Saying those words would go against the worldview he'd been raised to believe, but for her, he'd face the scorn of the townsfolk. For her, he was willing to change everything. For her, he was willing to be a better man.

Then it was there, his hand was on her leg, where it slid over her wet skin, his fingers hungry for her flesh. He couldn't believe he was touching her. His words were about to tumble from his mouth, the confession of his feelings, of his devotion to her, but before they could escape his lips, Cynthia screamed.

"What are you doing!?" She ripped his hand from her leg and flung it away. She squirmed towards the door, trying to get away from him. "Pull over!"

"Come on now... Ah know your kind!" he chided, talking of how promiscuous he knew women like her were but now he saw how his words were misconstrued.

"My kind?" she asked, spite filling her voice.

"Now hold on, Ah don't mean any offence; Ah just thought you felt-"

"Fuck whatever you're talking about, just let me out!"

"Ah *need* you, Cyn-thia!" With that, it was out. His dirty little secret. He glanced at her and noticed her eyes widening, panic ruining her face in an instant.

"Let me out... now!"

"Listen... listen to me! Ah don't want t' *hurt* you, Ah just want us to talk. Ah've seen the way you look at me when y'think no one else is watching. Ah feel the same way! We have a *connect-ion...*" Fleming stopped talking as he took in the look in her eyes. He'd been flicking glances at her, trying not to crash the car on the slippery road, but also not wanting to slow down and allow her a chance at escape before he'd said his piece. Her eyes... they were haunted, full of fear and hatred. She was utterly repulsed. In that moment he knew that he'd never be able to have her, love her, be with her.

Cynthia screamed at him in the tight confines of the car, "How dare you, I-"

Fleming didn't let her finish her sentence. He'd heard enough lies spilling from her mouth, and the beast that he'd be suppressing burst from the icy depths of his soul. He threw a fist at her. Hard. It struck her in the face, making her head snap back, bouncing off the passenger window. The glass fractured into a spiderweb. She was dazed, head rolling limply on her neck. One eye was already swelling.

"Ah could have *loved* you, Cyn-thia, if y'would've let me... but my momma surely was right. Your kind are *nothing* more than a bunch of prick *teases*, walking around town like the whole *world* owes you something!" he hissed. "Ah bet you do this often, don'tchoo? Hitchhike, wet and almost naked, and then it's *my* fault all of a sudden when you've had enough... we could have been *happy*, Cyn-thia." Fleming was sobbing. What had he been thinking, putting himself out there like that? The depth of rejection, and by a black bitch at that. He'd made himself vulnerable for the first and very last time. His heartbreak became blinding rage. "Ah'll show *you* who's the fucking boss. Does your husband have *any* idea how much of a slut you are? Probably how you snagged him in the first place, ain't it, being all *promiscuous* and shit! Well, Ah'll show *you* what happens to *sluts* who reject me, you women who take *me* for a fool... Y'ain't gonna walk right for a *week*! My momma was right about something else, too: no one's *ever* going to miss a no good nig-"

The words died in his throat as he glanced to his right. Cynthia had groggily reached for the handle. Even though leaping from the speeding car would probably kill her, she was clearly desperate to avoid what was to come. Fleming slammed the central locking just in time to keep her a prisoner. She slammed her palm against the broken window, trying to create a new opening, but it wouldn't give. There was no escape, she was trapped.

Cynthia tried to grab the wheel. Fleming hit her again, his forearm slamming against her, this time sending a claret spray of blood from her nose onto the window. He hit her again. And again. He wanted to destroy her beauty, wipe her teasing face from his mind, make her pay for making him want her, make her suffer for

188 | ROSS JEFFERY

rejecting his advances. He despised himself for allowing her to make him feel weak. He would never forgive himself for loving her when it went against everything he'd ever known. When one more sickening crunch of gristle and bone rang out through the car and her head hung low on her shoulders, arms slumped by her sides, Fleming realised he'd gone too far.

"Jee-zus Christ, look what you gone an' made me do! Look what you did!" He needed to get off the road in case someone saw his floundering cargo. The last thing he needed was for someone to notice him with her and brandish him a sympathiser too. He needed to get off the main highway, and fast. Fleming thought about where to go and within a split second a voice seemed to utter the answer.

He took the next right and headed up the hill, watching as the houses became less frequent. The trees grew thicker. He was almost there.

She'd taken the fight out of him. He had loved her, but now he despised everything about her. He wanted to destroy every last piece of her. If he couldn't be with her, then no one could, and he'd make sure of it. This goddamn bitch had a lot to answer for, and he'd make her answer for every single thing.

The things he did to her body kept him sated long after his drive home. The last thing he saw was her hair pillowing atop the water at the bottom of the well.

His deed was done. His secret would be forever buried.

"Ahh... you do remember!" Cynthia purred. Her eyes peered at Fleming's face, seeing the recognition of his actions. His facial expressions were like a landslide as horror washed over him. She snapped a frozen hand over his mouth and tightened her gnarled fingers around it, forcing his mouth into a fish-like pout. Dipping forward, she bit his fleshy lips, chewed on them playfully. "Do you remember doing this to mine? Laughing at their plumpness, calling me 'nigger lips?' Before you bit... them... *off.*"

Her face began to transform into the mangled, ragged mess he had made. Lips tore from their place, teeth fell out, one eye swelled to near bursting, her nose broke and a deep crater appeared in the side of her head where a grey sack pulsated within. He turned his head away.

"What's wrong? You once found me so attractive. Or was I just a piece of poisoned fruit you couldn't help but desire? Did you only want me because your inbred mother told you I was bad for you, like a candy bar you weren't allowed to eat but just couldn't resist?" She cackled and clawed at his entire body. "What's the matter, are you scared? Because you *should* be."

He shook his head violently. He must be dreaming. Soon he'd wake. He wasn't going to submit to her, he wouldn't let her have any advantage over him, not after he bared all just to have her throw it back in his face. "It's *just* a *dream!*" Fleming screamed into the night.

"Tut, tut... It's not a dream, sweetheart..." Her face leered towards his and he shrunk back from her chattering teeth. "This is your waking nightmare!"

Another lightning strike caused the room to blaze with light. It made Fleming wince. Then he glanced back at Cynthia's face and she'd returned to her tempting best "You prefer this?" Cynthia purred. She watched him with hooded eyelids, perfect in every way: her skin unblemished, chocolate mousse soft. He wanted to lose himself in her flesh again. Part of him was reviled but he remembered how good she'd felt that time at the well. He needed that again.

"I need you to do something for me."

Fleming groaned. The things *she* was doing appalled and delighted him.

"Can I count on you? When the time is right?"

He nodded in abandon. Fleming would have agreed to do anything in that moment with his body wracked with an unrelenting ache that was finally being soothed. "What... what is... hnnggh... you... want me... do?"

"I need you to get rid of that bitch. She's spoiling my appetite... I need her gone... can you do that for me?"

"Yes. Ah'll.. Ah'll do it..." Fleming stuttered. With exhaustion his head fell to the side and he saw her figure cast on the wall. It betrayed the siren straddling him.

A grotesque creature was hunched over him, nubs of bone showing through her back, drooping flesh hung like a fringe from her stomach. Then he noticed the tendrils rippling at the edges of her shadow, trying to break free. He turned back to her. Fleming saw that she was looking upon her own shadow, also. Slowly, she brought her eyes back to his.

"There are things you... will never understsssstand." Cynthia's mouth moved but the voice was not her own. *"There are many of... ussss..."* She leaned forwards again, her face gliding up past his cheek, her afro tickling at the side of his face, her sweet coconut scent stronger now, her hair still streaming water down onto his face.

"Now... listen carefully..."

CHAPTER 19

In the unlit library, a body sat hunched over in a chair in the darkest corner of the room. A soft blue beam from the moon created pools of light, tricking the eye to believe there were actual bodies of water on the floor. The real water trickled down the window panes, causing the light to shift and ripple, furthering the illusion. A cigarette lay in an ashtray, the ember blinking out. Smoke dribbled from the barely glowing end, snaking its way onto the maple side table, dancing across the surface, before tumbling off and undulating towards the floor, where it dispersed as if seeping into the floor itself, fleeing a different, ominous presence that was filling the room. A letter sat next to an envelope on the table and the smoke stained the edges of each sheet.

Stanley woke himself with a wracking cough. A lump of phlegm shifted from his throat to his mouth, where his tongue wrestled with the foreign foe. The cough forced his aching body up from his lounging and sent trembling hands searching his pockets. He pulled out a stained handkerchief and spit the contents into the silk, closing it around his mouth to ensure that he got it all.

As he moved to the edge of the chair, he reached out a hand and clicked the lamp on the side table into life. The space around his chair lit up like a spotlight had been turned on, the smoke from the now extinguished cigarette a haze in the air around him. He opened the silken hanky in front of him, like a child observing a butterfly print, but instead of wonder, Stanley was disgusted at what he found. A yellow stain, mottled and veiny with red streaks, forming a deep brown mess the longer he watched it mingle. The lining of his throat was raw.

A lightning bolt tore its way through his body as he coughed again, but he managed to cover his mouth in time with the silk. He was trying to breathe, but with each inhale he coughed again and again, an endless cycle.

When his coughing subsided, he felt assaulted, his fragile frame not used to the workout the coughing was giving him. Stanley knew the bouts of coughing were growing worse and it was only a matter of time before he wouldn't be able to breathe his way through it. He sagged in the chair, listening to the rain against the window. It sounded much gentler after his coughing.

A shuffling sound caught his attention. His eyes darted to the darkness of the library, and he squinted, trying to filter out the harsh light of the lamp. He could hear a subtle footfall, as of someone moving in the darkness. He threw the hanky onto the side table, the lamp revealing even more spatterings of blood and phlegm.

"Who's there?" His voice came out strained, as if his vocal cords were about to snap like a violinist's bow from overuse. His fingers delicately rubbed his throat, trying not to trigger the same searing pain as before. He tried to grip a blockage within... or was it a tear he was trying to hold together?

He stifled a couple of small coughs. The pattering of feet seemed to flit across the room and back again. Someone, or something, was running about in the darkness. "I said... who's there?" he managed to croak out. Stanley shuffled to the edge of the chair, placing his paper-thin fingers around the arms of it, and summoned all the energy he had to raise his bag of bones from the seat.

"*Don't...*" A growl emanated from the shadows, husky in its commanding authority.

Stanley crumpled back into the seat, as if pushed down by an unseen and powerful hand. He raised his own hand, blocking out the lamps light to peer beyond it into the darkness. Near the end of a bookcase, he saw It, peering out from behind the shelf's end like a child fearful of a coming scolding from a parent. The unmistakable tendrils of black that Stanley had grown accustomed to flowed from its edges, cutting small veins in the bluish light still filtering in through the window, each black vine dancing in the dark, clambering and wriggling toward the roof above.

"Come into the light," Stanley said. Never had he spoken so freely to It.

"*No,*" the voice spat back, the timbre deep and reverberating. Stanley thought he heard the ashtray judder on the side table. The butt of his cigarette fell from the edge of the ashtray and rolled onto the floor.

"What do you want?" Stanley's voice was weak.

"*I've come to tell you... your service is almost over... your debt almost paid. Soon... you will be able to retire... from our deal.*"

A wave of relief flooded him. It was as if his body had opened a dam and water rushed forth into the darkness. He was nearly finished.

The shape moved from its cover, stepping out into the room. It was still hard to distinguish where It finished and the darkness of the library started.

Stanley continued to watch as the indistinguishable void of

blackness seemed to swell, growing taller, blocking out the light from the window, stretching at the confines of the abyss. "Retire? Is my work here really done?"

"Yes. Your master... has found one whose... ssssssoul is ready... who can take things forwards. You knew this... was only temporary... that you could only sssssserve us... so long."

"But... what will I do?" Relief was replaced by panic. "I've nothing left. I've given you my best years, and now... now I'm just a shell, a bag of rattling bones. Please... please use me! I've still so much to offer." Stanley's voice cracked as it grew higher in pitch. He choked down another cough, but it escaped in a wracking fit. Blood sprayed into the air, tin red specks hovering for a moment before dropping onto the rug around his feet like dirty rain.

"Sssstanley... you have been ever... diligent in your work... in your service. But you have... outlived your usefulness... look at you."

Stanley wiped the blood trickling from the corner of his mouth with the back of his hand.

"You used to be strong... powerful. We moved unnoticed. You... were the vessel and you... bore us well. But the weight... of the burden... consumes the vessel. Your body wassssstrong and your mind was willing... and your inventiveness is sssssomething We... will never forget. You will be... remembered... when the time comes." The shape in the darkness moved closer, tendrils drifting into the light for a second before shrinking back, recoiling as if burnt.

A deathly silence filled the library; only the pattering of rain on the window could be heard. Stanley remained in his chair, observing the probing veins as they drifted into and snapped back from the light. He felt as though a weight had been lifted. His body felt younger, more alive than it ever had. The silence was growing more intense. Stanley uttered words into the darkness just to fill it with something. "Speak, please; I'm listening. Please... don't leave me."

"*Hushhhh...*" a hiss like a snake wrapped around his body. Stanley flinched in his chair. A tear escaped, rolling down his cheek. "*You've done ssso much... for us, Stanley... who would have thought... that words... were the way into the ssssoul? Your body has become... too decrepit to carry out our work... but take heart Sssstanley... you have done so much! There have been... many before you, and many... will come after you... all sssservants to the greater cause... but don't forget... it was you, Stanley, you... alone were the one able to create... the key. You'll be remembered... for all eternity... for your actions.*"

"I can do more! Please! Please let me?"

"*Each dog has... its day, Stanley. You've been ours... for longer than... most, but now... with the book... We can move with...out bringing attention. Of course... we will still need a... home to germinate and... grow, and one sssuch person... has come to our attention... one that is pure, so that when... we nestle within, when we... break him and force oursssselves upon him... he'll give us all... the nourishment we need. This town... this place... is like a fattened calf... for the slaughter. In our new host... we will grow sssstronger, and then... we will be ready to move... to the next town. And... the book... your book, Stanley, will go... before us.*"

"But I can help!"

"**NO!**"

The lamp burst. Darkness swooped in as the tinkling of glass fell onto the wood. It smothered Stanley, and he felt a hand at his throat, the pain instantaneous. He tried to raise his hands, to pull the assailing fingers away, but more hands came out of the darkness, an impossible number pressing his arms against the chair. "***How dare you de...fy your Master!***"

"But we've accomplished so much..." Stanley whimpered through his constricted throat.

"*And, we've still... much more to do. But remember...* **We can snuff you out***... in an instant!*" The hands from the void released their grip. "*Do not make us... regret using you... one lassst time...*"

Stanley breathed deeply, bringing air into his lungs that burned as it rushed through his injured throat. The cough began again. He raised a hand to his face, felt something sticky and warm on his lips, followed by a trickling down his arm. The moonlight shone against the black blood.

"*The mind is... weak, but we... are sssssure the body... is still willing... are you willing, Stanley?*"

Stanley nodded glibly into the darkness, more of a reflex than a conscious thought, not wanting to disappoint his master and suffer another correction.

"*Will you do... one last thing for usssss... Stanley?*"

Stanley nodded again, shaking uncontrollably like a beaten mutt crouching at its master's feet.

"*Goooood... now... lisssssten, as this... is your last action as one... of our acolytes... we will remember you... when the time comesss...*"

Stanley felt a breath at his ear, and a thousand voices uttered their final request of him. When they were done, he nodded a final time – sealing his oath and his fate.

CHAPTER 20

Fleming made his way rapidly toward the cell block, his breath ragged. Sweat dampened his brow and circles appeared at his armpits, matching the ones on his shoulder left by the rain. The urgency of his mission from his late-night visitor honed his focus. He had parked his car in the empty lot and then quick-timed it into his office, using his personal entrance off the side of the building so as to not rouse suspicion over his late-night arrival at JC. The way his heart smashed his ribs made him feel like he was two beats away from a heart attack.

The keys at his hips were clutched in his fist to prevent them from jangling and announcing his presence to those ahead. Once in his office, he had made sure to turn off all the cameras along the route he'd planned to take. He could have no evidence placing him in the prison with his target; no, especially not that. Nothing could be allowed to come back and bite him on his fat ass. On tiptoe, he'd left the office as stealthily as his scotch-riddled frame had allowed.

Fleming paused. Turning left would lead him exactly where he needed to be. He steeled himself for what was to come, taking deep breaths, trying not to look too flustered for when he finally came face-to-face with his target. The Warden peered around the corner, out onto the raised steel aisle before him. He needed to tread lightly, make as little noise as possible. He set off again, slowly approaching the cell. He placed one faltering foot on the mesh, before placing another slowly in front, creeping toward his final destination. He passed a few cells, inmates fast asleep, concealed in the darkness.

"Hey!"

Fleming froze. He turned and saw an inmate staring out of the darkness, eyes bright like white gemstones. It was Christopher, the soft-spoken Goliath of a man that reminded Fleming of John Coffey.

"Forget y'ever saw me, son," Fleming whispered. "If y'know what's good for you, you'll forget you ever did see me."

Christopher seemed to consider him a moment, then those eyes retreated into the dark and were extinguished.

Fleming crept on.

Ages seemed to pass but he finally reached the cell he was hunting. He placed his hands on the bars, pulling himself closer. Peering into the cell, he could see his inmate was asleep, turned towards the wall. Just as well really. A pair of white briefs and a pale sheet dangling off the end of the bed were the only other bits Fleming could make out.

He placed the key into the lock and turned it slightly before he felt the teeth bite. He could hear the faint grinding of the lock as it slid from the frame. He took a deep breath and turned it another quarter to open.

CLICK.

Fleming flinched at the gunshot-like sound but to those asleep it was nothing but a pin dropping, dulled by the sound of the rain and the snoring, or the mad babbling of those few inmates that were still awake. He pulled open the cell door, expecting a comical squeak of hinges, but was relieved when it swung open silently. With one hand clutching his keys, he turned and began to pull the door closed as quietly as he had opened it. Fleming took one last look through the grate into the floor below, taking in the guard station, where one of the guards had his feet up, reading the paper. All else was still.

He was one step closer to his plan. Reaching through the bars, he placed the key back into the lock and clicked it closed, locking himself inside. He'd gone unnoticed. Or so he thought.

Fleming was suddenly thrust up against the door, and in an odd moment, he was grateful that he'd managed to lock it or he and his pursuer would have fallen in one sorry lump right onto the concourse. Not only would his secret meeting have been over, quite possibly his life would have ended as well.

He felt something sharp press up against his chin, digging into his flesh. Another hand clamped over his mouth and nose, smothering him.

"Well now... look-ee here. To what do I owe the *pleasure*, Chief? Y'come by for a late night boo-ty-call?"

Henry pressed fully against Fleming and licked at the Warden's earlobe, flicking his tongue out against the pearl of flesh like a boxer hitting a speed bag. Then he sucked it into his mouth and gnawed on it, before letting it fall. "You like that?" Henry whispered.

Fleming shook his head, and the sharp object at his neck dug in further, his flesh dimpling. He changed his shake into a nod.

"Now, you done gone an' made a *big* mistake, Chief. I'm just gonna take them keys off'n you, and then I'm gonna wheel you outta here with my new friend, Pricker. He's real sharp, y'see. And you, you're gonna be the *perfect* gentleman and open every goddamn door for me. Innthat right?"

Fleming didn't move a single muscle.

Henry sneered. "Got somethin' you wanna say, then? Well I suppose I can listen. I'm gonna take my hand off your mouth so I can hear that bea-yoo-tiful voice sing. But you so much as inhale too much, and you drop 'fore them stooges down there even get to their feet... understand?"

Fleming nodded. As Henry removed his hand, Fleming smelled the nicotine from Henry's fingers, and part of Fleming wanted to suck those bones dry.

The hand loosened, disappeared, and then grabbed at his shoulder. Fleming was forcibly spun around. It all happened so quickly that his head swam, like the time he rode a rollercoaster when the circus had come to town. The shiv was pressed up into his side, nestled between some ribs, near where he assumed his lungs were. Fleming glanced down to study the object poking him. It was a tooth brush, the end of which had been melted and a scalpel blade inserted. Fleming had seen them many times, even confiscated his fair share during cell inspections, but he'd never feared them before. They looked so childish and puny when he had dumped them in trashcans after searching a cell. Seeing one up close and personal put a different perspective on things.

"Scream, I'm gonna prick you with this. Might not kill you right away, but I'm sure by the time I've stalled the guards trying to get in here..." Henry reached down, tracing a finger delicately down Fleming's arm, until he laid hold of the keys, where he tugged them, winking at Fleming playfully. "An' seeing as how you were *so* kind to bring me the keys... so, you gonna play nice?"

He reluctantly let go of the keys and said, "Yes." Before Henry could blink, Fleming fished out the taser from his pocket and pulled the trigger.

Henry's eyes went wide. With a *fut*, metal was embedded in his chest and he fell to the ground, spasming. There was no cry or noise, except his body hitting the floor in its writhing, which probably sounded to those in the neighbouring cells like vigorous masturbation. Fleming fixed his hair and straightened his jacket, wiping the sweat from his brow. He regarded Henry, twitching and frothing at the mouth. When the jerking was done, he stooped and picked up his keys.

"Ah do think we understand each other now," Fleming said.

Henry crawled towards his bed.

Fleming shocked him again for good measure.

When Henry was done kicking like a half-dead insect, Fleming propped his limp body on the bed. Henry's glassy eyes rolled beneath his lids. Fleming returned the shank, sliding it into the waistband of Henry's briefs. He patted Henry on the head.

As he stepped back, the vacant bunk above the one Henry was seated in caught his attention, making him think of the few times a bed had ever been empty. That particular bunk had been empty ever since Klein had killed Henry's cell-mate, and Henry had moved from the top to the bottom, sleeping where his lover would never lay again. The incident report still sat on Fleming's desk, and a copy of it had also been given to Dolores to add to the ever-increasing evidence that Juniper Correctional was failing its inmates.

"Now. Let's start this con-versation again, shall we?" Fleming said.

Henry nodded weakly. He reached over to a little compartment underneath the top bunk and retrieved a cigarette. He lit one with a strike of a match, a little flame flickering for a moment and revealing, of all things, a sly smirk on Henry's face.

"Somethin' amusin'?" Fleming said, grinding his teeth.

"I guess y'don't get t'be Warden without learnin' a few tricks. I mean this as a compliment: you really belong in here, y'know that?"

Fleming's lip curled.

Henry leaned towards the flame, the cigarette blooming to life as he inhaled. Henry shook out the match and dropped it onto the floor, and continued to sit opposite Fleming. One glowing amber eye stared in the darkness. "So *what* brings the big cheese t'my door, hmm?"

"Ah... Ah have a prop-osition for you."

"For *moi*? Oh, y'shouldn't have... What *is* it you want from me? Some darkies been givin' you a hard time? Want me t' get some new meat to bend to your au-thor-i-ty? Or what about-"

"Klein." Fleming said, cutting Henry off.

Henry tried to rise, but his nerves were still scoured from the taser, and so instead he made a kind of flopping motion. He grunted in annoyance as he settled back down. The smoke drifted up from the cigarette dangling from his mouth and danced towards Fleming, swirling into his eyes.

"That sonofabitch! Don'tchu be prick teasing me now, Fleming!"

"Y'wan' him?"

"Of *fucking* course I want him. I wanna make an example of that piece of *shit*. What he did, what he took from me... I'm gonna make that motherfucker *bleed* and-"

"Well that's good; we have some-thing to barter with, then."

Henry paused. "Whatchu mean, 'barter?'"

"Ah can give you Klein. He's currently in the sick bay, due back in general pop-ulation when Ah auth-orise it."

"What the *hell*'re you waiting for, Chief, sign the fucking papers already!"

"Ah need you to do one, *little* thing fo' me first. When that's done, Ah'll sign the papers and bring him to you myself."

Henry took another deep drag, smoke pluming into the air as he exhaled. "Name it! No one gets the best of me in here. I gots a rep-u-tation t'keep up! And I got... urges, since he took my dear bitch. I've been savin' up a special batch, just for him. I'll stick it in him, and I'll stick him, but in what order depends on him. I been reading about it, I think they call that necra... necro..."

"Nec-rophilia," Fleming said dryly.

"I knew that... why you gotta go and spoil it for?"

"Henry, whatever you do with him, that's up to you, but what Ah need from you is simple..." Fleming paused as if uncertain. "Can Ah truly trust you, Henry? Because what Ah'm about to say is somethin' of the *utmost* importance... and if you betray my trust, well. You'll never see Klein again fo' starters. Ah'll have him transferred and you silenced before you can whack another one off."

"Trust, Warden dear," Henry mockingly drawled, "is a two-way street. Now you made quite an entrance tonight. Get me Klein, and I'll do whatever you want; I'll even blow you for free..."

"Tha' won't be necessary, Henry. But you'll get Klein after you've done what Ah need. Are we clear?"

"Crystal... but don't'cha try an' fuck me over now, Chief. You of all people should know I'll be the one doing the fucking."

Fleming's face turned into a satanic snarl. "Ah could have fucked *you* right here, you miserable ingrate. You were so weak, Ah could have raped you *all night long*, and the other inmates would have cheered me *on*."

Henry's jaw dropped open, causing the cigarette to fall on his lap.

Fleming smoothed his hair again, in an attempt to calm himself. "When have Ah *ever* tried to fuck you over, Henry? You have been my *most* loyal servant in this place. You are my eyes and ears, my enforcer... We share a special bond, you and Ah. You'll get yours, just as soon as Ah've got mine."

Henry picked up the cigarette in his lap. His hand trembled, and Fleming knew his outburst had its desired effect. "So... whaddya need from me?" Henry stuck out his tongue and then extinguished the butt on the slippery flesh. There was a hiss, like a snake puncturing the air.

"We have a... situation here, as you know, with the Marshals. Well... what's left of them, anyway... But what Ah need you to do is make this situation... disappear. Do you understand?"

"What, y'want me t' kill that snooping bitch?" Henry cackled. "That's dark even for you, Chief. You *know* what will happen to me if I get caught, or you have 'a sudden change of heart...' Killing a law enforcement officer? Shee-it, I like to be pricked but not t'death! State'll overrule County in matters of murder of an officer of the law." He shook his head and waved Fleming away. "I ain't gettin' th'needle for doing your dirty work, no matter the reward. I'll just bide my time, get to Klein by my own means. Y'move him to another prison, I'll just send word to whichever shithouse y'send him to, and he won't see out the week."

Fleming was mildly impressed by Henry's legal knowledge. He chuckled. "Calm yourself, Henry. Klein is still on the hook here; all you need to do is reel him in..." Fleming reached out a hand in the darkness, placed it on Henry's knee. "Look, to make this go away Ah need a patsy and-"

"A patsy? What the hell is that?"

"You know, a scapegoat; a fall guy? Ah don't want you to kill her, that's surely not what Ah'm saying. Ah just need you to give her something... give her *someone* she can hang for the failings - all the suicides, the deaths... d'you understand? They'll think it's an inside job. Who knows, it might be, but *we* need to give *her* someone they can lay all the blame on."

"Who you got in mind?"

Fleming shrugged nonchalantly. "Well, Ah was thinking about Frank."

"Ah... good old Frank. You got priors with him, don'tcha?"

Henry reached down to Fleming's hand that was still on his knee, and delicately stroked it.

Fleming recoiled and tried to not shudder. "Ehm. No. Not at all... Ah just don't like that smarmy son-of-a-bitch walking around here like his shit don't stink, and Ah've been waiting for the chance to throw that lame dicked do-gooder under the bus for some time, ever since..." Fleming faltered, his voice quavered.

"Since?" Henry prompted.

"Never you mind. It doesn't concern you... just per-sonal history is all. Ah just want him gone. Ah want this fucking investigation over and Ah thought you, as my general, would be able to make that happen. So. Can you?"

"If whatcha say y'can deliver is right, then I'll do what y'need. When is this all going down anyhow?"

"Tomorrow. Ah'll escort Dolores down here; tell her that Ah have an *exemplary* inmate that has information about the murders, that you know *who's* been doing them *and* that you're willing to testify. Then all you've got to do is follow through, give her everythin' she needs to hang that *fucker*. We'll be in the home stretch, and you'll get your precious Klein. Understood?"

"Yeah... but we'll need a lot more'n a convicts word against a prison guard. Y'seen my record; who's gonna believe a guy like me?"

"Don't you worry, Henry, Ah have some... incriminating evidence." He pointed at Henry. "There are many cogs turning here; each one connected, each with a common goal, and you... *you* are the one that all these cogs fit into, right at the centre, driving us forwards. Don't you fail us. Everything is falling into place." And with that Fleming headed towards the cell door.

"Just don't go fucking me, Chief! I ain't gonna be one of your so-called pansies!"

"It's patsy, Henry... and when have Ah ever not followed through?"

"I don't know, I don't do your laundry. But you screw me on this, an' I'll get you. Maybe not t'marrah, maybe not the next day... But you'll be lookin' over your shoulder so much you'll break your fucking neck. I'm serious, Fleming. I'll get t' you, and *destroy* you. Now, put an egg in your shoe and beat it!"

Fleming considered tasering him one more time for insolence, but thought better of it. Henry was only trying to prove his toughness again. "You just make sure you keep your end of the deal and you'll get what's coming to you." He turned and let himself out of the cell as quietly as he had stalked in, disappearing into the shadows that welcomed him.

Fleming was sitting at his desk, a glass of whiskey in one hand, a cigarette in the other. He raised the glass and drained it, then placed it on the table. His head lolled back against the chair and he stared up at the ceiling. He couldn't remember if he'd gone home last night after talking with Henry or had spent the evening in his office, drinking the night into morning. A burning sensation flared behind his eyes and he rubbed them to erase the glaring light of his lamps. He dropped his arms over his stomach. The buttons of his shirt pinched across his gut, skin showing through the pulled fabric. He had a vague memory of digging into a cabinet in his office and pulling out an old shirt that no longer fit, but whether that had been when he'd first snuck in, or sometime after, he couldn't tell. All that mattered was he was in the office, and that bitch would be too, soon enough.

After catching a glimpse of his bedraggled face in the reflection of his computer monitor, Fleming began to brush what remained of his hair back into place. He glanced down at the table, to the manila folder that sat front and centre on his desk. The small tab at the side said "Whitten, Frank."

He brought the cigarette to his mouth and inhaled, the ash falling onto his shirt. As he leaned forward, ash fell to the floor, leaving a ghost of grey on the puckered fabric. Fleming paid it no mind, only realising his cigarette had burnt to the end when it singed his lips. He stubbed it out into the ashtray and reached for the folder.

Fleming began sifting through the contents. He'd been busy over the last few weeks, falsifying evidence, creating witness accounts from dead inmates, forging staff signatures and complaints. He paused on one document in particular: Frank's last appraisal. Fleming had created it only hours before, with mentions of Frank not being fit for duty, of negligence and inappropriate behaviour towards inmates, even assaults. There was a smattering of reprimands about his future conduct. A smirk broke out across Fleming's face. He was surprised at how good it was, considering how quickly it had been collated. For the first time in months, Fleming felt a spark of joy. It made him feel so *good* to finally be ridding himself of Frank, even if it meant throwing him under the bus. Fleming desperately hoped that in doing this, maybe the memories that plagued him every day would join Frank under the thick tyres too.

Dolores was looking for someone to blame for this mess, and Fleming was giving her a scapegoat, plus enough rope to finish the job. Then she could be on her way: gone, and operations at the prison could continue as before; but most importantly, his visitor would be satisfied.

Fleming scooped the documents back into order and slid them inside the file, and pushed it back towards the centre of his desk. He reached for his glass and raised it to his lips, only to discover that he'd finished that round of amber fuel. Fleming automatically reached for his drawer, but opening it, he rediscovered the book.

His heart juddered in his chest, like a car struggling to start. He reached in and grabbed the book, pulled it from the drawer. A bottle of whiskey rolled down into the void left behind. He laid the book on his desk. He hadn't looked at it for some time... not since Davy had given it to Fleming moments before he went outside and sat motionlessly within the inferno that consumed him.

Fear threatened to swallow his mind and he scrabbled for the numbness offered by the alcohol bottle. He twisted the lid loose and didn't bother to retrieve it when it fell to the floor. The liquid flowed into the glass noisily. Fleming poured until the scotch threatened to overflow. He sat the bottle on his desk but the trickling noise of liquid remained. He picked the up the glass thinking it had a crack in it but could find no leaking. It had to be his sleep deprived mind playing tricks on him. He dropped the bottle into the trash and took a sip of his drink.

He could still hear the sound of running water splashing. *The secretary must be cleaning.* Fleming took another swig of his drink and went to set his glass on his desk. The movement pulled his attention to the book. It sat there within a puddle of its own creation.

Fleming placed the glass down and pressed his fingers into his eyes until it hurt. When he blinked them open, he had hoped the vision would be gone... but the book was still bleeding water. It trickled out from within the pages, the mahogany table discolouring the clear liquid into blood. The first fingers of liquid had reached the edge of the desk and were dripping into a large puddle on the floor.

The light was dim in his office... Fleming was sure he wasn't seeing things clearly. It was just early morning; he was just sleep deprived; that was just it. But the clock on his desk read 11:43

AM, far later than it should have been. He reached out a trembling hand, watching as the water dribbled from the book. Tentatively, he touched the cover. It was slick, but it didn't feel like water. A memory of touching frogspawn as a child flickered through his mind, the gloopy, thick bundle of tadpole eggs having a similar slime to the book. When he opened the cover, there was a thick webbing connecting the cover to the pages within.

A new noise rose above the trickling and splashing of the watery puddle; a small murmur, as if someone else was humming in his office. It was... soothing... though he felt a coldness emanate from the back of his neck, a coldness that seeped into his body and chilled his marrow.

Two hands shot out from under his desk. In the faded light caused by the storm clouds, Fleming noted that the hands which clasped his thighs were onyx black. They reminded him briefly of Davy's that were attached to the steering wheel of his car, charcoaled and gnarled. They squeezed at the baggy flesh of his legs. He tried to slide his chair back but was held in place.

"*Good boy...*" The humming didn't stop and so the words had a haunting tremble within them. "You've been busy... haven't you? I bet you're *dead*... tired, why don't I help... *relieve* some of that tension?"

Fleming wanted to scream at the monster to stop but the words seemed foreign in his head, as though his tongue had been made alien to him. Revulsion and desire swept through him in equal force, but the desire to have *her* again made him stay.

The hands crawled their way towards the zipper of his pants and grasped the toggle between index finger and thumb. He could feel it coming undone one tooth at a time. A hand reached inside, cold against his flesh.

He was frozen, a swirling vortex of self-hatred and uncaring desire. A black sponge of hair began to emerge from under the desk. The anticipation of being with her again made him sit in the chair as if he were in the throes of rigor mortis.

RINGRING. RINGRING.

He jolted at the noise. The phone brought Fleming back to the waking world. Unsure of his surroundings, he glanced down under the desk, but there was nothing there. He looked to the book, still on the table. The water had gone.

RINGRING.

Fleming blinked at the clock as he reached for the phone. "What is it?" he barked. It had clicked to 9:57 AM. Absentmindedly, he reached down between his legs; he was still hard, but his zipper was firmly in place. It had all been... just a dream? Even the clock? It had registered in such a visceral way...

"Your 10 AM is here, Warden. Would you like me to send her in?"

CHAPTER 21

"**S**traight a-way, do you hear me?"

The secretary closed her eyes as she replied, "Of course, sir." She took a deep breath as she softly lowered the phone back to its cradle. "He'll see you-"

"Great," Dolores called over her shoulder. She was already halfway to Fleming's door. "Thanks, Neveah."

"Wait!"

Dolores didn't stop and strode into the office, the legs of her cream pantsuit swishing against her skin. Fleming squawked as he sat up straight. She heard the clinking of glass from the desk, and assumed he had just hidden another bottle of scotch. The smell of the alcohol and the constant cloud of smoke in his office were over-powering, but she had come prepared by basically bathing in her jasmine and coconut perfume. Dolores sat in the chair opposite Fleming and placed her briefcase on the floor, deliberately crossing her legs to angle her body towards him. Appealing to sex-obsessed men had been a tactic of hers when she'd been a police officer, and she knew that her body language could entice Fleming to share more information than he planned.

Fleming adjusted his shirt collar and leaned toward her, elbows on the desk. His forearms covered a folder. He opened his mouth to speak and, much as she had with Officer Barnes, she spoke first.

"It would appear congratulations are in order, Warden Fleming."

His piggy eyes squinted at her in confused suspicion. "What?"

"You seem to have lasted two whole days without another body turning up dead. Are you going for a personal record?"

"Ah would not be too sure about that."

Dolores shifted in her seat. "Is there something you've not told me? If this is something best left to the record, I can have Miss Collins brought from the waiting room."

"There'll be no need for that, Dolores, Ah've-"

"Marshal Fink."

"Em... yes... As Ah was saying, Marshal, Ah've arranged for someone to join our discussion. He should be here shortly. Ah think you'll find what he has to say, and to show you, of the utmost importance. In the mean while, this should help fill in some of the blanks." Fleming peeled the folder from under his arms and handed it across the desk.

Dolores reached for the folder, and the door to the office burst open. She paused and turned to see who the newcomer was. Her eyes narrowed slightly.

Officer Barnes glided into the room like a wraith and deliberately brushed against Dolores as he plopped into the seat next to her. Her lips puckered slightly and she couldn't help moving slightly away from him, recrossing her legs.

Fleming wore a bemused look. "We'll get t' this later," he said as he laid the folder on his desk again. "Thank you for joining us,

Off-icer Barnes. Do you have the in-for-mation for Dolores; I apol-ogise... I mean, for our resident Mahshal?"

A smug smile broke out across Barnes' face, revealing his nico-tine stained teeth. "Right here." Barnes raised his hand with a thin folder pinched between two fingers. Dolores reached out to accept it, but he pulled it away from her, like a child withholding a sweet in a teasing game.

"How hilarious." Dolores rolled her eyes and held out her hand. "Give me the folder."

"I's waiting for you t' say 'thank you.' Or don't -" Barnes glanced towards Fleming who shook his head slightly. "Well. Don't *you* say thank you for important information, where y'come from?"

"Please, *and* thank you," Dolores retorted. Barnes handed over the file and she smiled sarcastically.

In her thirteen years as a U.S. Federal Marshal, Dolores had seen a lot of horrid things. But nothing had quite prepared her for what lay within the two yellowed pieces of cardboard. She opened the top cover and immediately closed it. Her hand covered her mouth and her eyes closed while she took a deep breath. When she opened them, she saw Fleming watching her intently, almost greedily, as if her reaction was a feast and he was the only one at the banquet.

She could not let him win. Dolores opened the file again, slowly, peering at the contents, flipping pages and photos one by one. Inside, what remained of Alex Rose created a storm of nausea in her stomach. All the photos depicted various body parts found separated from the others - an arm lay in a field, hand severed inches above the forearm, fingers cut at each joint and laid out evenly; a leg was wrapped around a small tree, each joint and appendage again cut apart and spaced out. But whoever had killed Alex had taken a photo before the butchering, and as a black woman looking at a black man, that was the one that would haunt her nightmares. Federal Marshal Alexander Rose had been hogtied, *and* hanged. His eyes were cavernous holes, blood trickled down his cheeks. The rope was wrapped three times around his neck, so tightly that it had bleached his face. But it was clear to Dolores that Alex had not died from the hanging; something had scared him to death.

Dolores closed the folder and chucked it on Fleming's desk. She reached into the briefcase and found a tissue. Dabbing at her eyes she said, "My apologies for the emotional display. Alex and I have... had... worked together for a very long time." She blew her nose. "It's never easy to see another officer treated so disrespectful-ly." The folder had vomited some of its contents across the desk when she'd tossed it, and she frowned as she watched the Warden begin to shuffle them back together.

Fleming was casually looking through the photos, his fingers softly tracing their edges. It was like he was caressing a lover and Dolores was sickened by it. She blew her nose again, a little louder. Fleming looked up at her curiously. He watched her for a moment, then turned his gaze back to the other man. "You were ex-plaining, Officer Barnes?"

"Right. Since Mr. Rose's disappearance, and our discussions, Do-lores, I doubled the efforts of the police force in an attempt t' locate him. We were hopin' he might have been stumbling around injured after we found his car out on 701, fearing that it was a car-jacking gone wrong. Mr. Rose, being unfamiliar with the town, could've found himself in the wrong part real easy, a part that don't take too kindly to... well... you know what I mean. But last night we received an anonymous phone call. The tipper advised we search the clearing out by the old well. I sent a patrol right on up there first thing this morning, and we discovered the deceased Mr. Rose — as de-tailed in these photos of the crime scene."

"It's so barbaric," she whispered huskily. Her brow furrowed as she thought for a moment. "You said you had an anonymous tip..."

"Yes, sure did."

"And did you trace the call? Do you know where it came from?"

"We do indeed know, but we didn't need t' trace it as-"

"Why not?"

Barnes shrugged. "The operator announced it."

"What do you mean?"

"Came from here, Juniper Correctional. We were asked if we would accept the charges and then the operator connected the caller."

At this Dolores glanced from Barnes to Fleming. "Who was the caller?" Rage burned ruby red in her eyes.

Fleming was transfixed. He was clearly enjoying the show playing out before him, one that all parties hoped to draw to an end sooner rather than later. But there was something behind his eyes that unnerved Dolores other than him being just another horny white man. "Who was the caller?" Dolores barked again.

Fleming didn't blink as Barnes responded, "The police don't rightly know, ma'am, but that's why I came on down here today. I believe Warden Fleming has some more information to add. Is that correct, sir?"

The man positively preened before them. Dolores was disgusted by his need for attention, the way he craved to be the centre of attention. She watched as he slid his folder out from under the one of Alex's photos. In doing so, more photos flew out and floated to the floor of the office like dead butterflies. He lifted the folder as if putting on some type of magic show, waving it in front of him to partially conceal his face.

As he began to talk, he fought a smile that continued to try and break across his chubby cheeks. "Well, Do-lores, Ah seem to be doin' your job for you." Fleming tapped the folder edge on his desk. "This is all the information Ah've been able to dig up regarding what Ah believe to be the *cancer* eatin' away at this *fine* establishment. Ah believe Ah have identified the person de*stroy*ing this institution like Samson de*stroy*ed the temple. He has been tearing it down from the inside, right under my nose." He slapped the file on the table and slammed a hand on top of it for dramatic effect, as if the folder might grow legs and run away.

"When Officer Barnes contacted me about Mr. Rose's sit-u-ation, Ah did my duty and traced the phone records from the prison. Ah know who called you. And Ah'll take you to him. Ah conducted a little interview myself last night, and believe me, you'll really want to hear what he has to say. But here, in this fold-er," Fleming slid the file across the desk, his fingers splayed across the cover, "is the son-of-a-bitch that has been *deceiving* us all along. His thirst for destruction has even led him to commit some *heinous* crimes, and there is evidence to back these up. Y'll find written statements from prisoners *and* guards alike. Each one adds to the next, to make the evidence against him irrefutable. Ah have had my assumptions for a long time now, but Ah needed *you* here to spur me on in finding the rat within our midst. So *thank you*, Do-lores. Thank you for tryin' to make this place better, for having the safety and wellbeing of our inmates in the forefront of *all* the work you've been doing. Here, go on an' take it." Fleming edged the folder towards Dolores and removed his hand, leaving the ghostly imprint of his fingers on the cover.

She stared at the prints as she processed what she had been told. Her mouth puckered again, in thought. Dolores curled her fingers around the tissue and accepted the folder. She heard Flem-ing's chair groan in displeasure as he rocked in it. There was no doubt Fleming would be watching her as she flipped through this file, though what he would be looking for in her reaction, she could not predict. The situation with Alex had shaken her enough that she just wanted to be done for the day.

Her eyes flipped rapidly across the pages, astounded by the accusations within. She paused to look at Fleming and shake her head before she returned to reading the contents. Silence descended for a few moments. She became so absorbed in her reading that she jumped when Fleming called the officer's name. Dolores only half tuned in to the conversation and was more aware of the last parts.

"-case and put Frank where he belongs. Don't you agree, Dolores?"

She jerked her head up. "Hmm?"

"Ah said, don't you agree?"

"I didn't hear the conversation, Warden. What were you saying?"

"Ah was just suggesting to Officer Barnes that he go find that clerk of yours, Miss Collins and escort her to Juniper Police headquarters to collate the evidence he has for your investigation."

"Of course... Thank you, Warden..." Dolores paused and bit her lower lip. She inhaled, straightened her shoulders, and turned to Officer Barnes. "And Officer Barnes, thank you for your thoroughness with your investigation so far. It would indeed be best if we can get all the evidence together so we can move our plans forward, and I can eventually get out of your hair... I know you'd all be relieved by that."

Officer Barnes stood to leave, leaned over the desk and shook Warden Fleming's hand, then turned and, to both Fleming and Dolores' surprise, held his hand out for the Marshal. She saw Fleming steeple his fingers as he observed the strange stand-off taking place, but it ended quickly as Dolores shook Barnes' hand, and nodded her thanks to him, but remained silent. Neither

Fleming nor Dolores missed the way Barnes wiped his hand against his pantleg as he neared the door.

No sooner had the door closed behind Barnes than Fleming pushed his chair back to stand, and moved around the table. Dolores still remained in her seat with her head in the file. Something about this felt so... fake. But surely, no matter how racist and sexist Warden Fleming was, he wouldn't create an entirely fake complaint against the most competent guard he had...

Would he?

"Shall we?"

Dolores looked up from the file, feeling slightly lost. Fleming beamed. He knew she was on the hook, either to follow through with the accusations against Frank, or to potentially lose her entire career. What she held was a grand slam - a disgraced correctional officer; multiple murders; a vendetta against the establishment, all contributing from a mental psychotic break - and taking this to headquarters would all but guarantee her fewer field jobs in shit holes like Juniper. But her conscience would eat at her every night, because to accept this at face value, to push for Frank to be charged fully without use of an insanity pleas, would mean to shirk her duties as an officer of the law.

Either way, Dolores wasn't sure how she'd leave Juniper alive.

She slowly shuffled the papers back into the folder and laid it on the desk thoughtfully. "Yes... yes. Let's get a move on, shall we? Where is Frank right now?"

"Frank's not back on shift until tonight, which gives us plenty of time t' work out how we approach this."

She nodded and bent to pick up her briefcase. "So, who's the whistleblower?"

"Henry Crumb." Fleming strode over to the door, and rested his heavy hand on the knob, waiting for her to follow him.

"The head of The Sisters?" Dolores spluttered. She joined him at the doorway.

"One and the same. After you, Do-lores." Fleming held the door open and watched as Dolores walked out. His greedy eyes stayed trained on her hips as she clacked her heels against the tile.

Dolores was certain the file was fake. But how to convince Fleming she believed it, that she didn't care who had spilled the beans or how they'd been spilled, that was a matter she had to figure out on the very short walk to Henry Crumb's dark cell.

CHAPTER 22

Fleming fell behind Dolores as they walked on the gangway to the cells. He watched her ass swaying as she tottered in front of him. He enjoyed the view despite his intense dislike of her. She had stumbled slightly when she stepped from concrete to the corrugated gangway and the heel of her shoe had fallen through a gap in the metal latticework. Fleming had closed the distance, extending a supportive arm, and offered to follow her to keep her steady. Dolores had stiffened in unease but agreed. Fleming was positively giddy at the control he had gained.

The gangway forced Dolores on to her tiptoes as she walked and though she wobbled occasionally, she held steady overall. Fleming decided she must have firm calves. He assumed she played tennis or ran marathons to keep them in such a toned shape. Fleming reached out a hand as she hit an uneven patch of flooring, and held her elbow. He'd always found elbows to be quite an erotic area; he imagined himself placing it in his mouth and sucking on it... then he felt his cheeks grow warm. Dolores turned to him; he could feel her leaning into his grasp, thankful for the offer of support. But it was short lived. Once they made it across the gangway to firmer ground, she would pull out of his grasp and his fantasy would be over.

They reached Crumb's pen. Fleming brushed against Dolores as he stepped in front of her to access the door. She stayed on her toes, barely keeping her heels from sinking in the grating. He imagined those legs, strong and lean, wrapped around him, and almost stumbled into her as his vision momentarily consumed him with desire.

He pulled at the keys jangling on his large waist and fumbled for the key to the cell. Dolores tottered toward him, laying a hand on his arm once again. *You prick tease, how your tune has changed.* Fleming felt her hand gripping his shirt, her treacle-coloured fingers creasing the fabric. Her manicured nails pinched his skin slightly and he felt a twitch below his belt. He zeroed in on her wrist in an effort to ground himself. She wore a rather large watch. Gold faced, with a supple brown leather strap; it was magnificent. It looked older, and more masculine than her other feminine wear. Fleming assumed it was an heirloom. The red jewel paint on the hands, and the starry silver quality of the numbers focused his mind and he turned his attention back to the cell, inserting the key and clicking the lock open. "Inmate Crumb! Walk to the back of your cell, face the wall and kneel. Place your hands behind your head, in-ter-locking your fingers," he bellowed into the room.

Henry shuffled away from his bunk. Fleming felt relief that he was at least dressed, considering the last time he'd seen the prisoner. A grey pair of prison pants hung loosely around his thin hips, revealing the top of his ass crack. Crumb had cut a V down the front of a standard t-shirt and had ripped the sleeves from it to display his sinewy arms. Tattoos adorned one arm like a dark sleeve. As he reached the wall, he crouched down on the floor, bowing his head in what looked like silent prayer. But the ink on his neck caught the dusky light, and revealed the hateful iconography that carved his skin. Smudgy tattoos of white pride and Nazi insignia were etched onto his flesh in crude prison style ink as he interlocked his fingers. He left his hands on top of his head to show the ragged hole of his missing ear.

"Y'know, I'm more comfy down here, anyway." Henry winked saucily at Dolores as Fleming pulled open the cell door. It swung open freely, as it had the night before, and Fleming felt his pulse quicken, a flashback of his pact with Crumb striking him behind the eyes like a lightning bolt. He shook it loose and moved forward, holding the cell door open for Dolores to come through. She marched into the room on the more stable ground, oozing self-confidence now that she sensed victory at hand.

Fleming turned and closed the cell. He hooked his keys back onto his belt loop. His trousers sagged slightly, so he pulled them up over his muffin top of a waist before moving to join Dolores in the centre of the room.

She nodded to acknowledge the Warden before turning to the inmate. "Henry, I'm Marshal Fink. I've been told by Warden Fleming that you have some important information about what's been going on here at Juniper Correctional, and about a particular correctional officer?" She was met with silence.

"Crumb." Fleming prompted.

"May I sssssstand?' Henry uttered.

"Of course." Dolores gestured to the bed before Fleming could speak.

Henry placed his hands on the wall and leant forwards, walking himself up the crumbling brickwork. Once upright, he stood facing the stone. He twisted his neck to the left. A crack was audible in the cell. His head remained pointed in that direction while the rest of his body turned to face his two guests.

Knowing he had their full attention, he reached into his pants and adjusted himself. He sinuously moved towards them, his seduction on full display. Henry stretched out the hand he had removed from his pants, and offered it to Dolores. Fleming watched her as she quickly judged what to do. She reached out and gripped his hand with her thumb and forefinger, giving him only a little shake.

Henry offered it to Fleming.

Fleming turned and walked to the other side of the cell, leaving Henry's hand outstretched, rejected.

"No harm, no foul!" Henry said with a shrug.

Fleming reached the wall and glanced over at the photos stuck on there. A postcard of Hitler sat centred in a place of pride, surrounded by other photos and cut outs. He turned and leaned against the wall, Hitler the devil on his shoulder. Fleming watched Dolores wipe her hand on her leg. She moved to take a seat on Henry's bunk, but was stopped by some clutter. The Marshal placed some items onto the top bunk then sat down on the cleared mattress.

"What the *fuck* d'you think you're doing??" Henry spat at Dolores.

Dolores shuffled uncomfortably on the bed, her eyes searching out Fleming. It struck him that this woman was scared. She'd realised she'd been a little too trusting, a little too sure. He raised a hand and waved to her, an offhand signal not to worry, before turning on the prisoner.

"Henry!"

Henry turned to Fleming, his head bobbing on his neck like a bird. "Whaaat?" he asked innocently.

"We can quite easily turn 'round and leave; you'll do well to remember that. If you want *something out of this*, you will respect Marshal Dolores Fink. And hold your fucking tongue. Do you understand." He didn't leave it a question. The pact between them, was carried in the unspoken way Fleming looked into Henry's dead eyes.

Henry shrugged and turned back to Dolores. "Marshal Dolores, I am *so sorry* for my outburst... it's just... that there bunk..." Henry paused and drew the back of his hand against the mattress like he was stroking the softest skin. "...this bunk used to be my lover's... that was until that *roach* Klein put a knife'n him," he ended with a snarl. He whirled to point at her. "Y'all heard 'bout that, right? What that li'l *fuckin' asshole* did??"

"Yes, we did. It was in the reports that the Warden provided for us. It was written up by Frank, wasn't it, Warden?"

Fleming bobbed an affirmative. "That is correct, Do-lores."

Henry started to laugh maniacally, a high-pitched squeal. "Frank, that's *sooo* funny. He's dirtier'n them sheets you're sittin' on D... Y'don't mind if I calls ya, 'D,' do ya?"

Fleming kept stoic as Dolores floundered, pulling her hands into her lap, rather than resting them on the stained bedding. The fact she never corrected Henry on her name, like she constantly corrected him, confirmed his assumption - she wanted him, but she wanted to *dominate* him. He preened. Finally, finally one who could match his stamina and desire.

"'Dirty?' What do you mean, Henry?" Dolores asked, trying to keep up the professional veneer.

As she continued to fidget, Fleming watched Henry's eyes grow large when he saw the shine on her wrist. He was like a magpie, obsessed with obtaining any shiny object it saw. "Whassat there?" Henry pointed at her watch, edged his way towards her. "Is that real a Rolex?" Henry stopped and looked around to Fleming, to check he'd not overstepped the mark, unaware of Dolores shrinking away from him. Fleming only stared.

The Marshal ran her hand lightly across the device. "Yes, it is... it was my father's."

Henry blinked at her. "Was?"

"Yes, he died a few years back; a mugging. He'd left it to me in his will..." Her voice trailed off in silence for a moment. She awkwardly continued, "Do you like it?"

Henry purred. "Why yes! It's just *beautiful*, and we don't get *any* beautiful things to look at in here... the only exception your *exquisite* company, may I just say. So when we see somethin' like that, somethin' so out of place, well... it just makes your heart sing, don't it? It's the same feeling I used to get from my play thing, before... before that *sonofabitch* put a knife in his head only to have it covered up! Like it were some shit stained sheet *he* didn't want nobody seeing. 'Self-defence,' Frank said it was! I got somethin' to tell you, Dolores, it was damn *murder*! Cold blooded, *fucking murder*, and Frank... he should be in here, with us, for being an ac-cess-ory to the fact!"

"Let's talk about that-"

"Nu-uh. First, we're gonna talk 'bout what'ya gonna get me."

"Inmate Crumb, this is not a bartering game. You are going to tell Do-lores what she wants to know, and you are gonna tell her *now*. Are we clear?" Fleming snarled, irritated by Henry's games.

"Crystal, Chief... but I *do* like that watch. Say, if I were to get that watch, I'd sing like Judy Garland. I'd give you Frank seasoned and on a spit ready for bar-be-cuin'... but, y'see, without that watch? I might be - oh, what *do* they call it now... 'an un-reliable witness...' what with me being... a little cuckoo." At this Henry turned and ran towards the wall, smashing his face into it. He flew backwards after the impact, laid out prone on the floor, laughing like a hyena.

Fleming glanced over at Dolores, who looked as if she'd outrun the devil to escape this room. Henry writhed on the ground, rising from the floor like an eel with legs. His eyes fixated on Dolores. Fleming watched blood trickle down the inmate's face, flooding

226 | ROSS JEFFERY

into the curves and crevices of lips before dribbling in thick, red swaths to the floor.

Henry wore a rictus sneer on his face. "Now. Let's talk about that watch."

Dolores was struggling to look him in the face, her gaze flying back and forth between the monster before her and Fleming at the wall. It was as if she were silently pleading for Fleming to intervene, but he was enjoying watching her look so uncomfortable. *We're not in Kansas anymore, Dolores,* Fleming thought with delight.

"Nothin' t' say, D? Well... I guess I'd better take another go..." Henry turned to rush forwards when he heard a tiny squeak. He paused to see where it had come from.

"Yes. You can have it. But first, *first,* you need to tell me everything about Frank. And you need to keep your head. If you do anything else like this, anything to raise concern over your mental capabilities, everything will be gone. You screw me on this, Crumb, you'll end up committed somewhere far worse than Juniper Correctional. You have my word on that. Do you understand?"

"I do, darlin', I understand *real* good."

"Right. Let's begin. Tell me everything you know of Frank's misdeeds."

Henry slithered around the droplets of blood on the floor and sat next to Dolores on the bed. He began talking, creating a dazzling web of lies, that only the most skilled spider could have followed.

Fleming heard something trundling along the gangway outside. He peeled himself from the wall and walked over to the cell door. It was strange, being in here, looking out of these bars. He had never been on the other side of them before. He smiled at the irony; if he didn't follow through with his visitor's demands, he'd need to get used to this view; his life depended on these small things falling into place, like the scapegoat currently being prepared for slaughter. That would please them, the voices. The darkness and the pestilence. Fleming gripped the bars. He could hear the hushed talking of Dolores and Henry over his shoulder.

A rickety cart, the front wheel busted, squeaked along the gangway. *A right fucking commotion*, Fleming thought. Then it came into full view and he gasped. The librarian at the opposite end of the cart looked dead, his face sunken in so much that it looked painted on a skull. Even his temples were two hollowed out holes, a papery translucent film all that ensured his insides stayed where they were. Stanley's skin was so thin, Fleming could see how the joint of his jaw worked; he recoiled when he realised the bumps against Stanley's lips were the man's teeth. Grey irises that flickered deep within the caverns were all that remained of his eyes.

Stanley stopped outside the door to Henry's pen. A scuffle had begun behind Fleming in the cell: strained voices gasping, a thudding of heels on concrete. He continued to watch Stanley as the impossibly frail old man slowly glanced up at the Warden, his brow creasing as his dead eyes locked on to Fleming's. No words were uttered as Stanley reached down into the cart. The struggle reached a climax and began petering out. Something heavy landed on the floor, but Fleming continued to face Stanley, blocking the librarian's view, but also dreading the carnage behind him.

Stanley stretched his liver spotted hands into the depths of the cart and pulled out a guard's uniform. Fleming sucked in a short breath when he saw the name tag. Something was afoot that he had no comprehension of; many gears were working in a much larger beast than he had realised. Stanley passed the uniform through the bars to Fleming who took it from him, being mindful not to touch Stanley for fear of catching whatever was killing the man. Fleming went to turn back into the room, but stopped when he noticed Stanley reaching in for something else. He waited for Stanley to find the strength to lift what was hidden and bring it into view. When he slowly drew out a long, black object, he knew instantly what it was.

Stanley passed the baton through the bars. "The uniform," croaked Stanley, as if at any moment his voice would finish, "is from a mutual friend of ours."

"Ah thank you, Stanley."

"And that," Stanley nodded to the last item he passed through. "That's for our... other... mutual friend." Stanley nodded to the space behind Fleming, and then resumed his shuffling down the gangway, and passed out of view.

Fleming glanced down at the items. The light reflected off the polished metal of the plate bearing the name *Whitten*. He felt the weight of the stick in his hand, gripped the handle and held it down within the shadow of his leg. Fleming turned back into the cell.

Henry straddled Dolores, his body shielding the top half of hers from Fleming. Henry's arms pumped up and down. A wet *thud* rang out with each downward movement. Fleming edged his way around the room and saw that Henry was mashing Dolores' face into the concrete. He held her hair in his brutal hands. Her face was a bloody crevice where her nose and eye sockets should have been. Fleming looked at the lumpy puddle on the floor, and noticed tiny white stars twinkling in the thick broth. They were fragments of her bones, teeth, and cartilage. A small sack like a bloodied poached egg wobbled within the crimson gelatinous gunk. Fleming assumed it had once been an eye.

"Henry..." Fleming murmured.

Henry continued to pound the head into the concrete.

"Henry!" Fleming raised his voice, urgent and forceful.

Henry glanced up. A dazed expression clouded his face.

Fleming shuffled forward, still concealing the baton at his leg. He threw the clothes at Henry. "Bloody them up some. Ah'll get them put in his locker."

"In a minute. I gotta get what's mine first!" Henry let go of Dolores' head and it made one final wet *splat* as it fell into the mess on the floor. He skittered around the body to her outstretched arm, which was still clutching the bedsheet and twitching. He tore the sheet away and began to fiddle with the watch strap.

"Henry, just wipe the *fucking* shirt in the blood and Ah can get you what you want!"

Henry stopped fussing over the watch, glanced up at Fleming. The blood from his facial wound was now mixed with the spatter from Dolores' head-banging. His eyes were bloodthirsty and a smile broke out across his rancid face. "Klein..."

"Yes, Klein. Do this *right now*, and Ah'll go 'n have him released im-mediately from medical. Ah will *personally* escort him to your cell."

With that, Henry snatched the prison uniform and began to rub it in the blood, smearing the shirt and pants with what was left of Dolores. Carelessly, he flung them back towards Fleming and they landed on the floor. He returned to fiddling with the watch.

Fleming pulled a pillow from the top bunk and removed the innards, put his arm in the case and then drew the "evidence" up inside the bag like he was picking up dog shit. Fleming moved around the scuttling prisoner, making his way towards the door. Then he stopped, turning towards Henry, who was oblivious as his fingers were roving over Dolores' watch.

Finally, Henry held up his treasure. Flipping the watch over, he glanced at the back, where the battery cover was. He held it in the air, swung it like a pendulum. Henry brought it closer to his face, wiped a finger over the metal, removing some of the blood. "It's a *fucking* fake..." Henry hissed, then laughed, turning towards

Fleming. "Can you *believe* that rich ass bitch had a fuc-" Henry was cut off mid-sentence by the swinging nightstick of Fleming.

The swing almost cleft his head right through. Fleming was a heavy-set man, and had flung his fair share of nightsticks at rampaging inmates. But there was something about this strike, it was as if a secondary force was behind it, that made it all the more deadly. The baton was lodged in the side of Inmate Crumb's face.

Fleming placed a boot on Henry's twitching face, pushing down with the sole. He slid the baton from the face. It made a screeching noise as the plastic rubbed against crumpled bone. Henry's body fell atop Dolores, one bloody, sorry mess. Fleming thought Henry looked beautiful, much improved by the three-inch deep concave running from eye to jaw.

"*Finishhhh the job...*" a voice whispered from the corner of the cell; Fleming didn't have to look up to know who it was.

"Do it for me!" his deadly lover pleaded.

Henry was still alive, twitching on the floor, trying to speak but all that issued forth were bubbles of blood which bloomed from his mouth and popped over his face.

A minuscule part of Fleming was transfixed by the hold Cynthia had over him in death. It was much greater than any yearning he had had for her when she was alive. She was his new addiction. Without further thinking, desperately wanting to not disappoint her, Fleming lifted the nightstick and reigned all mighty hell down on Henry's head.

The darkness was appeased once more.

CHAPTER 23

F rank pulled into the parking lot of Juniper Correctional. It was 10:05 in the evening, but his shift didn't start for another twenty-five minutes. The past few weeks laid heavily on him - his talk with Klein, the death sentence that was the investigation into Juniper Correctional, the fervent need to talk with his wife. It was all hanging round his neck like a yoke. He sighed. Rather than mope around at home until the shit really did hit the fan, he focused his energies on work and trying to make things better for both prisoners and fellow guards alike.

He'd been able to make an AA meeting, at least. Listening to people unburden themselves seemed almost therapeutic to him; it helped him, too, in some way, the act of giving air to his fears, grief, and yearnings. He knew many of those who attended - it was a small town, after all - but there was the code, and he revered that. Where he could tell his secrets, and those uttered by others, remained just that, secrets. They could speak freely and not fear that someone would run their mouth off at The Dead Mexican or anywhere else in town. It was a weird type of family. All were hiding things they didn't want to get out, but airing them in that safe environment made them feel alive, that they were seen, that they would, and could, survive.

He put the car in park and as it lurched forward sluggishly, empty bottles of cola rolled around and clinked in the passenger footwell. Frank turned the ignition off and the sound of Patty Smith singing how "...the night belonged to lovers..." phased out to nothingness and his thoughts turned once again back to his wife. She'd been at the forefront of his mind all day. He couldn't recall the last time he'd seen her. What they had been doing? What had they said to each other? It ate him up that he couldn't remember. What kind of husband did that make him? He sat in silence, but that was soon filled with the cacophony of angry hammering on his car. It sounded like a machine gun firing on the vehicle, the metal barely stopping the drops before they had a chance of striking him down. Frank remained in the idling car, longing for the night to belong to him and his wife one last time, rather than his life belonging to this shit hole that he put first time and time again.

Through the torrent of water on the windshield, he noticed the lights in the library. It was as if he'd been dragged underwater and a ball of light pulled him towards safety. He hadn't really visited with Stanley in a while, and the warmth of the library was as good a place as any to be with his thoughts.

Suddenly, a vision struck him. Stanley, stacking shelves and preparing his cart for his late-night rounds, but another flash and he was collapsed on the floor, eyes wide and glassy in death. Thunder roared, jerking him away from his stupor like the shock he'd gotten from pissing on an electrified fence when he was younger. Frank shook the image from his mind. His eyes roved along the foreboding grey bricks of Juniper Correctional, drawn to another light, this one coming from the huge glass window of Fleming's office. It surprised Frank that the lights were on so late in the evening. The Marshals must have really run Fleming through the shit. Peering through the rain, he noticed a rather large blob illuminated by a small amber glow, like a winking demonic eye in a shadowed face.

Frank fiddled anxiously with his rearview mirror. Something was making his skin break out in goosebumps, such a crazy attack of them it was as if he'd been doused in ice water. They hurt his flesh as they peaked; his clothes felt too rough. *It's all in my head,* he told himself. He'd just seen too many scary films while trying to wait for his wife to walk in the door. There was no one lurking in the back of his car.

He jerked the mirror towards him, his face blooming in the reflective surface. He rubbed at his hollowed cheeks, pulled down the skin below each eye, leaned forward and looked at his bloodshot eyes. *These fucking night shifts will be the death of me for sure.* The rosary around the mirror jangled as he smacked it back into place, and Frank's eyes were drawn to the picture of his wife hanging from the beads. His fingers softly touched the photo. It was the closest he'd come to touching her, being with her, for what felt like an eternity by now. His heart swam with love for her, and he felt lightheaded at the thought of being with her again.

Frank's attention was snapped back to reality when two people in rain ponchos walked out of the prison pushing a bag atop a gurney. He turned the keys and the wipers came back on. He watched as another set of figures brought another gurney. The rain made the bags look slick. When the first set of figures opened the doors of the waiting car, Frank saw that it read *IPER GUE* on the door closest to him.

"What the fuck?!" His mind raced ahead, thoughts scattering like disturbed flies on a trash heap. Klein's face swam into view; had he finally met his demise? Had Frank and Juniper Correctional failed to keep yet another inmate safe? But there were two

234 | ROSS JEFFERY

bodies... *Who was in the other bag?* Frank wondered, before reaching across the passenger seat and grabbing his coat.

He pulled the keys from the ignition and bolted for the safety of the staff entrance. As he sprinted across the parking lot, he didn't bother stopping to ask about the bodies that were being tossed into the van. There was no time. It was as if Juniper Correctional were throwing out the trash under the cover of darkness so no one, not even the Marshals, would notice.

The corrugated roof of the loading bay offered a small reprieve, though the rain sounded like bricks thrown during a riot were landing on the roof. He shook, trying to dislodge the water and troubled thoughts. The rain from his body pooled around him, red droplets running off him. For a moment, he thought he'd been shot. But it was just the rain mixing with the dust from bricks, the bleeding, crumbling dust of a dying penitentiary. Frank sighed and patted the building as he walked. How long it would hold up against the unrelenting pressures of this world was another matter for another day.

Frank glanced back toward the hearse, thinking to ask the body loaders about what was in the bags, but all he saw were brake-lights staring back at him, large red eyes of a phantom throbbing in the complete blackness of night. It sent a chill down his spine. They blinked out and the van skidded off out of the parking lot.

"Poor sonsofbitches." Officer Barnes was standing near the door. Frank wondered how he hadn't seen him there. Barnes threw away his cigarette and it landed in a puddle with a barely audible hiss. Barnes sauntered towards Frank.

"What the fuck happened?" Frank was almost shouting to be heard over the rattling on the roof.

"Another failin', I s'pose. Whatever it is, it's being dealt with... *you* know..." Barnes tapped the side of his nose.

Frank had always known that Barnes was bent, but had never

known how far over. How long had Barnes been in Fleming's pocket and dealing with his dirty laundry? "Who was in the bags, Barnes?"

"Henry Crumb."

At the pronouncement of the name, Frank's stomach bottomed out. It felt like he'd been on a fairground attraction, his body swimming upwards as his stomach plummeted, about to hurl his dinner up. "'And the other? Is it. Was it... Klein?" A sickly pallor swept over Frank's clammy face.

Barnes moved closer, placed a comforting hand on his shoulder. "Y'feeling alright, Frank? Y'don't look s'good. Everything okay?"

Frank was dimly aware of Barnes rocking his shoulder. "Who's in the other bag, Eddie."

"Sure as shit ain't Klein. He's still holed up in the infirmary."

"Then who *the hell is it*?!"

"The lady Marshal; Dolores."

Frank looked dumbfounded for a second, then he hurled a steaming pile of puke onto the gravel.

"Shit!" Barnes said. "You *sure* y'need be here? I know you're... sym-pathetic to them fuckers locked up in here, but y'should go on home and rest."

It was something in the way Barnes had said *sympathetic* that made Frank think about the times he'd heard himself being called names in the break room and around the town. Frank began to feel a rage building within him. "What the *hell* happened??"

Barnes stepped back from the force of Frank's anger. "No idea, Frank! I'm in the same boat as you. Hell, I just gone an' took that mousy one back down to the office, and then I get a call to head on back here, an' for the second time today!"

"Why'd you take Miss Collins to the office?"

"Fleming sent her with me, somethin' about collectin'

evidence– maybe it was co-llatin'? But I can't rightly discuss that with you, what with you being the 'nice guard' and all." Barnes touched the side of his nose again and winked.

Frank wanted to punch the smug asshole right out and into the next day, but it wouldn't do him any good so he balled up his fists, digging his nails into his palms.

Barnes continued, "Last I heard, he was headin' down to Henry's cell to collect some last piece of the puzzle, a confession or somethin', that was gonna put an end to all this investigatin' bullshit."

"So, what happens now?"

"No fuckin' clue. There ain't no one left to keep goin' with the investigation, so I guess it'll just... go away? That little mousy girl'll be skippin' town as soon as the sun comes up. She was like a deer in headlights when they first got here, but after the big fella and, now that black lady? Sure as shit she'll wanna quit while the quittin's good!"

"Wait... you're telling me both Marshals are dead?"

"Yeah, that's why I came up here earlier, then... shee-it, all this happened. Not sure how the Warden is gonna spin *this*." Barnes began to walk past Frank, pulling the collar of his coat up around his neck, readying himself to step into the storm. He hesitated for a moment and glanced back over his shoulder. "Y'know... people sling a lot of shit at each other, but that man's always standing behind someone else, avoiding the 'spray' so t'speak... He'll come out of this smellin' of roses. Mark my fucking words!"

And with that, he stepped into the storm.

———

Frank walked into the locker room, the aftertaste of his vomit still in his mouth. He stumbled over to the sink and put his head under the faucet, twisting so the cold water splashed over his chin. He scrubbed his teeth with a finger, trying to clean out the rancid taste, but a stain of it remained. Only something stronger could remove it, and his thoughts turned to the bottle... but he couldn't, not now. He began repeating his mantra under his breath. "Lord, grant me the serenity to accept the things I cannot change." He turned off the water. "The courage to change the things I can." The groaning of pipework in the archaic building filled the silent void left from the water. "And the wisdom to know the difference."

He walked toward his locker to hang his coat up, and realised his shirt was soaking wet and more wrinkled than Stanley. His mind raced with the news of the three deaths as he mechanically unbuttoned his shirt to change. This place was cursed, he was sure of it. He couldn't even recall how many deaths the last few made – but his frantic brain latched on to the idea that they might all have some respite from this shitstorm. Surely the staff could be spared, their jobs secured, for the time being at least. He was unsure how this could be spun in any favourable direction, and for now ignorance was bliss. But he was damn sure going to find out what really happened, and he was damn near certain that heads would roll in the clean-up, one way or another. Barnes was right though; Fleming would have a scapegoat ready for the hanging.

As he stood in front of the wall of metal boxes, Frank spun his four digit code into place and unhooked the lock, placing it on top of the lockers with a clank. He was just about to open the door when he noticed something at the bottom of his locker had dribbled out and onto the floor. He knelt down to examine it more closely. The coldness of his belt-buckle pressing against his stomach triggered another icy chill attacking his body. Whatever the liquid had been, it was dry. Frank picked at it with his thumbnail, noting the brown flakes against his nail. Rust?

He rubbed some flecks into his palm, poking at them with his finger like a boy with an insect. A drop of rain fell from Frank's head onto his hand, ebbing its way toward the silt. Frank observed in abject horror as the solid brown turned to liquid red.

He flung the offending discovery from his hand, reached faltering fingers towards his locker and pulled open the door. His fingers tightened against the door. Realisations, like fourth of July fireworks, exploded in his head as his eyes roved around inside the locker; each image he took in hit him like a dentist's drill shredding a nerve, leaving him sucker punched.

The coolness of the metal against his hands was a relief to the heat breaking out across him. He could feel something trying to rise within his stomach once again, but it was empty, and the acid just burned at his insides.

He observed a bloodied nightstick, hanging by its strap in the corner of his locker from the hook where he had kept his own. It glistened with an oily substance, veiny almost, with whatever was stuck to its sides. The baton had white shards stuck in it, like porcupine spines. Frank unwillingly peered closer and then recoiled. There was a tooth lodged in the shaft.

A thick puddle of congealed gloop had pooled below the head of the baton. The hemmed edge of a pants leg, painstakingly stitched by his wife, dragged through the gore. His eyes travelled up the leg to the uniform hung up on a coat-hanger. He grasped the sleeve to pull the shirt into the light. His name tag was on the breast pocket. As he pulled, the shirt fanned out and he saw that the entire front was covered in dark brown smears that lead to streaks on the right arm, like someone had mopped the floor with it. The blood had begun to dry, causing some of the fabric to stick together.

He let go and the shirt fell back into the locker. The harsh light of the locker room reflected on something shiny at the bottom of the blood pool. He reached in gingerly, picking at it with his fingers, trying to draw it further into the light without touching it. The secondhand of a watch ticked behind a face of blood. *What is happening?* Frank thought, his breathing growing erratic, sweat caking his body. He saw black spots appear at the corners of his vision; he was sure that at any moment, he was going to pass out.

The door to the locker room swung open. Frank quickly slammed his locker shut, placed his hand over it, as if he could delete the contents from existence. He stood there nonchalantly, as Officers Petty and Larry walked into the room. They seemed oblivious of Frank, consumed in talking sport, or politics, whatever the current shit they were shooting was. They headed over to their lockers and grabbed their coats; it was their shift change which meant a chance to escape. Coats in hand they retreated back the way they came, not even registering that Frank was in the room.

Once the room was clear, Frank opened the locker once again, hoping for the briefest of moments that it was all a dream, his sleep-starved mind playing a despicable trick on him... but as he flung the locker open again he realised it was a nightmare. He slammed the locker shut. His hand reached for the padlock and secured it in place, hoping no one would see the false trail inside.

He turned and leaned against the locker. While he'd known there would be a scapegoat, he had never thought *he'd* be the one hung, drawn and quartered. Frank rubbed at his eyes with the heels of his hands, rubbed until they hurt and the black and white dots disappeared. He opened them to stare at the floor, noticed a fragment of something near his foot. He stooped down to cautiously pick it up pinching it between his fingernails so as not to get more DNA on anything; though, with the treasure trove of evidence in his locker, he wondered if there was really a point to being so careful. It was a torn piece of paper.

As he turned the piece of bloodied paper over, he noticed a

small number on the back. 189. Only one place had numbered pages that went that high.

"Stanley... what's Fleming got you messed up in?" Frank whispered to the room, before grabbing his wet shirt and heading for the door, vengeance burning brightly in his eyes.

CHAPTER 24

Fleming was biting what remained of the nails on his left hand, his right resting on the arm of his chair, the smoke from the forgotten cigarette wafting down towards the floor as if it were being pulled all the way to hell. He'd been watching the parking lot, where the bodies had been taken away, and the arrival of Frank had signalled the endgame. Even at the finale, Frank was punctual, arriving well before his shift started. There was never any doubt that he'd be early to his own funeral.

He continued to watch until the lights of the morgue van turned onto the 701 and disappeared toward the town. His nails were no longer able to be gnawed, so he began to chew at the flesh around them as his lamp cast the only light in his gloom-filled office.

Another job done, which left one remaining. Fleming lifted his cigarette again, inhaled, and then paused when he noticed blood running down his hand. A fat globule of red snaked down from his index finger and disappeared within the crease of his thumb.

Fleming spun his chair around, his portly stomach hitting his desk
as he reached out and extinguished his smoke in the overflowing
ashtray. He dipped fingers from his other hand into his drink and
began to massage the blood from the webbed space. Once it had
vanished, he wiped the moisture on his pants.

The bulb in his lamp flickered and died. Unrelenting static
filled his mind. He rested an elbow on his desk and placed his head
in his hand. The file he'd given to Dolores taunted him from where
it lay on the edge. He slapped a hand against it like he was killing a
fly, and dragged it across his leather desk protector. A frown
crossed his face as he flicked open the manila folder and began
sifting through the contents. Everything was done, yet he felt a
paranoid urge to go over it again... and again.

He heard it abruptly. A dripping sound. Faintly at first, but
then increasing in frequency and velocity. Soon, it was heavy, loud
trickles, cavernous in their echo around his office. He perched
stiffly in his chair, leaving the file in the centre of his desk, and
began scanning the room for the source. The last time he had
heard the noise it was from Cynthia, or rather, the thing that wore
her shape. He craned his neck up, imagining that he'd see the
opening of the well above him, its deep, inverted pit stretching up
through the ceiling and into the roof. But there was nothing there,
only the cloud of smoke he had produced.

Another drip began and his head moved instinctively to his
right. The source of the dripping remained hidden, moving around
the room. It was like trying to find a cricket in the long grass,
honing in on the noise only for it to fall silent and then start
sounding off from another completely different location.

Fleming pushed his chair away from the desk as he stood and
peered around his office. He began to shuffle in the direction of the
noise. He'd only taken a few steps before he felt, more than heard,

a squelch. Glancing down, he saw water oozing up from the carpet. He lifted his foot daintily. The water receded back into the carpet. He placed his foot back down and watched as the water regurgitated through the fibres. Dirty brown water pooled over his shoes. He dropped to his haunches, and reached a splayed hand down to press his fingers into the carpet. It felt drenched, the consistency of porridge. That night flooded his memory and he snatched his hand away. Muscle memory brought his fingers to his nose. Fleming gagged as he took in the rancid smell of putrefaction.

More water gathered in the puddle below his feet. He followed the flow to its source, his eyes tracing the increasing ripple up his desk leg and to his drawer, where the water was bubbling out of the cracks. He pulled at the handle. The drawer was heavy, but as it slid out, the movement caused a tide of water to cascade out, splashing onto the floor. Brown water continued to dribble out after the overflow had slowed. Leaves were carried on the waves like tiny boats before falling to the floor with the other detritus. He peered inside. *What the hell is happening to my mind?* He stared into the mini reservoir in his drawer. He raised a tentative hand toward the desk and paused. Fleming blinked and suddenly plunged his hand deep within. A fetid stench bloomed as he disturbed the surface of the water, one of rotting flesh and stagnant liquid, a thick swampy smell. He choked, and then his fingers latched onto what was within.

As he began to remove the book, he heard soft laughter. He glanced up quickly, but there was no one there. There was nothing but shadow.

"Am losin' my mind?" he whispered hoarsely.

"*Yeesssssssss... you are!*"

Fleming shook his head, as if to dislodge the voices. He pulled his hand out of the drawer. Grasped within his fingers was the book, but it had not been affected by its time in the water. It was dry, and as it nestled there in his fingers, he could have sworn that he felt it *pulsing* between his fat digits, a faint heartbeat.

"Come back to... *uuussssssssss...*" The darkness whispered again, but it was as if two voices spoke in unison. Fleming stood up just as lightning flashed outside his window, throwing a much needed light into the gloom of the room. For the briefest of moments Fleming thought he saw two figures standing in the middle of his office, the door framed between them. But as the flash died so did their images. They replayed across his eyes like a movie reel as he stared into the darkened room. Fleming glanced down at the floor. The desk drawer was still open, but the water – all the sopping mess – had vanished. He lifted his hand, half thinking and half hoping the book wouldn't be there and this was all another strange dream, but he could still feel it, the heartbeat at his fingertips.

"*Sssssit* down..." It was more of a command than a request, with the same simpering sibilance Fleming imagined a snake's voice to have.

He chaffed at being constantly told what to do. "What d'you want from me?" Fleming declared boldly. There was suddenly a hand at his shoulder.

"We said - *Sit. Down!*"

Fleming was suddenly thrust back into his waiting seat. Yet there was still no one there. All he could hear was the drumming of the rain on the window, and the faint *thudthud* of the book, but that could have quite easily been his own heart beating within his chest. Fleming threw the book onto the table, where it landed atop the incriminating file against Frank.

"What do you *want*? Ah thought Ah had done your bidding!"

Fleming's voice sounded like that of a scolded child, close to breaking. He leant forwards slightly, trying to peer into the darkness. He couldn't see anything, but he felt something moving beyond. There was the faintest rustling, as if feet were moving around.

Tendrils slid out of the darkness, each one licking the edge of the pale glow from the parking lot lightposts that offered a gauze of illumination. The fingers poked the soft light on the floor before vanishing away as if singed. *"You've almosssst finished your... work. But there is one... last pieccce of the puzzle... we need to find... the centrepiece of our... design. Our host... he's grownnnn... frail..."*

Fleming could identify the voice that was moving closer to him. "Cyn-thia... Ah have done what yo-"

"Sssssshut your mouth..." Fleming was struck across the face, the crack sounding like someone snapped a pool cue over their knee.

"Our host has grown weak." The voices flowed from one to another, sometimes Cynthia, sometimes one Fleming recognised but didn't want to acknowledge. "He's beennnnn... keeping us safe, helping... ussssss navigate from facccccility to facility, town... to town, and he'ssss grown tired... *There are so many of ussss...* he can't feed ussss all. We've grown hunnnngry... and he'ss just ssskin and bone now!"

Fleming felt a hand tickle the side of his neck. Fingers dragged up his face. Then it was gone again.

"What do Ah do?" Fleming uttered.

Cynthia answered, "We need a new host, someone that we can reside within, someone who can contain us all... This legion." There was a crack of lightning, three short bursts of bright white light. Standing before his desk were the two women, each in a posture like twin versions of the Colossus of Rhodes. Behind them tumbled a mass of bodies, writhing one over the other, limbs seeming to entwine, snaking together, crawling over the floor and up the walls. The whole space was alive with a thriving mass of contorted flesh and limbs. Then darkness engulfed the room again.

Fleming's heart was racing. He reached out and gripped the book, then held it up to the darkness, the faint heartbeat thrumming at his fingertips. "What is *this* for, then? Can you all not reside in here? *This* is how Ah came to know you... Why don't you all just..." His voice was high pitched, fearful and desperate, as it trailed off into silence.

"Shhhh my dear..." The voice continued to sound more and more like Cynthia, less corrupted, yet it did not encourage Fleming, but further disturbed him; was she about to wreck him like he had done to her? "Listen, carefully: the book is only the key. It was a tremendous idea from our host, a way for us to get *in*. The book picks the lock, and we move in!"

The two women stepped forward in unison, just at the edge of the rectangle of light that touched the feet of his desk. "T-t-take me... use me?" Fleming offered to the apparitions before him.

"*T-t-uttt*... t-t-tuttt... *tutttt*... does he seem, sc- sc-scarrrred t-t-to you?" The voice slurped at the words as if sucking in dribble. Her voice was constantly wet and ragged, as if it had trouble phrasing the words it wanted to speak.

"I don't think he *sees*... yet; shall we help him see?" Cynthia's words came across sweet but Fleming felt a barb of dread.

Two sets of hands reached out and laid hold of the desk's edge. Two sets of hands, four sets of fingers, mirrored perfectly. The ones nearest him were pale brown, the skin wrinkled from too much time submerged in water, bleached skin where a wedding ring should have been on the left ring finger. The other's fingers were the colour of terracotta, the nails neatly manicured, and a tan line from a missing watch. He could not run from what his heart already knew.

"D'lores?" His voice was small and inquisitive. The body with the manicured hands began to enter the pale light, inch by inch. Fleming was frozen to the spot, wanting desperately to look away, but like a car accident, he felt drawn to watch the scene play out.

Her torso dropped lower and then he noticed the jaw, hanging from a ragged thread, barely held together by bloody sinew and tendon. What was left of her teeth could be seen through the puckered flesh of her gaping mouth. But still she unfolded, spreading her hands out across the desk and leaned closer still, until her head was fully revealed. The left side of her face was a sunken bloody mess, remnants of brain throbbing, a cavernous hole displaying what was left of her intelligence.

She chuckled malevolently, her jaw flapping redundantly by the shreds of skin and sinew that stopped it from tearing off. "Itttt issss I, Wardddden... how prett-tt-tty do I look-k now?" Dolores spoke as dribble escaped from the various holes in her face, trickling down onto the desk, bloody trails like spiderwebs forming as her head rocked side to side.

"Ah... Ah did it for them!" Fleming spluttered, pointing a finger towards the hidden masses.

"There, *there*, my dear boy... We know you did it for us. Dolores... is just yanking your chain, she knows... how much you like that..." Cynthia slipped back into the conversation. She too had emerged into the light, her skin but a see-through membrane, flesh so close to splitting all her festering insides forth into the room and over his desk. The skin of her arms sagged and shone a greyish brown, the bags under her eyes drooping as if she were *becoming* water. "We have a purpose for you, Fleming, a use for you in our plans... I never want to lose you again... We have a connection, you and I... but a host? No... no, no. You're not... suitable for *that*. Besides, we have found our..."

"... man..." Dolores continued the conversation, sharing the singular hive mind. "And you... will bring him to us or face... our wrath!"

Fleming felt a thousand hands rush upon him from the darkness. He couldn't even scream. And then there was nothing.

CHAPTER 25

As Frank approached the library under the cover of darkness, he couldn't keep his body from shaking. His hands trembled so much, that his keys were gangling in his grasp and giving away his position. He didn't fully know what he was capable of, and strangling the sonofabitch that was trying to frame him for this shitstorm was high on his agenda, but he had to talk to Stanley first.

He slowed himself at the entrance and tried to calm his breathing; he didn't want to give away what he knew. As far as Stanley was concerned, Frank had just started his shift and had not yet discovered what was in his locker. The door, which to this point had been framed in soft lights of grandeur, now seemed less welcoming and safe. Frank continued to wrestle with his thoughts as he gripped the handle and turned it.

The door creaked open, and the light from within beamed brightly through the crack, like headlights on the road. A strong, decaying smell snuck out, forcing him back a step before he was able to regain his composure and push forward into the room.

Frank scanned the library the same way he did whenever entering a threatening cell: check all the corners, search for blind spots, identify potential hazards. His initial sweep of the library turned up nothing. He reached behind him and drew the door closed. The click of the lock made him flinch as it reverberated up to the vaulted ceiling. His element of surprise was completely eradicated in that one moment.

Frank waited for Stanley to peer out from one of the long rows of bookcases, but no one emerged. He gingerly stepped forward. The place smelled mouldy, the air bitter and damp. He made his way around the large desk, checking to see if Stanley was behind it and crouching out of view, but there was nothing.

He frowned and turned to the fireplace. At the far end of the library sat a collection of tatty chairs, and right in the middle of the group was a mustard coloured wingback, facing away from him. The back of the chair was so high he couldn't see if someone was sitting in it, and what with Stanley's hunch and how frail he was, Frank'd never see the man's head poking over the top in a million years. Frank glanced down below the chair and saw the shadow of two feet.

"Hey, Stan! Where are you?" Frank rolled his head around as he spoke, to make it seem like he was still searching and less cop-on-the-hunt. He took some steps towards the chair, calling louder this time. "Stanley! You here?"

Still nothing.

He could see Stanley's emaciated wrist resting on the arm of the chair. A piece of paper was clutched in his hand. Frank pressed on. He'd stopped shouting now, assuming Stanley had fallen asleep and he did not want to startle the old man into a heart attack. Frank wanted to confront him about the stuff in his locker, but he didn't need another body turning up with him present.

The closer Frank got, the thicker the smell of death became.

Frank lifted the crook of his elbow up to cover his nose and mouth. Flies had started dancing around his head, which he futilely tried to bat away with the other hand. He was within touching distance of the chair now. Stanley remained unmoving. *He finally gave up the ghost,* Frank thought with some sadness as he peered over the top of the chair and saw Stanley's bald head. It was cocked to the side as if reclining into a bosom for comfort. Frank moved around the chair and turned to face the librarian. "What... *the hell!*"

Stanley wasn't just reclining in the chair, he'd become fused to it, his skin dribbling off his bones and seeping into the fabric. What skin remained on his face looked like glue poured onto his skull. Stanley's chest had sunken inwards, his alien-shaped head stuck on a crumbling neck. There was a black mass in the centre of Stanley's body, writhing and humming. As Frank leaned towards the body, the mass burst into the air. An angry herd of flies swarmed out to investigate Frank, before returning to their feast. The seat of the chair was covered in a brown sludge that oozed over the edge: Stanley's decomposing, liquifying body. Amidst the bones were piles of waste and putrefied innards. The stench made Frank's eyes water, and he felt his throat closing as he dry heaved into the crook of his arm. Stanley's other arm, which was also resting on the chair, looked like it had been de-gloved, as the skin had presumably burst open from the pressure of bodily gasses.

Frank glanced down and saw it was not paper, but an envelope, stuck to Stanley's hand. He reached out and tried to take it, but it was as fused to him as Stanley was to the chair. Frank pulled harder, and Stanley's wrist twisted and dropped to the floor with a wet thud as a stream of fluid spilled from the sleeve of skin that remained. Frank took a step back as the liquid splattered onto the floor. If he had not already thrown up outside, he would have done so among the books. *Small mercies,* Frank thought, as he staggered

252 | ROSS JEFFERY

against the smell on his way back to the desk in the centre of the room.

He coughed up a nugget of food from his throat and spit it into the trash. The taste of death overpowered the residue of his vomit coated mouth easily. As he reached out and turned the envelope over, he noticed a flap of skin attached to the side; flesh torn from Stanley's fingertips. Just above it, written in a scrawl that was barely legible, were the initials *FW*.

How much strength had it taken for Stanley to even lift a pen when he was that close to the end? Frank traced his fingers over the ink before tearing the envelope open. The letter was folded in three and he smoothed it onto the flat surface to better see with the dim light. Frank began to read, as the rain continued to hit the windows and ceiling like a never-ending drumroll, filling him with tension and fear of what was to come.

Frank,

If you are reading this, then I'm sorry. It was never meant to happen this way, but I've grown too fragile to move on, and too exhausted to continue. But I'm too pathetic to take this darkness away from here, away from you. I'm stuck here now, but so are they. Evil has only the power we choose to give it, or I should say, Them. Unfortunately I've given my all. They hunger and thirst for YOU now, a continual longing that has no abating.

I've given up, Frank, but you... you still have something to lose. They ravaged me, and I've nothing left to give Them. They spoiled me from the inside out, a parasite of malevolent intent. Their teeth gnash at me in the dark, Their voices haunt the very fabric of my mind. You don't have to be a building to be haunted, remember that Frank. They'll come for you, as they came for me.

Frank, listen to me- these Marshals are more obsessed with

how much blood is on the wall, and not necessarily with how it got there. The suicides, they ain't nothing, just a waste product of the vengeful pestilence. Bodies get chewed up and spat out, and for the Marshals it's an easy diversion - if they focus on those suicides, they don't need to look at what's really going on. Don't be consumed with finding the 'who' of this atrocity; first find the 'how', and then you'll get the 'who'. And when you find them, you must kill them Frank; only by killing them will you kill It. Don't let Them then turn you into their new host. They speak deception that feels like a nectar that's sweet on the tongue, but don't fall for their tricks, don't let Them into your mind as I did. Only destruction await those who do.

They're in my head, Frank. They are like radiation, continually mutating my very soul. I shouldn't have helped Them but I did, they would not be denied. I told Them that although it's true that the way to the soul is the eyes, the eyes can be tricked. I helped Them with that. The book Frank, is the way to open any mind. I created it for Them and by doing so, I gave Them a way of having access to any soul in here. And not just here. That book has travelled with me from institution to institution and so they have travelled too. I offered Them a feast. I happened to unlock a dam and now I can't stop the flow. I know you've seen it, Frank. But please, do this dying man one last request: Don't. Read. It. Once you open that gateway, there is no way of shutting it. They won't ask for your consent to occupy you, they'll just move in.

Only one man has ever able to tame them; he cast them into a herd of pigs a long time ago, and the pigs drowned. The darkness feared him and the sheer utterance of his name brought wails and agitation and the gnashing of teeth. Some believe he is God himself. Knowing what I've done, I daren't even write his name for fear that doing so will bring the wolf closer to your door. But I believe a spiritual man such as yourself will know His name.

Before me, they didn't have the book, they'd just use anyone. Didn't matter if it were human or animal, but once worn out, they'd move on. It was slow, but like a rock falling down a cliff, it set off an unstoppable landslide. This darkness, it's older than you and I. Hard to believe when you see how old I've become, but it's older than this place, older than the trees, the earth – it was there in the beginning, even before that bible of yours said there was light – because for light to exist there had to be darkness.

I must be quick now, Frank. They'll return from their activity soon, looking to bed down for the night. They've been spending more and more time with Warden Fleming. They see the darkness in him... the murders he's been party to, not just here in Juniper Correctional. They see his corruption and the taste is intoxicating. I fear that he is their chosen successor, and so he must be stopped, Frank. They know all of his sin; the darkness he's hidden for so many years, fermenting, ripening in his soul. He will lead others to sin; greater and greater the dominoes shall fall, corrupting the very best of us, corrupting even your god-fearing soul, Frank. You must stay strong! Don't listen to their lies, but the truth will be worse for you... I'm so sorry.

I have resigned myself to acting as this pawn.

My time here is nearly over, my penance finally paid. Maybe I'll find peace? I know this may just be an old man wishing for the best. When they realise what I've done, they won't be happy. And if some deity waits for me after this atrocity of a life, I expect they will not look on me kindly, either.

I've carried this burden a thousand lifetimes. What have I done? What will become of this place? I've moved from place to place for so long to avoid detection, I've tried to cleanse places, move on when I felt they'd had their fill– but if I'm honest, Juniper is the only place I've really felt at home in. But what will become of Juniper without me to call time on their feasting... what will become of you, my friend? I'd pray for your soul, but They wouldn't allow it. Would God even hear me? At least I can cling to hope that he knows your voice when you call on him.

I leave you with hope . Destroying the book may destroy Them, but be prepared for the cost.

I'm truly sorry, for I know what is to come.

Yours,

Stanley

Frank remained motionless at the desk after he had finished reading. Eventually he turned the pages over, his hands shaking as he laid them back down. He glanced over his shoulder, toward Stanley. The burden the frail librarian had carried, and no one had ever known.

Frank folded the letter, placed it in his pocket, and headed towards the door. Rage and sadness burned like a wild fire within him. And there was only one way to let it out.

CHAPTER 26

Juniper Correctional was a cesspit. The place took on another form as Frank headed towards Fleming's office. His veil was pulled aside and he saw the prison for what it truly was. What had been paint chipped walls revealed themselves to be barely painted cracks and crumbles. He saw how filthy the place had actually become. Just a few steps from the supply cupboards, a dead rat lay shrivelled and curled. How long had it been there, and how long had it been since these hallways had been cleaned? How long had Frank been pretending that everything was fine?

He rounded the corner and saw the sign for the infirmary, another unsanitary place. His thoughts briefly turned to Klein. He didn't know why he felt such a connection to the man; he'd only known him in passing, really, and just had the one conversation with Klein in the infirmary bed where he'd seen the true broken soul beneath the harsh veneer. There *was* something in him that was good, Frank was sure of it... but it was stuffed down deep, shrouded within a cloak of darkness. He turned right, away from the infirmary and his thoughts of Klein. Only one thing could be done right now, and that was confronting the sonofabitch that was trying to frame him and was responsible for countless murders, if Stanley's letter was to be believed.

Frank approached Fleming's imposing office. He banged on the closed door. The sight of the golden name plate erased all rationale left. Frank was done with pomp and ceremony and trying to follow the rules. He grabbed the handle and forced the door open, storming into the darkened room with anger and justice in his heart. The door flung wide and knocked a potted plant from the top of a filing cabinet. It crashed to the floor, earth and splintered china spilling across the rug. The noise did not register as he stepped forward into the dark. Something tickled his neck, as if he'd walked into a spider's web. He waved an arm around his head and felt a ribbony something, but when he pulled at it to relinquish its sticky touch, there was nothing there.

After shrugging the sensation off, he approached the desk. He reached out and pressed the lamp switch and the office burst into light. He glanced over his shoulder, sensing that something was fleeing the light, but again, only nothingness was found. Frank turned back to the desk. An open file of incident reports, statements from inmates and officers, and photos of the suicides, lay in the centre. Frank saw a handwritten statement to the right of the pile. Reaching across, he picked it up and read it under the lamp's light. It was a statement from Henry Crumb regarding behaviours he had seen Frank take part in, and was signed by Warden Fleming as true.

Every ounce of control he had left was poured into not roaring from rage. His hands curled around the lies and forced them into a crumpled sphere. Frank threw the balled-up letter into the trash-can, then scraped all the paperwork into the manila folder and tossed it into the trash too. He stalked around the desk and slammed open the drawers one by one. It only took three before he found the small, cardboard box he was hunting. He tore out a stick and struck a match. It hissed at him like an angry cat before falling silent. The flame flickered as if caught in a breeze. He dropped it into the trashcan.

The paper quickly ignited and began to curl in on itself. Frank wasn't worried about the smoke alarms. They'd been wall decor for years, ever since Obadiah had been interned with his predilection for setting things on fire. The guards had just disconnected the fire alarms. It was easier not having to evacuate the prison every few days because he'd again set something on fire. And as Frank now knew, Fleming allowed anything if it made for smoother sailing.

Orange tongues licked hungrily out of the basket. Frank watched as the fuel of the fire disintegrated, and the flames slowly died. The paper was less than cinders, orange veins glowing over its surface before turning grey, then black, and finally becoming smoke in a last exhale.

When Frank glanced at the desktop, he noticed a note taped to the cover of the lamp. He reached forward and pulled it off.

I'll be waiting for you in the loft.

Frank threw the note into the trash and headed for the door. "I'm coming for you, Fleming!"

As if in answer, something rapped against the window. He wheeled around, anticipating a trap, but saw that it was just the pulley rope, swinging back and forth in the wind. That ancient damnation that Junipereans had used to hang the guilty and innocent alike, once upon a time. He gritted his teeth. If he had to, he'd hang Fleming.

Frank slammed the door shut and headed down the hall to the stairwell.

"FLEMING!"

The roar reverberated through the dusty apex. Frank jumped up the last few stairs leading to the loft. It was a secret space that ran the entire length of Juniper Correctional, all the way up to the rafters above the cell block, but Frank knew there was a window at that end. From the loft, it was like looking down into a beehive, watching each inmate gestate in their own private comb of hell.

Frank stood on the small landing, slightly out of breath. He paused at the last barrier between his justice being exacted. The old wooden door stood ajar and blue paint flaked around the handle hanging limply on an aged hinge.

Frank realised that his right hand was balled into another fist; he opened and closed it, flexing his fingers, feeling the bones grinding within. An urge to grind them into Fleming's face took over him. Vengeance coursed through his blood. He felt cold, felt as if he were having an out of body experience. He could have sworn he heard whispering in the dark. Idly, he thought it could be the rain, with its constant thrumming on the roof, the tinkling of the water running into the gutters. But there was something to it that sounded distinctly like children's laughter. No, that couldn't be. His mind was playing tricks on him. Fleming's treachery and sense of theatre had him spooked. He rubbed at his temples and the sound subsided into nothing.

"Fleming!" Frank yelled again. The floor below his feet groaned as he stepped forward. "I'm coming in there and we're gonna have this out, but one way or the other, you'll be leaving here in cuffs! You hear me?! FLEMING!"

Nothing came back. He wondered if his words had been snuffed out by the rain. He stepped towards the door and pushed it aside, where it collapsed against the wall, the top hinge giving way to years of rust. Frank waved off the cloud of dust as he moved into the musty smelling loft.

As he walked into it, he noticed the open delivery window at the far end of the cavernous space. There was moonlight spilling into the room, rain splashing in, wind rushing at him. The pulley rope swung to and fro, like a mighty pendulum. Frank turned to look down the other way towards the window overlooking the cell block. There was no one there. A couple of rats scuttled around in the distance, silhouetted against the backdrop of the lighting from inside the prison, but no human form. He turned away from his former home. Glancing back towards the delivery window, he was momentarily confused. The flooring, so slick with rain, looked like blood had penetrated the tiles. Even the building screamed with haunted visuals of the murder scenes Fleming had hidden.

Frank slowly began to stalk toward the open window. He stopped dead in his tracks as a body emerged from the darkness, silhouetted like an outlaw from those Western films Cynthia loved so much. A smirk broke out on his face. In this domain, he was the sheriff who knew something very bad was going to happen; blood was going to be spilled, and it wouldn't be his own. He had no idea who the shadowy persona was but he didn't fully care. It didn't look like Fleming; it was too small in the surrounding light. And there was something else odd about the figure. It was as if this shape had been cut out of the astral plane – a void in human form.

Part of him wanted to move forward, but something held him in place. His feet were anchored to the floor, as if his toes had grown roots and buried themselves. Frank glanced down. In the pale light that only just reached him, he was sure he could see two hands, one each clamped around an ankle. Just as he was about to reach down and break those fingers, a voice came from the void.

"We've been waiting for you, Frank."

Frank's head snapped up, and he fixed his eyes on the dark shape. "Fleming, you godforsaken sonofabitch... what have you done?"

"Godforsaken..." A voice came from Frank's left, hidden only an arm's reach away. He turned to face the new speaker, and heard the childlike laughter again. It moved to his right. He whipped his head in the other direction, momentarily seeing the figure he assumed was Fleming still standing guard at the end of the space.

"He said *godforsaken*..." There was more giggling at this. Frank wondered how many people were in here with them, and recalled Stanley mentioning a legion. The patter of tiny feet scuttled around in the darkness, disorienting him to their location. He wished it were mice, but that was naive; he didn't know how, but he knew there were children up here. Visions of a sick and twisted paedophile ring, one where Fleming had a penchant for young children and kept them locked away filtered through his mind. If murder was the tip of Fleming's iceberg of darkness, and sex trafficking the next step down, Frank had no wish to keep learning what lay below the surface.

"Don't be *ssssilly*..." a young girl's voice came from the darkness. It seemed to have heard Frank's thoughts. "We're here for the *ssssshow*. We're... orphanssss... we're just waiting... for a way home!"

A round of cackling broke out on all sides of Frank. It was deafening, and he placed his hands over his ears, but still he could hear the raucous laughter, as if it were being streamed directly into his brain. There was no way of stopping it. "GET OUT OF MY HEAD!" His voice was hoarse, and he felt a prickle in his throat as if his vocal cords were about to snap and unfurl down his throat, bind him up from the inside, so he'd have no way of screaming when whatever it was came for him.

"We're only trying to help."' It spoke as a young boy. "We're helping hands!" His voice was singsong and seemed to float over the darkness.

Frank tried to move one of his feet again. He managed to lift the left one slightly before it was slammed back down, restrained by yet another hand.

"Siii-lence!" Fleming shouted. His voice seemed to echo and grow with intensity as it worked its way over to Frank. He felt himself hit by the force of the command. The tiny feet were scuttling around him, small black shapes, skittering out of the shadow and running into the edge of the light, only to be lost in the blackness on the other side – the darkness claiming again what it had birthed.

"So he talks," Frank said sarcastically, his voice not betraying the dread he was feeling.

Something like a sigh wound its way across the space. "Frank, how long have we known each other? How long have Ah *suffered* your presence... Ah could have snuffed you out in an *instant*, but Ah needed to keep you... close. So please, talk to me with a little respect."

"I'll talk to you how I goddamn please, you sonofabitch. You tried to frame me!"

A phlegmy laughter broke forth from the dark. Fleming coughed, and Frank heard a lump of something hit the floor. *"Frame* you? No... Ah would not say that. Ah have been trying - or should Ah say *we* have been trying - to get your attention, Frank. You would not have come quietly. We had no *choice* but t'force your hand... make *you* search *us* out. The things we've *seen,* Frank! We only wanted to open your eyes... guide you into knowing."

"He still doesn't see..." The boy's voice came as a whisper crawling across Frank's shoulders.

"Si-lence!' Fleming barked.

"He doessssn't know..." A girl's voice now whispered so close to Frank's ear he was fearful of what he might see if he turned.

A chorus of voices began speaking like a group of unruly school children, tumbling over each other in their question, "Shall we tell him?"

"SILENCE!"

Frank stumbled backwards, but a hand pushed him back to his feet before he could topple over. When he had found solid ground for a moment, he asked "What? What don't I know?" His voice was wavering, fearful of his request, not sure that he wanted to know the answer.

"Frank... *you* have been *chosen*. Consider it the pro-motion of a lifetime. My... *friends*... have chosen you to be their new dwellin' place... Ah have been their most astute helper but Ah, *unfortunately*, cannot go much further. They will have no more need for me once they have you. We share... what shall Ah call it... a connect-ion!" The last word came out through a giggle, as if Fleming had found his choice of words amusing.

"A connection? I don't think so. You're deluded, Fleming. You're not well. Why don't we just-"

"Hush now, Frank. This part is important." Fleming took a step forward, the rain behind him picking up in intensity, hitting the floor around Fleming's shadow like hail, a growing drumroll for a punchline. "They *sym*-pathise with you, with everything you've suffered. You're a good man, Frank... you even found *God*, not at the end of the bottle as you had hoped, but within these groups you've been going to, through the pain you've been working through. It is *admirable*, Frank! Now don't be so shocked - we know *everything* about you and what's going on inside you."

Fleming tapped his temple "You are good, Frank. One can-not deny it."

Frank was perturbed by that sentiment leaving Fleming's lips. "I don't think you know what 'good' is, Fleming. I'm going to take you to the authorities, have you tried for the murderer you are. They'll believe me. I have proof; a written confession from Stan. But all you had on me, every single thing, is ash!"

"None of that matters. You... no longer have a choice..." Fleming had come closer, standing only a few feet away.

"We always have a choice... even you, Fleming!"

"Fuck choice. You *must* obey."

Frank spat at the faceless head standing opposite him, the light around it like a halo.

Fleming wiped the spit from his face, or at least, appeared to; his shape still remained shadowed, as if the light was unwilling to reveal it. "How *is* your wife, Frank?" Fleming turned away and headed back to the open window.

"What?" Frank was puzzled at the sudden turn of events.

"Can we tell him?" The childlike voices uttered in unison.

Fleming continued to walk away, his footfalls echoing around the din of the loft space.

"Tell me what? Out with it, stop all these parlour games!"

"You can tell him..." Fleming tossed a hand into the air, a gesture of casual boredom.

"Oooooo! Goodie!" a girl's voice rang out.

"*Cyn... thia...*" Another child sang into the darkness.

Frank's head turned to the left, trying to find the voice, but then a boy uttered the name from the other side. Frank's head swung from left to right as if he were taking strikes to the face. A flagellation of the cold hard truth.

"Do you miss her?" a boy squeaked.

"How long's it been?" a girl whispered.

"Do you know where she is?" another voice from the dark. That question began the round of overlapping voices, all asking "Where is she, Frank? Where's your wife?"

He screamed as the noise overpowered all rational thought left. "She... she's... she's dead... stop it! She was... mu... mu... murdered!" Frank stammered out, tears streaking down his face.

Instantly there was silence. Admission of the reality he had been avoiding was more painful than a beating. Only Frank's sobs could be heard beyond the door to the loft.

"She's here, with us... Would you like to talk to her?" a child offered from the darkness.

Frank curled into himself, forced to stand as his body tried to drop from the weight of his confession, his tears dropping to the floor like bombs. Was it not cruel enough to make him listen to this? Must they tease him with what was lost?

From the darkness, he heard someone approach from behind. A hand touched his shoulder. It snaked down to his chest. A breath kissed his neck, lips touching his ear.

"Frank... you're home."

CHAPTER 27

"It can't be..." Frank choked out. The awful mourning in his soul spread through his body. He blinked rapidly to dislodge the tears that prevented him from seeing her. "'You... you *died*! You were dead and gone and I was alone! I've missed you s-s-so much..." Snot ran into his mouth; hiccups kept interrupting him; his muscles twitched as if he were having a fit. But the many hands kept him standing. "Every day's been a nightmare I can't wake from. Why didn't you come to me sooner?? I've been praying every day that I'd get to see you again. Where were you?!"

Cynthia's head retreated and appeared at his other side. "It wasn't the right time, my love..."

He felt her walk away, her hand snaking across his shoulder as she disappeared into the darkness.

"She can't serve *two* masters, Frank!" Fleming spat from the end of the loft.

He whipped toward the Warden, anger beginning to burn again. "Fleming! What did you do to her? What have you done?!"

"Don't you know?' the little girl whispered. "*He* took her from you. Bashed her head in after he raped her... or did he rape her after he caved her skull in?" The voice fell away, disappearing to join the others, the slapping of feet marking her retreat.

Frank choked on his snot as he tried to scream. "You sick *motherfucker*... how could you?! All these years! All the times..."

"S*shhhhh*... it all served a *purpose*, Frank! You just don't see it yet." Fleming's voice turned warm, appreciative. "She was a credit to your love. She did not come willingly! She was faithful to you until the very end... but Ah had to keep you around, Ah had to know if you *suspected* anything; and in keeping you at my side, Ah kept her memory alive. The *love* that I had for dearest Cyn-thia was real."

"Don't you dare mention her name!"

"What - *Cynthia*?" Fleming snickered.

Frank felt a rage burn through him, a wildfire that eclipsed everything rational. He fought to move, but other hands came from behind him, holding him in place. He raised a foot but it was pulled back down, shadows holding him fast. Frank wanted nothing more than to break loose. *I'm gonna smash your skull in!*

It was a thought, but the voices answered. *"Not yet..."*

"Come." Fleming turned, holding out a hand. A shadowed hand emerged from the dark beside Frank, quickly followed by an arm. It was a dainty sapling, and he knew instantly it was Cynthia. Fleming reached out and took hold of the hand. "Come in-to the light, so Frank can see us, together *at last*." Fleming pulled the arm and a body followed, seemingly thrown out of the shadow, staggering on high heels. Fleming punched the shadow in the face, and her head recoiled, rolling on a thin neck. Then the body slumped to the floor. "Ah would have treated her like a *queen*, Frank! But instead Ah treated her like the *whore* she was."

"Stop! What are you doing... stop! Fleming!! God help me, if I get out of this I'm going t-"

"What? What *are* you going to do? Smash my head in?" At this Fleming struck the fallen figure in the head. Again and again and again and again.

"Stop!"

Fleming reached down and caressed Cynthia's face, lifting her up by the chin. They were both silhouetted in the window. Fleming leaned down and murmured, "Ah shall *always* love you, my dear." He planted a kiss on Cynthia. She moaned, enjoying his caress. Frank could only watch as the fragile outline of his wife was abused. *Was this how it played out?* Frank thought.

A voice answered from beside him. "*Yessss.* This is how he... stole her from you... how he corrupted her!"

Frank closed his eyes.

OPEN THEM! A voice shouted in his mind.

He could not resist it. He opened them, and watched Fleming kissing the ghost of his wife.

Fleming looked at Frank. "Do you want to know how Ah did it?"

Frank shook his head, but he was lying – deep down, in some dark abyssal part of himself, he *did* want to know.

Fleming sensed this truth. "Ah en-*joyed* her until she was broken," he said. "And then Ah picked her up and *snapped* her neck like she was a Thanksgiving turkey. Y'should have *seen* her, Frank! How she looked, naked in the moonlight. Did you *ever* know her outside, under the stars? God, she was *irresistible*... and Ah *feasted* on her."

"Stop! I can't hear any more..."

Fleming looked through him, staring into a chasm only he could see. Frank watched as Fleming reached down to pull Cynthia into his arms, as if he were carrying his bride across the threshold. Then a small voice seemed to break through the cacophony of rain and chattering teeth and scuttling feet that surrounded him.

"Frank? Help me..." She sounded so lost and afraid. "Please... please, don't do this! I won't tell any-"

Fleming focused back on Frank. "That was what she said. Before Ah dropped her into the well."

"She was still *alive*?"

"Barely. But yes... she was fully aware. She would not stop *moaning* for hours," Fleming said mildly as he dropped the apparition of Cynthia from his arms.

Frank watched helplessly as she tumbled down into a hole, down into the well, down into her never-ending grave. Her wailing echoed around the rafters.

"He could have done something," one of the children said. "But he just sat there, waiting for her to die, listening to her plead for you."

"But why is she here *now*?" Frank screamed. "Why does she answer to him? *Why*? Why have you made her into this... this... monstrosity?"

Frank knew there was a heaven for good people no matter what they suffered in this life. But whatever this was... wherever his wife was... one of the only truly good people in all of Juniper, her afterlife was reduced to this? All her vibrancy of life peeled away to remain in service to Fleming? Would she always be a play thing to the dark forces at work here, trapped along with all the other innocents that skulked in the shadows?

"Would you like us to end it?" a frail voice intoned. Frank painfully noted it sounded like Cynthia, if she'd been given the chance to grow old.

He could hear her every moan. It felt as though her pain was being poured into his bones. "Yes, oh please, stop it! Please!" Frank sobbed.

"Would you like us to... do your bidding? We feel the... *rage* in your ssssoul, the *wrath* against... injustice..." The hands began to loosen around him, he felt himself falling towards the floor. "Just make our... vow, and we'll stop... it. Say the *wordssss* and we'll *end* her suffering. *Say the words and... finish this!*" The hands again pulled him upright.

Cynthia's voice was failing; all he could hear were gurgles and whimpers ringing out like a wounded animal howling for the hunter's rifle which would finally put her out of her misery.

"I beg you... please... I... I can't stand this..." Frank felt the rage rising within him again, overpowering his anguish.

The shadows were a baying mass of voices feeding off the anticipation of his action. Years of longing to be with his wife. Years of loneliness. Injustice at her disappearance, of reliving the day she had left and never returned, over and over... and all this time the evil monster that killed her was parading himself in front of him. "I'll do whatever you want... please just make it stop!"

"*Anything?*" a chorus of voices asked.

"Anything! Name it... Make it stop!"

"Do you want him dead?" The voices offered.

Fleming looked up from the well at the utterance. "What? What are you saying? Silence!" he spat. He took a step into the centre of the room trying to regain control.

"*Ssshhhh,*" the voices said, sounding like a pit of snakes. "Seize him."

And with that many arms reached out of the darkness, laying hold of his arms and legs. They stretched him out across the expanse of the loft like they had stretched Antonio, each one pulling at Fleming's limbs.

"If you don't kill that abomination, I will," Frank spat.

"There is no need... we shall do your... bidding, and you, in turn, *will... do ours.* If you remain ssssympathetic to our cause,

Frank, you... can *command* hordes. Will you give yoursssself to us... or shall we let her... *ssssssuffering continue?"*

Cynthia's cries burst from the well into the room, making his fillings rattle in his teeth.

"Kill him!" Frank screamed as tears swam in his eyes. "Have me! Take me! *Use me...* just make it stop!" At the utterance, Frank felt something twist in his gut, something pulling deep within the tightness of his chest. Something had gripped his lungs, breathing was difficult, but it was something more. Whatever it was had his soul within a vice-like grip; it felt like a coming heart attack. Frank wished it was...

What had he done?

"As you wish!" The chorus of voices whispered. Their unified declarations roared into a raging wind. Frank's hair stirred. He felt the tightness in his chest loosen as his eyes locked onto the suspended man before him.

Fleming's arms and legs began to tremble, as if he were on an electric chair, his limbs flailing but still restrained. Then Frank heard the pops over the top of the wind as bones were pulled from sockets. The suspended body began to droop, sagging at the dislocated joints. An ominous pause filled the air, broken only by the machine gun of rain. And then the tearing started.

The left arm disappeared into the darkness, as a crimson waterfall baptised the floor of the prison loft. A leg from the opposite side ripped away from the torso. Fleming's body seemed to turn in the air as the hidden things pulled at what remained of his other two limbs. And with one final sickening rip, his torso landed on the ground with a wet thud.

All that was left of Warden Hezekiah Fleming was a head and a birdcage of flesh that housed his internal organs. The shadows cast by the light through the window concealed some, but not all, of the horrors that had played out before him. Darkness crept along the unwaxed floor towards him, but Frank knew it wasn't one of the shadows. It wasn't even one of the many voices still whispering around him. There was a thick wetness ebbing toward him that glistened. Blood.

Cynthia was on the floor again. The well had vanished. Frank wanted to run to her but he couldn't. The blood seemed to flow around Cynthia and then she began to sink into it. Drowning, going down, down, down, until she was gone from sight. Something inside Frank broke as he realised she was gone for good this time.

The mound of flesh that had been Fleming slowed their spasmodic death twitches. Two long arms reached out from the darkness and dragged what remained into the abyss. Frank heard the gnashing of teeth begin and the room grew cold. He no longer had the capacity to feel the horror he should, knowing it was a grizzly frenzy.

The hands that anchored him released their grip. One even nudged him forwards.

Frank took faltering steps as he tottered closer to the spot where Fleming had been standing mere moments before. His foot slid on the blood and he nearly fell into the mess.

Something was vomited out of the void. It landed hard in the centre of the room with a thud. At first, Frank thought it would be a grisly trophy, part of Fleming that had been tossed aside in the frantic consummation. But as he stepped closer he saw it was angular.

A book. *The* book. The book that Stanley had mentioned he had returned, the one that Stanley had warned him not to read. He bent down and picked it up. As he turned the book over in his hands a hush descended upon the room. For a moment, Frank thought even the rain had stopped. The voices were completely silent.

Frank moved to stand in front of the open window, drawn by the rope twisting within the storms surging. The metal winch at the top tapped against its anchor, ringing out a death knell. He crouched down and touched the sodden tile, his fingers slick with blood and filth. Frank knelt and began scratching at the edges of a broken piece of flooring, trying to uncover Cynthia. He scratched until his nails split. His heart was heavy in his chest. He had lost her, again, and he began to sob.

"What's wrong, Frank?" It was a little girl's voice, worried and compassionate.

"I... I..."

"Would you like to see her again?"

He stilled. "You can do that?"

"Yes, Frank. Cynthia is with us, and we can get her for you, if you'd like."

"Please... I just want to see her one last time, tell her that I never stopped looking for her, that I never stopped loving her, and that I... I... I'm sorry I couldn't save her."

"Now, *husshhh*, child..." It was a man speaking with a thick drawl. "Ain't no good cry'n over spilt milk... she'll be along now in two shakes of a rattlesnake tail. But why don'tchu go on 'n read that infernal thing in your hand while you're a-waiting?"

Frank lifted the book. A force inside was urging him to open it, to look at the words within. It felt like a puppeteer had invaded him and was making him move. But Frank knew what waited for him in that book if he read it - the same thing that had consumed Stanley and butchered Fleming.

A piece of scripture fell into Frank's mind, one Cynthia used to say. *Do not be afraid of them, because the LORD your God, will be with you.* Frank would not fear this horde, this mighty legion that was vying for his soul.

Everything else had been taken from him. But he still had free will, and they couldn't force his hand. He had to *choose* to read the book, to participate freely in its calling, to let the darkness that stalked over the earth in. "I'll get to it soon," he said, carefully. "But I need to see my wife again, see my Cynthia, make sure she's okay. Please..."

As the words left Frank's mouth, he felt a hand drape around his neck, followed by a body near his side. He was still kneeling and so he leaned into the body, his head resting on its leg. The hand moved up and ruffled his hair, the same way Cynthia had used to do when he was goofing or wisecracking around the house. *It's you... It really is.*

"Of course it's me. Who else did you think it was gonna be?" Cynthia's voice was crisp and fresh.

Frank reached an arm around her legs, hugging her to him. "I'm so sorry, Cynthia, I tried... I never gave up looking for you, you know. And our house, it's the same as the day you left, when you didn't come home, and each time I wake up there it's like I'm reliving that morning, and each time I go back it's like a nightmare I can't escape from. Every night you never come home, it's... it's agony. I'm so sorry. I should have protected you, I should have kept digging, who knows if I might have caught him before-"

"Don't you fret, honey; we're together now, aren't we? And we can be together forever, just you and me..."

A whisper from the shadows raised the hair on his arms as it ghosted past. *"And us..."*

"But it won't be just you and me, will it, Cynthia? It'll be them, too."

"Look, darling, why don't you read me a little something from that book; you know I love it when you read to me. It'll be like old times!"

Frank felt a frisson of dread in his soul. His fingers reached for the book, thirsty to open it. It took every last fibre of self-control he had left not to look at it as his fingers clutched the cover. Both hands held it open in his lap. It felt as though gravity were crushing him, trying to pull his eyeballs down into the now open pages.

"No!" Frank uttered through gritted teeth, straining, pained.

"Oh, c'mon, darling... you *know* I... love a good *story*..."

Then, from the darkness came another voice, a deep and soulless garble. "**READ IT**!"

Frank stood up. He turned and with the moonlight coming in over his shoulder, he beheld Cynthia truly. She was no longer human. Her face drooped to the side as if her skin was pooling and falling off, her entire body covered in dark green and blue veins. Her legs were knock-kneed, just skin and bone covered in abrasions. Two pool balls stuffed under the transparent skin on her legs served as swollen and arthritic knees. Her hair gushed water from within the hive of her afro, coursing down her skin and running off in a greyish sludge. She reached out a hand, her skin hanging on the underside of her arm like fat dribbling off a grille. There was nothing left of the woman he had fallen in love with. No gypsy personality, no ethereal beauty. Just another tortured soul.

"Come back to... me, *sssweetie*, you know I love it... when you *read to me*..." She seemed oblivious to the fact that Frank could see her in truth. He glanced to the rafters and saw faces, hundreds of faces, all peering at him with eyes wide and teeth bared a true vision of the gates of hell. He turned and became aware of the numerous bodies huddled together, all revealed by the moonlight, and all hungry for him.

"Why don't you *read*... the book... it'll mean *sssso* much... to me if you just..."

Frank managed to peel one hand off the book, whilst his other hand cleaved the book to his chest. He could feel a steady pulse within it. Then he thrust the book out in front of him, waving it from side to side, as if trying to stave off an attacker. "I don't want this... I don't want you... take it."

"*It's yourssss, Frank... you read* it to... me and then we can *be together. You want that,* Frank, I... know you do. Don't deny *yoursssself; don't deny us.* Listen... I forgive you!" Cynthia scuttled forward, her legs wobbling as she approached with each faltering step.

Frank edged backwards towards the window. He felt the rain at his neck. "Get away from me!"

"*Come back to me, Frank...*" continued the thing that pretended to be his wife.

"Never! You're not *my* Cynthia." Frank turned and reached out into the darkness. He only had one option, one way out of this. There was no way he'd let them corrupt him into one of their pawns, become soulless like them. His flailing hand eventually took hold of what he was searching for. He glanced back into the faces of the horrors that awaited him, the faces of abominations which reminded him of the Book of Revelation. "My Cynthia *died.* There's no coming back from that. You're a deceiver, the greatest deceiver!" With that proclamation he pulled the heavy rope inside to him.

Frank wrapped it around his neck. "The only thing necessary for the triumph of evil is that good men and women do nothing! You'll not have this victory! Without a host, you'll just cease to exist!"

"***STOP HIM!***" the voices cried in unison. A thousand hands reached out to grab him, epochs of layered malice charged with stopping him. Frank felt the clawing at his back as he left the window. Tendrils tightened around his neck like vines. He was suspended for a moment before they snapped and sent him tumbling through the air, giving in to the welcoming arms of gravity and his God. Frank was the most free he'd been in years in those two seconds before his neck snapped.

He swung below Fleming's window, outside the infirmary. His body swayed back and forth, hitting the windows as he rocked, blown by the wind and battered by the rain.

In his clawed hand was clutched the final testament.

EPILOGUE

SOME YEARS LATER...

The guards walked Klein along the corridor to the Warden's office. As one, the group halted in front of the door. Klein stood, shackled and manacled, and waited to be allowed in.

Not that he'd needed the restraints. Since his early incarceration at Juniper Correctional the only real blot on his record was the altercation that lost him the sight in one eye, which had become a milky sphere in its socket. The other casualty of that night had been a fellow inmate, but it had been recorded as self-defence, and that was what he'd pleaded. The Powers That Be had agreed.

In the eyes of the law, he'd been cleared of any wrongdoing. He'd been the perfect inmate since his release from the infirmary following that incident. Many of the guards attributed the shock of finding Frank's body hanged outside his window as the scare needed to set Klein straight. The story circulated well enough - how Klein had been awoken by a banging noise, how he had looked out the window to see Frank's body twisting in the ever-raging storm and how the wind blew the body into the glass so the face stared right at Klein until impact. Even some of the inmates touted his bravery when he spoke of having tried to open the window to pull the man inside to save him. In the aftermath of two more deaths at the prison, Klein was heralded by authorities as a model of steady mindedness.

Klein's lips twitched as he mused on what had really happened that night. He had pried the window open as far as it could go and slipped his hand out toward the body. The air had seemed so cold it felt like he was scalded when the breeze slashed at his exposed arm. He had felt the edge of the object Frank had died clutching with his index and middle finger. It had taken several pushes, first with his index finger, then several fingers rocking it, trying to build momentum to get Frank swinging again. Little by little, Klein had managed to get a rhythm going. When the body had swung back and into his grasp, he grabbed the object, and with one final tug, he'd pulled it free.

At first, he had decided to pretend he'd seen and heard nothing. He had been a fairly unobservant prisoner up till then so it wouldn't have been unusual for him to say he had slept through everything. But there was something about the book in his hand that whispered to him, something that said he should read it. And so, Klein opened the small, leather bound-tome and developed a partnership with a source he had never expected. In time he grew accustomed to the sinister presence in his life, a constant companion that would see him through the rest of his time at Juniper Correctional.

The warden's door opened from the inside, and the guards pulled Klein back as an inmate was escorted out. The other prisoner hissed at Klein, as if sensing the true nature behind his changes. In the eyes of the other inmates, Klein was not so spotless.

There had been rumblings of incidents that Klein was suspected of being a part of - maimings and deaths, scratches on cheeks from unknown sources in the night - but nothing seemed to stick to him. He was untouchable. Guards liked him too much, and even some of the more powerful gang leaders knew they could call on him if the time arose. The majority, however, knew to give him a wide berth, and so trouble and strife seemed to ebb and flow around him, as if he were a conduit for it. He remained a rock in the prison stream that vengefulness passed around; or perhaps, the eye of a storm where true wrath raged and destroyed anything that got too close.

His reputation went ever before him. There was something always going on inside him; a glance could make a person's skin run cold and not because of the dead eye. There was a chill he exuded. A mere *tsk* of his displeasure could play on the mind. Terrible things seemed to happen to those that crossed him, but he was never found guilty of any wrongdoing. After all, how could a person be in two places at the same time? And even though they mostly liked him, he made all the guards on edge whenever they had to deal with him. Fear of a shank to the back kept them polite and distanced from him.

Personally, he thought it was all a bit much. He was merely the messenger for the true power. But he never failed to use his reputation as a weapon when the occasion arose. Outside the office Klein never blinked as his head slowly swivelled to follow the inmate in front of him. But he clasped his talisman with fingertips turned white. A murmur made him focus on Officer Petty at his side. Petty was glancing between Klein's face and the stranglehold he had on the book with a peculiar concern, and so Klein gently released the pressure he was exuding on the tome in his grasp.

"Sorry... I was thinking of my wife!" Klein said with a laugh. Petty chuckled nervously.

"Come," a voice boomed from inside the office. The guard that had knocked held the door open while Officer Petty gripped Klein by his bicep and escorted him in. Klein almost had to shield his eyes from the light pouring in through the large window in the centre of the far wall. He tried to lift his hands, but the guard pulled them down, so Klein cocked his head to the side and squinted.

"Come, sit down," the deep voice uttered. Klein was led towards the desk. The other guard pulled the chair out and the inmate collapsed into it. The desk was positioned so the window was to his left and by turning his body slightly, he found a reprieve from the brightness and could see the Warden better. As he laid the book on his knee, he took in the office. The wall opposite the window held photos of the other wardens that had steered the floundering ship of Juniper Correctional, but there was a blank space before the newest photo.

"So, Klein... You don't mind if I call you Klein, do you?" Warden Abraham raked a hand over his bald head, which was shaved and not lost to age.

"Not at all, Chief. You can call me whatever you want, as long as this goes the way I hope," Klein cracked with what he hoped was a winning smile.

"Well then. Klein, you've been interned here for a long time now. You arrived almost the same time I did, and you were here during that time we don't really need to drag up..."

Klein nodded.

"I've seen your record, seen how you've become a changed man within these walls. You've given yourself to reading and there is no better way to escape one's circumstance than in a book. Finding yourself taken away from this place and your duties, and for a fleeting time you reside in another world. Your help in the library has been a real jewel in the crown of your time here. We've been pleased to see that place, and the inmates, grow under your tutelage. You'll be leaving this place having left your mark in the best way possible."

"Sorry... you mean... I'm getting parole?" Klein was taken aback. His mind swam, trying to count the time he'd served as the slashes on the wall of his cell flashed across his memories.

"That is correct. We feel that there is no need to prolong your incarceration. You are a credit to yourself and this facility. We cannot see a reason to delay your reintegration with society and so you have been granted parole – three years have been deducted off your sentence for good behaviour. But promise me you will not let us down! If we find that you breach your parole, fail to turn up to your meetings, run a red light, hit your wife? You'll be straight back here, recalled to serve the rest of your time. Understand me, son?" Abraham stood and came around the table. He dwarfed Klein, who was like a school boy in Abraham's shadow. Abraham held out his baseball-mitt sized hand. The inmate held up both of his hands, as they were still shackled together. Abraham instead moved his outstretched hand to Klein's shoulder and gripped it, shook it slightly. "Do I make myself clear?"

"Yes, Chief - er, Warden – I understand perfectly, thank you; thank you so much! When do I leave?"

Abraham moved back around the desk and began to fuss with some papers. "Well, we've a few things to iron out here. We need to contact your wife, and then once we've crossed all the T's and dotted the I's, you can be on your way. I do, however have one question."

Klein barely kept the anticipation of completing his mission with Janet off his face. "Sir?"

"How would you feel about working as the librarian? You'd have some income, and the inmates already have a fondness for you. And with you being here, we might be able to work something out with your parole officer, ease up on restrictions a bit."

"I'll have to ask... Janet, sir. May I think on it?"

"Of course." Abraham waved his hands in a *tidy this up* gesture to the guards. They stepped in and began to usher Klein to his feet.

Klein reached forward and picked up the book from his knee, before he was hoisted to his feet. The shackles jingled as they shuffled him out of the seat and across the room.

"Klein!"

Klein began to shuffle around. His face was open, eyebrows raised in a nonverbal cue.

Abraham pointed with the pen in his hand at the book. "What's that book about? I've never seen you without it."

Klein was crushing it between his fingers again. He blinked at the question and looked down at the bent object, stroked it gently. "Oh... well... I wouldn't want to spoil it for you, Chief."

"That good, huh?"

"It's... *to die for*... Here, take it. I won't be needing it, so it's only right that it should stay here." Klein handed the book to Officer Petty, who in turn passed it to the Warden. The guards started to usher the prisoner out of the room, his chains jangling.

As he was escorted from the room, he turned back to catch a glimpse of Abraham through the closing door.

The Warden had flicked open the book and had started reading.

AFTERWORD

Firstly I would like to thank you all for returning to Juniper.

And to those who are discovering it for the first time, welcome. I hope you enjoyed your stay!

Secondly and on a more serious note, please remember that Tome *is* a work of fiction - the racist and derogatory language used by my cast of characters and the dark undertones held within are no reflection on how I view, act or see the world (*or the people within it for that matter*), but it is used in Tome as a tool to show the darkness in our world, this story and the characters that populate Juniper.

As a privileged white male I was overtly aware that I needed to seek guidance on the content of this book and I had a great early conversation with Richard Thomas (*a fabulous writer, teacher and friend*). Richard recommended I reach out and get some advice from POC readers / authors and ask for their honest opinion and advice on the language and the larger story I was trying to tell.

These BETA readers really helped me as I started to shape the novel in the latter stages of editing. One of these POC readers said:

'I've not had any real problems with the different ways people speak of people of colour in Tome. I think that's because it is usually either in the characters' thoughts or dialogue. The truth is that, unfortunately, no matter where we are in the world, there are people who are going to use racial slurs, ethnic denigrations, and so forth. But if I were you I'd put a disclaimer in the book to let people know and remember that this is a work of fiction and not at all your own voice!'

And so here I am.

I wanted to make sure that I took the views and opinions of those POC readers on board before I went any further (*also Gemma Amor - thank you for your insight!*), because I wanted to ensure that with writing these words, that I would not be inadvertently glorifying racism in any way; but instead shining a light on the whole abhorrent business.

As writers we need to use our words and our various positions in the field to carry this fight and I hope that in someway that this book aids in showing what the world is still like and how repulsive and how deeply rooted racism is in our societies and the hugely destructive force it is to the world around us and the next generation, if it goes unchecked.

Those POC readers have helped me to showcase the dark underbelly of racism and racist thinking that still exists today without shying away from the meat and bones of it all - and I thank you all for your assistance.

We only have to look at George Floyd to see that although Tome is a work of fiction - we *are* quite possibly living in this fictional racially divided town of Juniper already - some of us just don't know it.

So, I wanted to shed a light in the darkness and I hope I've done that.

Tome is the scariest book I've written, some of the scenes and themes played on my mind for days after writing them and one scene in particular - when Cynthia falls onto Fleming's bed literally kept me up at night (*it didn't help that I was writing it alone, in the dark, whilst it was pouring down outside*).

I think that what made this book so challenging was that I was trying to face (and question) what makes monsters of men and women. What makes people take the actions they take? As a believer in Jesus I also believe heavily in the spiritual realm of good and evil and the way 'evil' appears in various guises to various people. That said, I firmly believe that it is not always a clear-cut business of what falls on the good side and what falls on the 'dark'. Certainly, I want to clarify that I don't believe for a moment that all of our 'bad' choices are the result of evil's presence in our lives. One thing is for sure though, and that is that I believe that despite what it may seem at any one moment in time, there is a bigger story being told and there is much more to life than simply what we see in front of us.

I don't claim to be an expert on it (nor would I want to be, I don't imagine) but I think it has to do with the deliberate causing of suffering and the intentional misdirection of power. It is a complex and contentious topic and one that I am still working through myself.

So I cannot deny my belief that there is a darkness which exists; evil, the enemy, satan, sin, the demonic; there are many ways to describe it. Whether this darkness sinks its claws in through thoughts of: inadequacy, suffering, temptation, pornography, unforgiveness, bitterness, money, addiction, racism, grief, homophobia, loneliness, self-hatred, violence or self-harm; it lies in wait to creep in any way it can, it just needs us to open the window and let it in; it wants to strangle anything that is good before it can sprout, and so it tells us lies and deceives us, telling us that we're simply not enough. It always starts with a thought. And I believe it is how we choose to respond to the thoughts that matter.

In the bible, satan is called the great deceiver, an evil that looks to bend and manipulate us to its leading. If we allow it, then it grows - like the book in Tome.

It feeds and festers like a necrotic wound until it destroys us from the inside out.

This is not a preach or a sermon, this is not me trying to win souls for the Lord, this is just me telling it as I believe it to be; the spiritual realm is real and if I believe wholeheartedly that there is goodness and light in the world in the form of Jesus, I also need to believe that there is evil and darkness too - to rubbish one would make a mockery of the other.

I draw a lot of inspiration for my stories from the bible and I also use it as good yard stick to judge if I've gone too far - but having read some pretty horrific things of late in the Old Testament - Tome might seem pretty tame seeing as in the books I've just read, you have mothers eating their children during a famine (2 Kings 6:29), Lot sleeping with his daughters (Genesis 19:30-38), rape and abuse of daughters (Judges 19:24), slavery and abuse (Exodus 21:20-21) and a good many other things too.

One of the things I've always had a fascination with since I became a Christian is the spiritual realm and spiritual battles – and Tome is my answer to this dark and very real fight.

'For we are not fighting against flesh-and-blood enemies, but against evil rulers and authorities of the unseen world, against mighty powers in this dark world, and against evil spirits in the heavenly places.' Ephesians 6:12

My good friend Mark once told me about a time he was praying for a friend, he'd asked if he could pray for them as he'd had a feeling that something wasn't quite right. As I recount this now it still sends a shiver up my spine. His friend said yes and so Mark laid hands on him (which is a way of unobtrusively making physical contact as you pray). Whilst he was praying he could feel something evil, a spirit or other entity rising up in his friend. Something fighting with the spoken prayer and the laying on of hands. There was a spirit that was trying to push him away, a physical act that his friend had no idea was taking place – but there, in that kitchen a battle was raging, and eventually after a struggle Mark finished praying.

He said that he felt something flee; something rise up and out of his friend and scurry away. Mark said that his friend looked different and more at peace – his friend recounted that he'd felt immediately lighter and better.

Mark concluded and I'd have to believe him, that this was an evil spirit that had attached itself to his friend, showing that the battle between unseen forces is real and alive today. I've not seen this in person; I've not witnessed this type of *'possession'* for want of a better word. But it's something I believe in nonetheless, and I wanted to show this type of spiritual battle within Tome – that evil *can* use us, manipulate us and control us for its gain without us ever knowing what has attached itself to us.

One of the pieces of scripture I kept returning to during the writing of Tome was Luke 8:26-37 – I have always been fascinated with this passage ever since I first picked up my bible to read, and I have no idea why; it just seemed to spring into my consciousness and kept rattling around in there, as if it were waiting for me to use it some day... and Tome might just be me honouring that passage.

Luke 8:26-37 - Jesus Restores a Demon-Possessed Man

26 *They sailed to the region of the Gerasenes, which is across the lake from Galilee. 27 When Jesus stepped ashore, he was met by a demon-possessed man from the town. For a long time this man had not worn clothes or lived in a house, but had lived in the tombs. 28 When he saw Jesus, he cried out and fell at his feet, shouting at the top of his voice, "What do you want with me, Jesus, Son of the Most High God? I beg you, don't torture me!" 29 For Jesus had commanded the impure spirit to come out of the man. Many times it had seized him, and though he was chained hand and foot and kept under guard, he had broken his chains and had been driven by the demon into solitary places.*

30 *Jesus asked him, "What is your name?" "Legion," he replied, because many demons had gone into him. 31 And they begged Jesus repeatedly not to order them to go into the Abyss.*

32 *A large herd of pigs was feeding there on the hillside. The demons begged Jesus to let them go into the pigs, and he gave them permission. 33 When the demons came out of the man, they went into the pigs, and the herd rushed down the steep bank into the lake and was drowned.*

34 *When those tending the pigs saw what had happened, they ran*

*off and reported this in the town and countryside, 35 and the people
went out to see what had happened. When they came to Jesus, they
found the man from whom the demons had gone out, sitting at Jesus'
feet, dressed and in his right mind; and they were afraid. 36 Those
who had seen it told the people how the demon-possessed man had
been cured. 37 Then all the people of the region of the Gerasenes
asked Jesus to leave them, because they were overcome with fear. So
he got into the boat and left.*

You see, Juniper is a godless place but I've tried to populate it
with God-fearing people (*Janet in Juniper and Frank in Tome*) –
they are my moral compasses for the telling of my tales – but both
are far from perfect.

I wanted Tome to show someone who was broken, who had
made mistakes but who was trying to fight the good fight even
though they were limping their way through it. The bible is full of
stories of broken people who find wholeness in Jesus, in his goodness and love. God can create beauty from the ashes of our lives.

Frank was a character that I very much enjoyed writing; he
was my sacrificial lamb. I wanted the conclusion of the story to
show that even when good triumphs over evil in this world of ours -
it never really goes away, an echo or a ripple of that darkness
remains. We put out one fire only for another to spark up
elsewhere.

After witnessing the actions of the police officers who were responsible for killing George Floyd whilst he was begging for his life, I
heard of further horrors which spilled out of this initial tragedy.
These ripples, spreading out from the epicentre, brought with
them more racism: lynchings, hangings, shootings, police brutality
and even more murders - the ripples moved on and evil continued
to find a new host. This is what I was trying to put across in Tome,

that there is a darkness that wanders the earth, feeding and feasting and destroying lives.

———

The initial spark for this story came to me out of the blue, as all great ideas tend to do.

I have on my shelves a signed copy of Chuck Palahniuk's 'Survivor'. It's a copy which was signed during a book tour and if you know Chuck he likes to add little embellishments whilst signing books on tour; to make these treasured items even more special (*sometimes he gives away signed severed plastic arms or blow up dolls or he'll add a unique inscription or stamp adorning the title page of your book*) and well this book had various stamps inside the cover relating to numerous facilities in America and this was the spark that set the fire raging in my mind.

I'd had an idea about writing something about a suicide plague for a while (*I'm fascinated with the book of Exodus so my thinking was a plague of biblical proportions*) but I needed something (*excuse the pun*) to hang this idea from and that's when I decided to have a book be the catalyst for this ongoing plague, this monumental battle of good vs evil – a book that can pass through establishments without raising concern, a vessel to carry this malevolent intent and so Tome was born.

I needed more though as I wanted to develop the spiritual warfare side of good vs evil. So I came upon the notion that a simple book could be the gateway to polluting the mind of those who read it. A book that pulls out their inner evil, their past sin, their murderous or treacherous acts; things that were long since buried or recently covered over - all these things a fragrant offering to this evil, and now all exposed in the cold light of day, drawn out like puss from a wound to fester and be consumed - misery loves company as they say.

The book to me worked like a parasite, feeding on peoples darkness and using the reader as a pawn in a much larger game, a game that has been going on since the dawning of time.

So I'll leave you with this;

'All that is necessary for the triumph of evil is that good men do nothing.'

- Edmund Burke -

ACKNOWLEDGMENTS

I have been lucky enough with Tome to have worked with not one, but two fabulous editors Joseph Sale and El Mealer - thank you both for helping me whip this project into shape and challenging me to make it even better than I could have ever imagined!

I wish to thank the following: Richard Thomas, Kealan Patrick Burke, Clennell Anthony, Priya Sharma (*thank you for always reading my words*), Gemma Amor (*I appreciated the heads up regarding the opening and our continued friendship*), Tracy Fahey, Joshua Marsella (*I can't wait for the next book!*), Joseph Sale, Gabino Iglesias, Tomek Dzido, Anthony Self, Christa Wojciechowski, Steve Stred, Sadie Hartmann & Night Worms, Kevin (*AKA Well Read Beard*), Brad Proctor, Chris from the Basement, Books of Blood, Kendall Reviews, Dan Soule, Mark Jefferies (*our conversations about the spiritual realm helped drive this story forwards - thanks for the continued prayers brother*), Kev Harrison and Christopher Stanley (*keep doing your thing guys and I'll keep supporting it, buying it and reading it*) and lastly a huge slice of thanks to the very supportive horror community of which I now seem to be a part of. Everyone mentioned above and probably many I've forgotten have all helped me write this book or have inspired me to make it the best it can be, you've championed me and believed in my words, so I thank you all from the bottom of my heart!

I wouldn't be writing today if it wasn't for those teachers I've had along the way, so thanks should also be given to those amazing authors who have inspired me and entertained me over the years: Stephen King, Cormac McCarthy, Philip K Dick, Chuck Palahniuk, Bret Easton Ellis, Peter Benchley, Donald Ray Pollock, Jodi Angel, Matthew Baker, John Bowie, Denis Johnson, Charles Bukowski, Hubert Selby Jr, Ray Bradbury, Neil Gaiman, Kelly Link, Yiyun Li, HG Wells, Margaret Atwood, Lucy Caldwell, Patrick deWitt, Jess Hagemann, Adam Nevill, William Peter Blatty, Courttia Newland, John McGregor, Sara Maitland, Angela Readman, Irvine Welsh, Bryan Washington, Xuan Juliana Wang, Carmen Maria Machado, Miranda July, Benjamin Myers, Roald Dahl, Sally Rooney, Sarah Hall, Wendy Erskine, J.G. Ballard, Knut Hamsun, Naomi Booth, Adrian J Walker, Max Porter, Lucie McKnight Hardy, Sarah Lotz, Dan Fante, Hunter S. Thompson, Joe Hill, Justin Torres and Aliya Whiteley.

To my amazing family: Anna thank you for always believing in me and for your never ending support and encouragement whilst I pursue this crazy dream of writing - I can never tell you how much your support means to me but I can keep trying.

Eva and Sophie - keep on being the trailblazers you are, keep on inspiring me and keep on being you, no matter what the world keeps telling you you should be!

And lastly, you the reader. Thank you for taking this journey with me, for buying this book and supporting this indie author's crazy dream.

If you're reading this then you made it to the end of yet another of my books - please do consider leaving a review on Amazon or Goodreads (*or both*) these are like gold dust and I read every single one!

ABOUT THE AUTHOR

Ross Jeffery is the author of the novella Juniper and the novella-in-flash Tethered. He is a Bristol based writer and Executive Director of Books for STORGY Magazine. Ross has appeared in many print publications and has a great deal of work in online journals and literary zines. Ross lives in Bristol with his wife (Anna) and two children (Eva and Sophie).

'ROSS JEFFERY HAS BIRTHED THE LOVECHILD OF
STEPHEN KING AND CORMAC MCCARTHY.'

- PRIYA SHARMA -

JUNIPER

BY ROSS JEFFERY

Available from Amazon

In eBook, Paperback & Hardback

FROM THE AUTHOR OF JUNIPER

TETHERED

A NOVELLA IN FLASH

—— ROSS JEFFERY ——

TETHERED IS A SHORT, INTENSE PORTRAIT OF A
TROUBLED FATHER-SON RELATIONSHIP AND AN
EXAMINATION OF THE 'STRANGE LABYRINTH' OF
PARENTING.
ROISÍN O'DONNELL AUTHOR OF WILD QUIET

Available from Amazon

In eBook & Paperback

ABOUT THE PUBLISHER

 The Writing Collective (TWC) is a band of writers who have a passion for writing and getting fabulous works of fiction into the hands of readers.

We have an author centric approach to publishing and work hard at providing authors a platform for their works and a publishing model that ensures that they get paid for what they write.

Here at the TWC we are continually reading and discovering new and talented writers who deserve that little push into the publishing world and with our unique model and collected experiences we hope to help get your book out into the world and into the hands of readers.

Turn over to discover our other titles.

SAVE GAME
セブ ゲム
TO SAVE HIS FATHER HE HAS TO WIN THE GAME.

JOSEPH SALE

Save Game by Joseph Sale. Levi Jensen is, by all accounts, a loser. He failed sixth-form, never got to university, and works at a no-future fast-food restaurant. The only thing he's good at is gaming. When his father starts dying of a new type of cancer, only treatable privately and at impossible expense, Levi's one hope of saving him becomes the million-dollar cash-prize for winning the dark-fantasy video-game Fate of Ellaria. But Levi isn't the only one with motivations beyond money for winning. And the price of success in Fate of Ellaria might mean the destruction of what little he has left in the real world. Available from Amazon.

Lost Voices is a horror collection of tales left by the wayside: stories recorded on abandoned VHS tapes, horrors found in lifeless towns, voices silenced by the encroaching darkness. Born from a conversation about screwed up stories that'd been rejected from various anthologies, magazines, and callouts for being too weird, freaky, and dark, Lost Voices dredges these lost tales from a past better forgotten. Stories by Joseph Sale, Emily Harrison, Christa Wojciechowski and Ross Jeffery.

Available from Amazon.

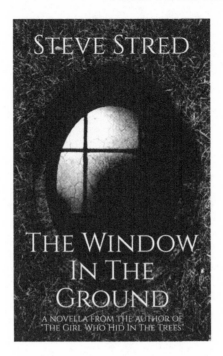

The Window In The Ground - Hidden on the outskirts of town hides a secret. If you follow a path through the trees, read the rules (always twice) on the sign post, go up a hill and across a grassy clearing, that secret will reveal itself. You see, for hundreds of years, this seemingly normal town has done its part, kept the balance. But on this day, a rule will be broken. This will set into motion a series of events that will continue to escalate, to cause chaos and ultimately lead to a devastating conclusion.

Available from Amazon